Front Page Affair

Jennifer Morey

HARLEQUIN® ROMANTIC SUSPENSE

ISBN-13: 978-0-373-27831-2

FRONT PAGE AFFAIR

This edition published by arrangement with Harlequin Books S.A.

For questions and comments about the quality of this book, please contact us at CustomerService@Harlequin.com.

Printed in U.S.A.

Books by Jennifer Morey

Harlequin Romantic Suspense

**Special Ops Affair* #1653
**Seducing the Accomplice* #1657
Lawman's Perfect Surrender #1700
**Seducing the Colonel's Daughter* #1718
A Rancher's Dangerous Affair #1740
***Front Page Affair* #1761

Silhouette Romantic Suspense

**The Secret Soldier* #1526
**Heiress Under Fire* #1578
Blackout at Christmas #1583
 "Kiss Me on Christmas"
**Unmasking the Mercenary* #1606
The Librarian's Secret Scandal #1624

*All McQueen's Men
**Ivy Avengers

Other titles by this author available
in ebook format.

JENNIFER MOREY

Two-time 2009 RITA® Award nominee and a Golden Quill winner for Best First Book for *The Secret Soldier,* Jennifer Morey writes contemporary romance and romantic suspense. Project manager par jour, she works for the space systems segment of a satellite imagery and information company. She lives in sunny Denver, Colorado. She can be reached through her website, www.jennifermorey.com, and on Facebook.

For Maddie, my beautiful, sweet yellow Lab who I lost to cancer in August 2012. Petunia is likened after her in this story, and in the next of this miniseries. My baby girl.

Chapter 1

Braden McCrae left work in a hurry. Pushing through the front doors of the building, he strode toward the parking lot. There had been a tremor in his dad's voice when he called. He wouldn't talk over the phone, only insisted on meeting him and Mom at his house. What had happened? Had one of his grandparents died? Were his parents all right? Or had his sister gotten herself into more trouble? Whatever it was, it couldn't be good. His dad never asked to meet in person if he didn't have something serious to tell him.

Reaching his Subaru, he hesitated before getting inside. A white BMW was parked in the outer lot. A couple of days ago, one just like it was parked down the street from his house. Was it the same SUV? Immediately on the offensive, he took in all the details he could from this distance. Someone was sitting inside, probably a man. He couldn't see the license plate from here.

A long-buried instinct emerged, the fighter in him. Life had taught him to be ready for anything. And he was now.

Driving out of the parking lot, he turned onto the street and watched his rearview mirror. Sure enough, the BMW pulled out of the lot. Who would follow him and why? Would his ex-wife go to such extremes? She'd been angry he'd appealed the divorce terms. He was only disputing the credit card balances, but she had thrown a fit. She'd never liked being married to a mere engineer. She had high hopes of him soaring to the top, running the company and earning an equally top salary. He wasn't opposed to making lots of money; he just didn't want the job that went along with it. Certain executives he'd observed were only as good as their ability to warp the truth. Only one line needed to be on their résumé—how many years of experience they had warping the truth.

And Serena had expected him to become that. It had led to their demise. Why did some women think they could change a man? What was wrong with the version they married? Braden didn't get it. He didn't get women.

Engineering was in his blood. He'd spent countless hours taking things apart and putting them back together when he was a kid. He was a natural at math and enjoyed blowing things up. He was happy with his job. But Serena didn't care about that.

He checked the mirror again. The BMW was several cars back. Serena was many things, but he didn't think she was the type to hire a thug to scare him into dropping the appeal. And there was only one way to find out who was in that BMW, and why. When he was a teenager, he learned how to avoid bullies and was afraid of defending himself. Now a grown man, he was no longer afraid and knew how to defend himself.

Turning a corner, he drove slowly until the SUV ap-

peared, and then went into a parking lot of a small, organic market. Leaning over, he opened his glove box and took out a big flashlight, covertly seeing the BMW park along the street.

Braden got out of his Subaru and headed toward the vehicle, careful to keep cars within close proximity in case he needed to take cover. There was a man inside. He was wearing a baseball cap and a dark blue, lightweight jacket. He was a big man. Seeing his approach, long, solid flashlight swinging at his side, the man stared at him a second or two. He hadn't expected his prey to become the predator. He also didn't appear afraid of that. Calmly, the man restarted the BMW engine that he'd presumptuously shut off. Then he looked at Braden again, as though making sure he hadn't misinterpreted his approach.

Nope. No misinterpretation. Braden fully intended to use this flashlight if he had to. But the man wisely decided not to go up against him. The man steered out into the street.

Braden jogged to the sidewalk and read the license plate. After memorizing the number, he headed back toward his Subaru. Whoever the man was hadn't anticipated Braden would notice the tail, much less take action. Not many knew that side of him. To most, he was an average guy. But he was also someone who couldn't be pushed around. Ever since he was a kid, he'd worked hard at that.

But this was a situation that could go beyond kickboxing and target practice in his free time. Why was someone tailing him?

Back inside his car, his father's tone over the phone reclaimed him. Was the reason the man in the BMW had singled him out related to whatever he'd go home to find out from his parents?

Fifteen minutes were too long. As he turned onto

his street, he saw his parents' car in the driveway of his middle-class, three-bedroom house. They had a key and must be waiting for him inside. A sense of foreboding kept him on alert.

After going through the garage, he stepped into his open kitchen, spotting his parents across the island counter. His mother stood rigidly beside the bulky, round pine table and his dad rose up from a chair, pushing it in and standing behind it. In their late fifties, they looked a decade younger. His dad was tall and fit, wearing jeans and a long-sleeved white, pink and gray finely striped shirt. His hazel eyes were heavy with apprehension and his salt-and-pepper hair uncombed. His mother kept her hair dyed the chocolate brown of her youth and her petite body in shape. As usual, she was put together in big, stylish silver-and-blue earrings, a matching necklace and designer slacks and blouse. The whites around her green eyes were red from crying. Braden had gotten his eyes from his mother and his dark hair from his father, although his dad wore his shorter.

It was difficult to see them so shaken.

"We have something to tell you," his mother said, her still-beautiful face ravaged with strain.

"It's your sister," his dad finished for her.

So, it was his sister. Her trouble wasn't over. "What's wrong?" he asked.

"She's gone missing."

Missing might mean dead. She had gone to the British Virgin Islands on vacation last week. Now she was missing.

Damn it. What would he do if he never saw her again? He and his sister were close in age and had done a lot together. They lost contact when they went to college, and

then he'd gotten married. She hadn't married and was the top executive he'd never be.

"How long?"

"She hasn't answered her phone in two days." His dad leaned on the back of the chair, his hands gripping the top, pale wood bar.

Why hadn't they called him sooner? He subdued his reproach. They probably didn't want to worry him unnecessarily. Now it was necessary. His parents hadn't achieved success by being impulsive. His dad was an architect who'd started a log business that provided well for his family. His mother didn't need her psychology degree, but she practiced out of their home.

"Has she called you?" his mother asked, looping her arm with his dad's.

"No. Not since before she left." She'd been upset over losing her job. "Have you talked to the police there?"

His mother began crying softly.

Freeing his arm from hers, his dad pulled her closer. "According to them, she never checked in at the Frenchman's Point Hotel, but the manager there said he saw her get into a taxi."

That offered a small glimmer of hope. "Where did the taxi take her?"

"The detective didn't know. Neither did the hotel manager. He only saw her get into the taxi."

"Have they questioned the driver?"

His mother's crying deepened into a wrenching sound.

"He was found shot to death later that night."

Murdered? The sting of shock bled into deflated hope. Tatum could be in serious trouble.

"The airline confirmed she boarded her plane," his dad said unnecessarily. If she was seen getting into a taxi, she must have made it to the island. "The detective assigned

to the case said she didn't rent a car," his dad rambled on, a father distraught. "He couldn't find evidence that she took a cab there. The other taxi drivers there didn't have a record and didn't recognize her picture."

Frenchman's Cay was an island off the coast of Tortola. "Who is the detective?"

"Monty Crawford."

At least he was intent on searching. "Did Tatum mention she might meet someone there?"

"No." His dad shook his head, barely hanging on to his composure. "We've searched through her things here in Denver. Nothing is missing and nothing is out of place that we can tell."

Braden contemplated telling them about the BMW and just as quickly decided to hold off. They had enough trauma to deal with right now. He'd go search for his sister and keep them informed as much as possible. The detective may seem to be doing that for them, but Braden could not stay here and wait. He had to do something. Finding a missing person wasn't his area of expertise, however. He wasn't proficient in this sort of thing, especially on foreign land, but he did know someone who was.

Halfway through their Monopoly game, Arizona Ivy had had enough. "I'm twenty-five. I can make my own decisions."

At her sharp tone, her brother's blue eyes lifted from the board game. Blond-haired, tall and muscular, he had Viking good looks. All of her brothers and sisters had that Scandinavian appearance. "You aren't thinking it through. As usual, you're being impulsive."

She didn't respond. She had a real shot at making a good career for herself and Lincoln was stepping all over her toes. She wrote the latest gossip for a not-so-great enter-

tainment rag. Who was divorcing whom. Who was cheating. Who was gay. She could do better than that. Her dad had helped her get a lead on a job, and Lincoln thought she was setting herself up for failure. She should stick with what she was good at, and that was entertainment.

Just because their father was a huge success as a movie producer didn't mean his kids were destined for entertainment careers. She had her own aspirations. And that was a much more serious career than the one she currently had. If only she could find a way to prove she was capable.

"It's still your turn," Lincoln said.

She didn't feel like playing anymore. "I have to go now."

While he protested with a brotherly "Aww, come on," she stood. Tucking her shoulder-blade-length blond hair behind one ear, she grabbed her car keys.

"Don't be a big baby, Arizona. I tell you these things because I don't want to see you get hurt."

"Then support me." She left his 1950s, newly remodeled kitchen. *Big baby.* He always treated her like a kid. His little sister. She was tired of that, too.

"I do support you. I wish you would listen to me," he called from his seat at the table.

"I do listen to you," she called back. "I wish you would listen to *me!*"

It wasn't fair. He was her only sibling out of eight that she could talk to. Guess not anymore. He was the oldest and she was the youngest. She was an adult now. She didn't need guidance. She could guide her own way.

Through his living room, the lack of feminine touches further sparked her ire. No flowers. No frilly decor. Just furniture and trim. She sure wished he'd find himself a woman. Then maybe he'd be too preoccupied to stick his nose in her business!

With snowballing energy, she swung the door open and

came face-to-face with a man standing there, his finger poised over the doorbell. The first things that struck her were his lean, hard biceps and broad chest. Next was his military-short, dark brown hair and sexy stubble that peppered a square jaw. And last were his intense green eyes. Something about them ignited warm embers.

As he lowered his hand, his bold gaze went down her body and back up again, brushing her with tingles. She'd worn jean shorts and strappy red high heels, which showcased her long legs. A metallic-beaded, sleeveless pink top did the same for her breasts and small waist. Her aim wasn't to be overly sexy, just fun. Some people didn't take it that way. Was he one of them?

His pique polo shirt was wrinkle-free and tucked neatly into his jeans. His shoes were leather. He was clean. Smelled that way, too. He appeared a lot more conservative than her. But she'd felt what lay underneath. It was in the green fire of his eyes.

"Hi," she said.

At her flirtatious tone, blinds shut tight over his emotions. Rigid control. Big, giant, thick wall.

What had caused his withdrawal? She hadn't mistaken the chemistry.

"I'm here to see Lincoln Ivy."

His deep voice melted through her.

"Braden, is that you?" Her brother appeared with a big smile on the porch. "Good to see you." Arizona stepped aside as he reached forward and shook his hand.

"It's been a while," Braden said.

"Yes. Too long."

Arizona stuck her hand out. "I'm Arizona. Ivy. Arizona Ivy. Lincoln's sister."

Braden reluctantly shook her hand. "Braden McCrae."

She felt silly for being so awkward. Why was she trying

so hard to get his attention? Normally, she was uncontrollably picky when a handsome man crossed her path. She looked for flaws and held back until she either found them and had an excuse to walk away, or didn't and dated them until the threat of more sent her scurrying.

"How do you know my brother?" He had smooth skin, and yet not. Strong. Slightly calloused.

"We went to college together." He let go of her hand.

As before, her skin tingled as though he'd caressed her intimately.

"What brings you here?" Lincoln sent her a curious look, obviously having noticed her reaction to his friend.

"I wish I could say it's just to pay a visit. Unfortunately, it's urgent."

"What is it?" Lincoln was perplexed now. His college friend had come for a reason and it wasn't to catch up.

"My sister is missing. She went to the British Virgin Islands on vacation and said she was going to call my parents but never did. The police are saying she was seen getting into a taxi in front of Frenchman's Point Hotel."

Arizona felt a one-two punch as Braden dropped his news. Missing. In the Virgin Islands. Plummeted back in time, she struggled with sobering memories and the ever-hovering sense of helplessness she could never quite shed.

"Are the police looking for her?" Lincoln asked.

"Yes. They've done some investigating, but nothing has turned up so far."

We're very sorry, but there's nothing more we can do...

The St. Thomas police hadn't known where Trevor's abductors had taken him. They'd demanded money, and her father had paid, but they'd killed Trevor anyway. To this day, they hadn't been caught. The injustice of that had stayed with her.

Arizona was vaguely aware of Braden glancing over

her before saying to Lincoln, "I'm going down there to look for her myself."

"And you came to me for help?" Lincoln asked, still perplexed.

"You're a bounty hunter. You know how to find people."

Lincoln fell into an undecided silence.

He hadn't been a bounty hunter when Trevor had been kidnapped. A few years had passed since that traumatic event. It may as well have happened a few months ago. Arizona's heart went out to Braden, and especially to his mother. She well understood what they were going through.

Except, all she sensed from him was determination to find his sister. He hadn't experienced the awfulness of losing someone close, knowing how horribly that person must have suffered before dying. She hoped he never would have to. "What if she decided to go somewhere else?" she asked. "Maybe she's having fun and not thinking about calling her mother." It's what Arizona would do. Calling home would be the last thing on her mind. "How old is she?"

"Twenty-nine. She would have called. And she would have returned my mother's calls. I hope she's only having fun. But I can't wait to find out. If I wait, it might be too late for her."

Arizona lowered her head as that struck a raw chord in her. She had waited until it was too late. Her fiancé had been kidnapped right under her nose. And no one had been able to do a thing to save him. That was the worst part. The helplessness. How many times had she wished there had been something she could have done?

She caught Braden watching her fully now, soft curiosity over what had changed her mood. Her brother's scrutiny

was far less empathetic. Braden's plight was beginning to circle her heart, close in and compel her to act.

"Did she go there alone?" she asked Braden.

He nodded. "She'd been dealing with so much after being asked to resign from American Freight Forwarding Services. She went to get away. That's why Mom was so worried. With all that happened..."

Dawning sprinkled down on Arizona. "Your sister is Tatum McCrae?" The female executive had allegedly allowed several unlicensed arms shipments to a prohibited country and had been asked to resign amidst a scandalous government investigation. She'd claimed she was being blamed for something she hadn't done. Luckily, the government had agreed and hadn't charged her. Export violations rarely made big news, but Arizona had been fascinated by the story, by the woman. Her reputation was solid. She was charitable and respected, a role model for young women.

If something had happened to her, it would make a great story. News of a woman like that vanishing in a place like Tortola would stir up a decent amount of public interest. This could be just the story she needed to boost her career. It would probably wind up in the news eventually, anyway. And Arizona never turned down a chance to fight for victims.

Noticing her brother's now very acute discord, she cocked her head in challenge. He was going to try to stop her again.

Lincoln turned to Braden. "I'll go with you to Tortola."

Surprise drew Braden's head back. "You will?"

Clever. So that's how he thought he'd stop her.

"Lincoln..."

"I also know some people I can call—" Lincoln talked

over her. "We'll look into her latest credit card use and other indicators of her whereabouts."

"That would be great."

Her brother was going to make this difficult for her. She wasn't going to let him ignore her. "Michael Benson said if I brought him a writing sample, and it was as good as Dad said it would be, he'd hire me."

Michael Benson was editor in chief for a prominent news magazine.

Lincoln sighed as Braden followed what must surely seem a strange turn of conversation. "That isn't the real reason you want to go."

"You want to do a story on my sister?" Braden searched her for answers, disconcerting her. He didn't sound pleased with the idea.

"Benson isn't going to hire you," her brother interrupted. "He's just saying that because he owes Dad a favor."

And the favor was reading her writing sample. Nothing more. "If I give him quality work, he'll hire me."

"You write about fashion and gossip. Nobody would ever take you seriously."

That hurt. Braden's brow had lowered enough to put a crease above his nose. He didn't like where this was headed.

"It's not what you think," she told him. "This is an opportunity to do something worthy."

"Why are you pushing this, Arizona? It's not what you really want."

She turned to her brother. "How do you know what I want?"

"This isn't about being taken seriously. This is about losing Trevor. Anytime you hear someone is being victimized, you take leaps without thinking. It's what made you

have the harebrained idea of becoming an international news reporter."

Braden looked from one to the other. "Who is Trevor?"

"Her fiancé. He—"

"Lincoln," Arizona stopped him. It was too personal.

Braden studied her a moment and didn't press for details. "I won't let you exploit my sister for a news story."

He said it so matter-of-factly that there was no doubt he meant it. "It's going to get in the news anyway. Why not let me break it? Besides, I could help you. Publicity will put pressure on police to work hard to find her."

"I don't need that kind of help. This is a private family matter."

"You heard the man. You aren't going," Lincoln said.

Now she was getting mad. "Why do you always think whatever I do is a bandage for what happened?"

"Because everything you've done since then has been exactly that."

She had to find a way to convince him he was wrong. "Define *everything.*"

"You've gone overboard in the last few years," Lincoln said. "If you aren't saving puppies or volunteering to help natural disaster victims, you're jumping out of planes every week. Slow down."

"I don't jump out of airplanes every week."

"You know what I'm saying, A."

She loved it when he called her A. It had begun when she was in school and received the one and only A in twelfth grade. That's when she'd aspired to go to college. That one A, and her brother making her feel so good about it.

"I need a good story," she said simply, pleading.

"Maybe I shouldn't have come." Braden turned to leave and then froze.

Arizona looked to see what had stopped him. A white BMW was parked across the street. A man sat inside.

"Who is that?" her brother asked.

With all three of them staring, the man in the BMW drove into the street and disappeared under the canopy of trees down the road.

Braden swore.

The rough sound captivated Arizona. So did his edgy profile. The translucence of his eyes radiated strength. So did his straight, proportioned nose, for some unknown reason to her. A mouth worth exploring. She didn't understand the potency of her response to him.

Who are you? she nearly asked.

He turned to her, caught what must be her rapturous look, and the tension along his brow tightened. "Do you really jump out of planes?"

"Occasionally." She was still drowning in his sex appeal.

His eyes scanned all over her face, nothing showing as to what he thought of her favorite sport. "Then go do that instead of a story on my sister."

While the affront doused the heat simmering in her, he glanced up the street once more.

Lincoln noticed. "Are you being followed?"

"I shouldn't have come." He started to walk away.

"Wait."

Reluctantly, he faced them again. Arizona began to feel contrite. He'd come for help from Lincoln, and she had interfered.

She sighed her exasperation. "All right. I'm leaving."

Kissing her brother's cheek, she said to Braden, "Nice to meet you."

He just watched her, surprise emerging into his nearly unreadable eyes. He hadn't expected her to back down.

Well, she lived with aggressive reporters all the time. While she intended to do a serious story, she couldn't inflict the same torture on Braden and his sister. She'd just have to find another opportunity.

Making her way down the narrow driveway, she started for her car. The street in this old neighborhood wasn't wide, leaving little room for cars to pass. The houses were big and close together, with mature trees towering above. All part of the charm.

At the driver's door, she looked over the hood at Braden and Lincoln, both in an involved conversation. She had to force herself not to go back and insist on Braden allowing her to join him. She could help him. Even if she didn't do a story, she could help him find his sister. It killed her that she wouldn't be able to. Not doing anything filled her with that familiar helplessness. She hated that feeling. And she'd do anything to make it go away. Usually that meant being proactive. But she couldn't now. Braden—and her brother—wouldn't let her.

She hoped they found Braden's sister. Maybe there was a way she could help from here in the States. She'd do something. She had to. She couldn't back off and do nothing. Not when there was a woman who'd disappeared in the Caribbean. It was too much like her fiancé's situation to ignore. She didn't know Braden's sister, but that didn't matter. Trevor was gone forever because she'd done nothing to help him. If she could help Braden, in any way, she would.

Hearing a car approach, she waited for it to pass before opening her door. When it didn't, she looked back to see that the white BMW they'd seen earlier had stopped in the middle of the road and a man was coming toward her. Large and muscular, he wore a black, long-sleeved shirt with black jeans and boots.

She began to back away but she wasn't fast enough.

He pounced on her, grabbing her arm and pulling her toward the BMW.

"Let go of me!" She struggled, her resistance hurting her arm where he held her roughly. He opened the passenger's door of the BMW.

He was taking her.

She put her foot against the doorframe to keep him from shoving her inside, screaming.

Where was her brother?

Just then, the stranger's grip vanished and she fell to the pavement. As she bumped her head on the rear fender of her car, she heard gunfire. Scrambling to her feet, she took cover behind her car and searched for her brother and Braden. The stranger was firing at both men. Braden had ducked behind the tree in Lincoln's front yard. Lincoln lay on the ground, gripping his knee in agony.

The man backed toward her, gun aimed toward the front yard. Arizona moved to the other side of her car as Braden crawled to Lincoln and dragged him to the cover of the tree.

Arizona froze as the man aimed his gun at her. He grabbed her arm again, methodical and sure. Terrifying. Fleetingly, she wondered if this was how Trevor had felt when he'd been taken.

She stumbled as the man yanked her back against his chest and forced her with him around the rear of her car. He put his gun to her head just as Braden emerged from the cover of her car. Somehow he'd made it from the tree to there. She strained to see Lincoln. He must have seated himself up behind the tree.

Something whizzed by her ear, disturbing her hair. She realized it was Braden's foot when the gun went flying. The man released her to face his opponent. Arizona stum-

bled with the abruptness of it and landed near the curb on her hands, yelping with the hard, rough contact.

Hurrying to her feet, she saw swinging legs and blocking hands as the two men fought between the vehicles. The gun was on the road behind her car. She started for it as Braden delivered a well-planted kick and the stranger fell closer to it than her.

The man took the gun and rolled to aim it at Braden.

Seeing Braden lunge for cover on the other side of her car, Arizona crawled along the sidewalk as the spray of loud gunfire erupted.

The next thing she heard was the squeal of tires and the revving of a fast engine. Climbing to her feet, she braced herself by the front fender of her car. Braden rose from where he'd crouched in the front as the BMW disappeared down the street.

Lincoln.

"Lincoln!" She ran for her brother, who still held his shot and bleeding knee, leaning against the tree.

Braden was already calling for help.

"I'm okay," Lincoln said. "Who was that?" He looked up at Braden, who shook his head, still breathing heavily from exertion and adrenaline.

"He was going to take me," Arizona uttered, unable to believe it. Why her?

"To use you for leverage," Braden answered her silent question, his face grim but set with resolve.

"For what?"

He only stared at her, having no answer, at least none he would give. Not only was he gorgeous, he wasn't the kind of man who could be controlled. Neither was he a man who scared easily. His sister was missing and the man who was following him had just attempted to kidnap Arizona.

Whatever he wanted, he was willing to go to great lengths to get it. And he believed he could get it from Braden.

Did Braden know what that was? Did he know why his sister had disappeared?

There was no time for her to ask questions. Lincoln needed a hospital and the sound of sirens was approaching.

Chapter 2

Braden watched Arizona pace the emergency room in front of the uncomfortable seat he occupied, chewing her thumbnail. Still in those shorts and colorful top, she had the same effect on him as the moment he'd seen her when she'd opened Lincoln's door. Grapefruit-sized breasts. Hooker shoes that he would not complain about. Ever. Her legs made him imagine R-rated things.

She stopped when she saw a tall, thin doctor approach wearing a white uniform and rectangular glasses.

"How is he?" Arizona asked anxiously. He got the feeling she was close to her brother.

"Fine. The surgery went well. Give him the night to rest. By morning he'll be able to go home."

"Thank God," she breathed.

Braden stood while the doctor finished explaining Lincoln's condition. He'd have a long recovery but he'd regain full use of his knee. Lucky.

When the doctor left, she slowly turned to him, weary with relief. But then a new light entered her eyes. Fresh panic.

"We have to get out of here." She grabbed his arm.

What was her hurry? He stayed where he was.

She gave up with a breath of exasperation, dropping her hands. "Any minute now, the press is going to descend on this place like flies at a food festival."

"Why?" What would draw the media here?

She cocked her head. "You try being one of Jackson Ivy's kids and stay out of the news."

Her father was a famous movie producer. Now he understood her urgency and felt a little of it himself. If he was going to search for his sister, he didn't need the press announcing his arrival in Tortola. He also wished there was a way to leave Arizona behind. She might attract too much attention. But he had no choice. Someone had gone after her, and the police had nothing to go on. Even if they found something during the investigation of their attack, it would take too long.

He started for the exit. "I would think you'd welcome the press."

Her pinched brow told him she didn't understand his meaning. Everything she did was so animated. Was she aware of that?

"The press hounds my family."

"The way you want to hound my sister. She's had enough of that already."

Shock rendered her speechless for a second, and he couldn't tell what she was thinking. "No, I wouldn't. The kind of news I'm after is different than that, but I understand you not wanting me to do any story. What you don't understand is I can still help you."

She wanted to help him? Would she do a story anyway?

Was this a way of getting him to let her go with him? He was taking her, but not because he needed help.

Outside, he steered her toward his car. “Why would you want to help me?”

She shrugged “Because I can.”

He looked over her petite frame in her girly outfit. “How?”

Shooting him a lowered brow with eyes full of affront, she said, “However. I can help you.”

“It could be dangerous.” He took in her long, slender legs as she walked beside him. Damn, they were hot.

“Then maybe you shouldn’t be going, either. Maybe you should let the police handle it.”

“The police aren’t getting anywhere, and I can’t leave you here.”

“What?”

He stopped at the door of his charcoal-colored Subaru, turning to face her. “Trust me, I’d rather not, but someone tried to kidnap you. What if there’s another attempt? I can’t allow the chance.” And she had no idea how unbending he was on that subject. She could argue all she wanted, he wasn’t letting her out of his sight.

“My brother won’t like that.” But she looked pleased as could be with the prospect of going with him. To help… or get a story?

He’d have to watch her. Stealing a glance at her breasts in the beaded, sleeveless pink top, he realized he wouldn’t suffer much doing so. “He just wants to make sure you don’t get hurt.” Or worse.

“Yes, he *is* very overprotective.”

“Probably a good thing in this case. What would have happened if that man had succeeded in taking you?”

She didn’t reply, the flicker of horrible imaginings crossing her eyes as she scanned the parking lot.

The white BMW wasn't around. He'd already looked.

At last she returned her gaze to him. "Why is someone following you?"

Why was she asking? "I have no idea."

"What do they want from you?"

He shook his head. He didn't know. The man in the BMW would have let him know once he'd had Arizona. After Braden had gone after him with the flashlight, he must have decided he'd have too difficult a time overpowering him, and then he'd seen him with Lincoln and Arizona. He would have used Arizona as leverage. It was disturbing. What did the man want? And how was it related to his sister?

Where had his life intersected with Tatum's to draw him into the fray? Tatum had come to see him during her trouble with the government. She'd told him then that her movements were being tracked. Now she was missing, and he'd have to take Arizona with him to find her. She was eager enough for that, which caused him to wonder why.

"What happened to your fiancé?" He was sure that was what drove her. Lincoln had indicated as much. She had a compelling motive to involve herself in this, and it was more than getting a story.

Deep pain sobered her eyes before she caught the reaction and stubborn determination returned. "Didn't you say our flight departure was in two hours?"

The fact that she refused to discuss her fiancé only convinced him further of her resolve. The story was an excuse, a small part of what moved her. The mystery of her fiancé intrigued him; her determination made him nervous.

Using his fob, he unlocked the doors of his Subaru. Why didn't she want to tell him about Trevor? Was it still too painful or did she think it would give him an edge in

fighting her on the story he wasn't convinced she'd completely abandoned yet? It had seemed so important to her.

This woman had so many facets to her, and it disconcerted him that he was beginning to want to learn every single one. Intimately.

At last, it was time to board. Braden couldn't stand the waiting anymore. Their flight had been delayed and being with Arizona in her blue cotton sundress had tested him long enough. He moved with her toward the jet bridge. Pulling out his wallet for his boarding pass, a picture fell out and fluttered to the commercially carpeted floor.

Arizona knelt to pick it up.

Seeing his ex-wife smiling in what used to be his favorite photo of her and now was merely something he'd neglected to remove and destroy, Braden snatched it from her.

"Your wife?" she asked.

Did they really have to go down this path? "Ex. The divorce was just final a few months ago."

"Oh." She looked at his still-open wallet and saw more pictures. "You have kids?"

He crumbled the picture of Serena and tossed it to a trash can near a thick concrete column. He made the hole. "A son. Aiden. He's six." That was a topic he could discuss all night.

Arizona glanced from the trash can to him. What he could only call a grimace crossed her expression.

"I don't want any pictures of my ex in my wallet," he explained.

The hint of a smile began to push up her mouth. "I'm the youngest of eight. Everyone but me got to hold babies growing up."

So, it wasn't throwing out the picture of Aiden's mother that bothered her. "Never been exposed to children, huh?"

"They're little aliens who poop and scream and don't stop wiggling."

"Most women love kids." They moved up in the line toward the jet bridge. Wasn't it a natural instinct for women to nurture? In the office he often saw groups of them hovering around newborns, cooing and coddling.

"I'm not most women."

"You don't want kids of your own some day?"

Arizona's eyes popped in appall. "Oh, God. No." She shuddered, her bare shoulders shaking a little.

Well, wasn't this an interesting highlight. Arizona Ivy couldn't stand kids. It reflected badly on her, and he welcomed the barrier. "What's wrong with them?"

"They're on another planet?"

Although her sarcasm was obvious, he took the message literally. He had a son. She didn't like kids. It would never work out for them. Good to know right from the start.

"They're just kids," he said. "Innocent. A clean palatte ready to absorb information and grow up to be an adult… just like you."

"Great. Introduce me when they're adults."

He chuckled. "What happens when you encounter them?" He'd love to see that some day.

"I find an excuse to leave the room."

"Don't you mean planet?" She could be a science project. What made some women gush over babies and others turn cold?

She sighed, no longer joking. "I guess I don't relate to them."

"They're kids." Nobody was supposed to relate. Not on the same level.

"They're loud and obnoxious."

"Kid. Not adult."

"Right."

Braden shook his head. She really didn't get it. "You're missing out on a big part of life."

"Yeah? What's that? Exhaustion that leads to unhappiness and lack of sex?"

"No. The moments you remember for a lifetime. The words they say and how they say them. The questions they ask. The first time they tell you they love you."

Feeling her watch him, he realized he was smiling fondly, thinking of Aiden.

"I can live without all that."

"Right, because you have a serious career to go after." And sex.

He wished that thought hadn't entered his head.

"Which is precisely why I prefer other women to do the childbearing." She walked forward, hauling her carry-on.

Braden felt better and better about her going along. Whatever had transpired when she'd bumped into him at Lincoln's house, it was brief and over now. He could concentrate on finding his sister and not worry about Arizona attracting him into bed. Best to avoid any chance of getting her pregnant and forcing her to become one of those childbearing women.

Sitting next to Braden in first class, Arizona was thankful for the spacious seating. His lean body was far enough away to prevent contact. Contact was dangerous with him. He may inflame her physically, but he'd failed the intellectual test. Flawed, to be sure. Son. Recently divorced. That was plenty to convince her he wasn't her type. Especially the kid part. A shudder wracked her shoulders. And it wasn't all from revulsion. She couldn't stop thinking about the look on his face when he talked about Aiden.

Beside her, Braden noticed, his perceptive eyes cynical.

Opening her *People* magazine, she tried to pay attention to that. Braden's presence was too strong.

She watched him remove his laptop and survey the cabin of the plane at the same time, as though expecting the driver of the BMW to pop out of nowhere. He was as vigilant as Lincoln. As fearless, too. The combination of nerd and superhero was a curious mix.

"What do you do, anyway?" Lincoln had never told her.

"I'm an engineer for Hamilton Corporation." As though on cue, he pulled out a pair of reading glasses and opened his laptop. Arizona watched him for a bit, disconcerted over the unbelievable comparison to her fiancé. Tall, handsome and an engineer for a high-tech corporation.

She kept that to herself. "What kind of engineer?"

He turned from his laptop screen, green eyes behind the anti-reflective lenses of his glasses. Still handsome.

"Advanced technology for the military. Countermeasure equipment. That sort of thing."

Vague reply. "Oh." She nodded through her discomfort. "Design and development?"

"Most of it's classified."

Her fiancé had worked in research. Top secret clearance, just as she was sure Braden had. She struggled to minimize the coincidence.

Then something dawned on her. "Do you think it's possible there's a link between what you do and your sister's disappearance?"

He turned with a lifted brow. Clearly, he doubted that.

"You do weapons designs for the military," she explained further. "Your sister was a freight forwarder accused of shipping weapons to a prohibited country."

"Where's the link? She didn't get the weapons from my company."

"Are you sure?"

"Very. The arms her company exported weren't ours."

His defensive response spoke loudly of his conviction, but it seemed forced. He refused to consider his sister could have been involved in anything sinister. In this case, Arizona agreed. It didn't seem likely that his job had anything to do with the accusations that had ruined his sister's reputation. The coincidence was unnerving, though.

A baby cried from somewhere in the back of the plane. The whine of jet engines and airflow muffled voices and the movement of flight attendants.

"Were you curious about my job because you were fishing for a connection or did something else prompt you?" he asked.

Prompt her? What had prompted her? She registered his reading glasses.

"I could tell you were—" a nerd, she almost said "—a college graduate."

He stared at her. "A college graduate?"

"Yeah. You know, the office type." His big chest and arms challenged her claim. So did the amusement in his eyes, entirely too...she'd rather not allow the word into her head.

"You could tell that by looking at me?"

She took in his stubble and the green of his captivating eyes. "Well, there are some deterring factors, but yes. I could tell."

"Deterring factors?"

Never one to shy away from confrontation, she let propriety drop. "You have this masculine look about you, and yet you wear Gucci loafers and smudged reading glasses. It's like Louis Vuitton clashing with Aeropostale."

"Stereotyping, are you?" He removed his glasses and wiped them with his soft shirt.

Another non-office thing to do. Who wiped their glasses on their shirt? She smiled with an exhaled laugh.

"While we're on the subject, I agree with your brother. You don't seem like the international reporter type."

She was having too much fun to be insulted. "You think I'm much more suited for tabloids?"

"It's just an observation. Sort of like the one you made about me."

Smart-ass. "Hey, I'm not the one who wears smudged glasses."

"No, but you write entertainment news and are the subject of entertainment news, like what you're reading about in that magazine." He gestured toward the *People* magazine in her lap. "An interesting dichotomy, don't you think?"

"Quite." She wasn't sure she liked his observations. She knew a lot of the people she read about. It was sort of like social media to her.

"Why'd you get into it anyway?"

"Jackson Ivy's daughter...?" Her levity fell flat. The fun was over.

This was getting too close to personal pains she'd rather not stir up. If she explained why she'd made her observation and where it had come from, she'd have to tell him about her fiancé.

"The media will follow you no matter what you do," he said. "So why not do something you love?"

What did she love? She thought awhile and nothing came to her other than her undying desire to be recognized as herself rather than Jackson Ivy's daughter. "My brother thinks I should start a nonprofit organization that takes crime victims skydiving or other high adventures. His version of entertainment that would suit me. Dad would back me."

"I'd get in on that," Braden said.

She took in his profile as he typed on his laptop. Would he? Which part? The organization or her dad backing it? "I want to make it on my own. You skydive?"

Pausing in his typing, he turned his face toward her. "I love anything outdoors."

That was different from Trevor. He'd been chained to his desk and his idea of physical exercise was taking the stairs. "Wow."

"That surprises you?"

"It's just..."

He angled his head, green eyes curious and prowling. "You think engineers are boring?"

"No..." He definitely wasn't boring her right now.

"You've banned all engineers, is that it?" His flirtatious grin muddled her senses further.

"No...I..." She struggled with what to say. Engineers reminded her of Trevor. It didn't matter what type of engineer, or how different they were, for some reason just the association hit a raw nerve. Except with him. Right now.

She had to stop all this focus on her. "Why are you so curious? Do you want to date me or something?"

Now he was the one speechless.

"No? Too soon after your divorce?"

"I don't want to date you." He was a rigid wall again.

His divorce had affected him profoundly; a man who'd loved his wife only to discover she didn't love him back. Or was it only that? She sensed something deeper at work.

"What happened? If you don't mind me asking..."

He averted his gaze to the front of the plane. "I wasn't what she expected."

Did all men answer questions so vaguely or were there only a few? The injured ones. "Did she cheat on you?"

"No. It had more to do with my title, or lack thereof."

What was wrong with engineer?

"Her parents are rich. She has a trust fund. She'll never have to work a day in her life. When she met me, I think in her mind she was giving me a chance. And when she realized I'd never advance to executive management, she served me and left."

He said it so simply. All that emotional baggage wrapped up in a few sentences. Discovering his wife's lack of caring had to have been difficult on him. How could some women be so shallow? Did they have no consideration for the men they married? They thought they loved them at one point. Of course there were always exceptions, but didn't the past they shared mean anything? To Arizona, that was like erasing a relationship as though it had never happened. What a waste. She planned to cherish every second she was alive. There was no such thing as mistakes. Everything happened for a reason. Good or bad. The mistakes were just things that happened to correct the course of life. The catalysts of fated change.

"She wasn't what you expected, either," she said quietly.

They shared a long look.

"Was Trevor what you expected?"

"I think he would have been." She stared over the top of the seat in front of her, falling into what-ifs. What if they'd gone to Paris instead of the Caribbean? What if they'd stayed in the hotel room all day? What if…

"Did he die?"

Braden's question brought her back to him. "Yes." Odd, how it didn't bother her to tell him this time. "He was kidnapped in St. Thomas. His captors demanded money. My father gave it to them, but…"

"Were his killers caught?"

She shook her head, angry all over again.

"Lincoln never told me."

"We tried very hard to keep it out of the press." Her entire family had. For her. She wouldn't have survived Trevor's death otherwise. "We succeeded somewhat."

"Private family matter?"

His meaning drove straight through her. She'd experienced what too much press could do to a person during a time of grief. Could she inflict that on Braden?

"I said we succeeded somewhat," she said.

But could she go against his wishes? If his sister turned up dead like her fiancé, would she be able to do it?

She wouldn't have to.

The news would leak out. One way or another. She'd been approached by reporters once Trevor's kidnapping and murder had gotten out. The same would happen to Braden. Wouldn't he rather it be her than a stranger?

She'd convince him he would. And not by giving in to her attraction. Getting mixed up with a man on the rebound was a risk she wasn't willing to take. Like his ex, her parents were rich. Like his ex, Arizona didn't have to work for a living. And if that wasn't enough, Braden was an engineer with a six-year-old son. No way.

Braden went into the bar for a drink. It was off the only restaurant in their hotel, a historic fort remodeled in the early sixties. There was little they could do until morning when they planned to go to the police, and it was too early to go to sleep. He wouldn't be able to sleep anyway, wondering where Tatum was and whether she was all right. Was she frightened? Hurt?

Just the thought made him curl his fist. "I'm here, Tatum," he murmured. "I'm coming to get you." And whoever had taken her would pay.

He just hoped Arizona wouldn't make that harder than it already would be. And not just while he was making bad

people pay. More and more he thought he'd have to keep her out of his heart, too.

"You're ruining my perception of you as an engineer."

He twisted to see the object of his thoughts standing behind him, holding a bottle of beer. "Mine of you is still intact."

She humphed at his witty response and sat on the barstool next to him, a grin tugging her kissable lips. "You drink?"

"Not every day. You?"

"Not every day." Laughter lit her stunning blue eyes, clear and light. Mysterious. "Couldn't sleep, huh?"

"It's early."

"You stay up late, too?"

"Yes."

"Don't engineers need their sleep?"

He leaned close. "Depends on what's keeping them awake."

She held her forefinger up. "Stop that."

"Breaking your stereotype?"

"I'm afraid it's already obliterated." She didn't seem happy about that. And then, she did.

If she was warming to him, he wasn't sure how he felt about that. "How long has it been since your fiancé died?"

"Four years."

Plenty of time for her heart to heal after someone she loved died. He surveyed her flawless skin, glowing a healthy tone, free of lines. Soft. "How old were you?"

"Twenty-one."

Did anyone know what they wanted in a spouse at that age? He sure as hell hadn't. "Young."

"You say that as though it was *too* young."

"I was twenty-one when I first got married. Divorced a year later."

His divorce record left her silent for a while. “Does that make this your second divorce?”

“Marriage must not be for me.”

“I can see how two divorces would make you cynical.”

Bitter. Resentful. Giving up on love. Yeah. Her apparent understanding threw him off, though. “You’ve been divorced?”

“No. Everyone chooses the one they marry. And in some cases, we have to choose more than once.”

In other words, he chose badly. It wasn’t far off what he thought himself. “Thanks.”

“I don’t mean it as an insult. I don’t believe in mistakes, that’s all.”

Divorces weren’t the result of mistaken choices. Interesting take. Simple. And guilt free. He liked it.

“You married young and it didn’t work out. It wasn’t meant to. Your second marriage ended, but you have a son. Where’s the mistake in that?”

For someone who didn’t like kids, she sure had a soft spot for them. He fought the warmth swelling in him. “Is that how you feel about your fiancé’s death?”

She turned away, sipping her beer.

She didn’t believe in mistakes, yet she avoided men who reminded her of her fiancé as though she meant to prevent one.

“He never should have been killed,” she finally said.

Nobody should have to die like that. True. “But it must not have been meant to be.”

Her head whipped toward him.

“You marrying him, I mean.”

“I would have if he hadn’t been killed.”

He said nothing, just let her fill in her own blanks. It was her philosophy. There was no such thing as mistakes.

Everything happened for a reason. Change happened for a reason.

Seeing how much she resisted what he'd forced her to think about, he decided he regretted making her feel that way.

"Come on, let's get out of here." He flagged over the bartender and ordered two waters and charged their drinks to his room.

He needed a distraction. Anything to stop imagining Tatum being held against her will. If she were still alive. He couldn't even bring himself to go there. She had to be alive. She just had to be.

All he had to do was get by until morning. What better way to do that than get a taste of the adventurer in Arizona?

Braden wouldn't tell her where he was taking her, but Arizona suspected he was only doing this to pass time. They couldn't talk to the police until morning. She needed this, too. Searching for Tatum brought back a lot of painful feelings. If they failed and Tatum wound up dead, she'd relive the agony of losing Trevor all over again. Success was a necessary ingredient each time she had an opportunity to help someone in need.

She walked with Braden toward the beach. When they reached it, she removed her sandals. A small group of people gathered near a building, lights from two posts shining on them. Down at the dock, a boat was ready to motor out to sea. Night diving.

She smiled big. "I haven't done this in years."

Braden went to the building where three people were being fitted with gear.

"How did you know there was a trip tonight?"

"I called when I got to the hotel. I thought it would take my mind off Tatum."

Just as she'd thought. But instead he'd opted for a drink. "It's more fun with a partner."

Now he was the one who smiled. A sexy grin that gave her an unvarnished glimpse of his thirst for adventure. She loved it because she could so relate.

He spoke to the man in charge, who nodded and set them up along with the others. She and Braden needed all of the gear. Dressed in a warm-water wetsuit, she boarded the boat after Braden and put on her gear. Now she understood why he'd asked the bartender for water. They'd each only had one drink but hydration was important when scuba diving.

Sitting next to him on a stern bench seat, she watched the three other passengers, a trio of men in their late thirties talking excitedly and paying them no attention. Two crewmen manned the dive.

"When did you learn to night dive?" Braden asked.

"I started by going to my parents' house in California. I swam in their indoor pool with the lights out. How did you learn?"

"In the ocean. Now it's one of my favorite things to do." He tipped his handsome face up to the moonlit sky. "It's pretty dark now." He looked back at her. "But if you dive at sunset you can see creatures getting ready for the night, some settling in, some preparing to feed. Sunrise is even better."

She fell into the images he created. "Seeing everything wake up. The sunlight brightening the water." She sighed. "Yes, it's beautiful."

She looked over at him and met his eyes, as lost as hers in the wonder. And then the wonder changed to something else. A connection, deeper than the physical chemistry they

shared the first moment she saw him. A real connection. And then that fizzled when the reason they'd come here came back to her.

She shouldn't be enjoying this so much. While Tatum either suffered or was already dead, they were living it up on an excursion. A glance at Braden made her think he felt the same.

But there was nothing they could do until morning. They needed to talk to the police first.

The boat slowed. One of the crewmen dropped anchor, and the other began instructing them on how to proceed with the dive. When it was their turn, Arizona dropped off before Braden. She turned on her headlamp and swam down, taking note of the anchor line to make the return easier. He caught up to her and they descended together, slowly. A crewman swam ahead of the group. Light from every diver's lamp helped with navigation. Light from the moon illuminated the surface just enough.

The sea bottom came into view. Colorful fish scattered and regathered. The reef inhabitants swayed with the ocean current. Lobsters crawled along the bottom. Waving her hand, she saw phosphorescent plankton lighting up the darkness.

Arizona looked at Braden and wondered if he could see her smiling. His eyes creased as though he were, too.

Kicking her feet, she navigated along the reef, checking out the flourishing life. There were signs stuck into the ocean floor that said Do Not Touch!

She wished she had a camera.

Feeling Braden take hold of her ankles, she stopped kicking while he swam up her body and pointed.

Looking ahead, she saw a big, long shark swim by, barely visible in the sphere of light. Ghostlike. Exotic. Her heart beat faster with a flash of apprehension. But

the shark passed the group of divers, probably having already fed at sunset.

Arizona rolled to swim on her back, facing Braden to convey her excitement. With his hands on her hips, eyes smiling, no words were necessary, especially when his gaze lowered to the way the straps of her vest plumped her breasts. She breathed deeper through her mouthpiece.

His green eyes glowed in their headlamps, excitement flaring to passion. She didn't mistake that. He felt it, too.

Then a crewman poked him on the arm, jarring them both back to attention. He jabbed his thumb upward. Time to surface.

Braden released her, and she surfaced with him, finding the anchor line in the moonlit sea. When her head broke into the night air, Braden surfaced in front of her. He removed his mouth pieces and then moved his mask down and slid it around to the back of his neck. Why he'd done that gleamed in his eyes. He was impassioned enough to kiss her. She hoped he did. Removing her mask, she slid it to the back of her neck as he had done. Braden's eyes smoldered hotter.

The others surfaced on the other side of the boat, talking excitedly about the shark. Their reason for coming to this island dropped away.

Braden reached up to hold on to a ladder. His intensity hadn't abated since touching her underwater. Hers hadn't, either.

Angling his head, he kissed her. Wet mouths melded. The way his strong arm held her, the way his other held them both above water, heated her already swirling senses. The exhilaration of the dive only added to her desire, spontaneity and a dash of danger with a man who had fallen under the same spell.

Wrapping her arms around his shoulders, she gave everything she had into the kiss.

"All right, you two, it's time to head to shore," one of the crewmen said. A chorus of chuckles passed across the boat.

Braden lifted his head, green eyes shadowed and hungry. She shook herself back to the present and turned. He pushed her rear as she climbed into the boat, making her laugh.

Sitting on the bench seat, watching them approach the shore, her levity faded as the weight of what had just happened came down on her. He was recently divorced. He had a *child.* And he was an engineer, even though she couldn't think of him that way anymore. She couldn't remember if it had ever felt this way with a man before. This quickly. It had never felt scary, that was for sure. She'd always cut it off before it got to that point. This felt scary.

Sneaking a glimpse over at him, she saw him staring off to his right, not smiling. Tense. Regretting, like her.

"It was just the dive," she said. It had served its purpose. It had taken their minds off Tatum and passed time.

But a little too well. They were here to find his sister, not have a steamy affair. His sister needed them. There was no time for anything else.

Chapter 3

Braden walked slightly behind Arizona, unable to stop looking at the seesawing sway of her butt as she moved. Those khaki shorts didn't help. They conformed to her shape, sloping up over slender hips to give way to a floral cotton tank that followed her curves to her plump, round breasts. Last night had been as unexpected as it had been memorable. He still couldn't get his mind past the enchantment.

It was just the dive.

She'd said it as an excuse. Like what she really felt was that it was a lot more. He was afraid he felt the same.

Braden reached the police station doors and opened one, standing aside as Arizona entered. Kissing her had been a big mistake.

Arizona didn't believe in mistakes.

Not what he intended, then. Diving had served to take his mind off his worry over his sister, but now every min-

ute couldn't be wasted. Once they talked to the police, he'd take the investigation into his own hands. He couldn't afford the distraction of sexual attraction to interfere.

Inside, Arizona asked to speak to someone about Tatum McCrae.

The dark-skinned woman in a black uniform appeared confused. "Who?"

Braden stepped forward. "We're here from the United States to find a missing person. Tatum McCrae." He pulled out a picture of her. "Her last known whereabouts were in Frenchman's Cay."

The woman looked at the picture and then back at Braden. "Sorry. Never seen her before."

"May we speak with Monty Crawford?" That was the officer his parents had spoken with.

"Have a seat." The woman went to find the man. It was a small police station.

Braden watched her cross the open room of four desks and stop before a tall, thin man with a big nose and a severely receding hairline standing just outside an office beside another, heavier man with a less dramatic hairline. The woman spoke to the big-nosed man, whose gaze shifted over her shoulder toward the front of the building. He responded with something and then turned to the heavier man, who nodded once and left to go sit at one of the desks in the open area while the woman retraced her steps back toward the front desk.

"You can go on back," she said.

Braden led Arizona through a swinging half door and approached the officer, the sound of fingers tapping on keyboards accompanying them.

The officer wore a grim face as he waited in front of an office.

Braden stopped before him. "Officer Crawford?"

The man nodded, extending his hand. "You're Tatum McCrae's brother?"

"Yes." He introduced himself and Arizona, who stood beside him. "I was told you were the one looking into my sister's disappearance. "

Crawford nodded a few times, still grim. "I've spoken with your parents. Anytime a tourist goes missing, we take it very seriously."

"Have you received any more leads?" No matter how small.

"I'm afraid not. She was seen getting into a taxi. That's the best we've got so far."

Which wasn't much.

"Are you sure she didn't mention anyone she might be meeting down here?" Crawford asked.

Braden shook his head.

"Do you think she might have met someone?" Arizona asked.

"She got into the taxi willingly. That suggests she at least went somewhere on her own. What happened after that is a mystery. The driver was killed, and none of the others we spoke with could tell us anything. There wasn't even a record of him picking her up."

"What do you know about his murder?"

"He was shot late that night. Hours after your sister was seen getting into his cab, and nowhere near Frenchman's Cay."

"Any leads on his killer? Any witnesses?"

Crawford shook his head. "None that help. He stopped at a coffee shop about an hour before that, but didn't say anything to connect his murder to your sister's disappearance."

This was discouraging. "How do you know he was the driver?"

"We've questioned all the others."

"Are you sure you didn't miss any?"

"As sure as I can be. We're still looking into it for that very reason."

He appeared to be doing everything he could.

"Are you sure she didn't meet someone she knew and doesn't want to be found?" Crawford asked.

"She would have called our mother," Braden insisted. "She knows she would worry."

The detective nodded again in that same somber way.

Braden pulled out a card and handed it to Crawford. "Will you call me if anything changes?"

Crawford took the card. "Of course." He pulled out his wallet and removed his own card. "I can understand why you traveled all this way, but I should caution you that this may take some time."

Braden put the detective's card in his back pocket. "All I want is my sister back."

"We'll find her."

Dead? Or alive?

Riding in the back of a taxi with Braden to Frenchman's Cay, Arizona ignored her building attraction to him. The urgency of finding Tatum superseded everything else. Entering into a relationship with him made her shudder as much as the idea of having kids did. She would concentrate on the task at hand instead.

Located on a twelve-acre peninsula a short drive from Road Town and connected to Tortola by a bridge, Frenchman's Cay was a sleepy island community. Restaurants and shops in Soper's Hole were colorful and well maintained. Bougainvillea, poinsettias and hibiscus abounded. White sandy beaches beckoned. And a lucky few called the for-

ested foothills home. On Frenchman's Point, Braden drove to a stop at the Island Hotel.

Arizona stepped up to the white-painted porch. It wasn't a large hotel. Twenty rooms, maybe. Inside, the lobby opened to wide expanses of light-colored tile. Custom art hung on the walls.

They approached the stone registration desk.

A young girl looked up from a book. Braden asked to speak with the general manager. The clerk went into an office behind the counter and emerged with a dark-skinned man with cropped white hair.

"What can I do for you?" he asked.

Braden showed him a picture of Tatum. "We're looking for this woman."

"Oh, yeah. Police came asking about her. Pretty lady. That's why I remembered her."

"Did she check in?"

"No."

The clerk's gaze shot from Braden to the manager.

Why would she get a taxi here if she hadn't checked in? Did the clerk find that odd, too?

"Are you sure all you saw was her getting into a taxi?"

The manager nodded once. "I was inside. Standing right here."

Arizona looked behind her. The doors and windows offered a fairly clear view of the covered passenger drop-off and valet parking area.

"Did anyone else see her?" Braden asked.

"No. Just me."

When Arizona faced forward again, she saw the girl quickly avert her head away from the manager and then her gaze flitted off Arizona and Braden.

"Did she talk to anyone before she got into the cab?"

Braden continued with his questioning, not appearing to notice the girl's jitteriness.

"Sorry, I saw what I saw. I wish I could help more. Missing." He shook his head regretfully. "Hope she's all right."

Braden took some time before giving up. "Thanks."

"Good luck finding your sister." The manager turned and went into the office, shutting the door behind him.

The girl behind the counter kept stealing glances at both her and Braden. Acting on her hunch, Arizona took the picture from Braden's lowered hand and went to the counter. Showing the picture, she asked, "Do you recognize this woman?"

The clerk's eyes darted toward the office and back, wariness holding her silent.

"Please," Arizona coaxed. "We just need to know where she went."

Still, the girl remained silent.

"If this woman is in trouble, you could help her." Arizona moved the photo closer.

The girl studied it for a while and then glanced fearfully at the office door again. When she faced forward, she leaned closer and said in a low voice, "I was coming in to work when she was getting into the taxi. I heard her tell the driver to take her to Julian Blake's house. She gave the driver the address, but everybody knows who lives there." She gave them a conspiratorial look. "Richest man on the island."

Everyone knew the man? He had a reputation. A rich reputation.

"Why didn't you go to the police?" Braden asked.

"I didn't know she was missing until right now. I took a few days off after that day. The police never questioned me."

"Did you know your manager was questioned?"

The girl shook her head.

Arizona shared a look with Braden, finding that piece of information suspicious.

"Can you tell us where Julian Blake lives?" Braden asked.

"On the other side of the island. Big house. You can't miss it." She told them how to get there.

After thanking the girl, Arizona turned with Braden.

"I wouldn't go there if I were you."

Stopping short at the sound of the girl's whisper, an urgent warning, she turned with Braden.

"Mr. Blake doesn't like uninvited visitors," the girl continued.

"Why doesn't he like visitors?" Braden asked.

"*Uninvited* visitors. Guess he prefers his privacy." She glanced at the office door again.

Why did he need privacy? So he could hide what he was doing? Arizona rubbed her arms, sensing danger rising. How far would Julian go to preserve his privacy? The last place Tatum was known to be is his house. Was he hiding something sinister?

"What does he do if someone comes to see him anyway?" Arizona asked.

"Escorts them off his property. That's what I hear anyway. Rich people live in their own world."

The way the girl said *escorts* gave Arizona an image of being forced away at gunpoint. "Thank you. You've been a tremendous help."

The girl glanced at the office door again. Why was she so nervous? Didn't she want her manager to know what she'd heard on her way into work? And if not, why? Were they both afraid of Julian Blake?

Arizona walked with Braden out of the hotel. "This is really getting weird."

"We have to go to Julian's house."

"Should we talk to the manager again?"

"Not yet. He probably won't tell us any more than he has, and I don't want to cause trouble for that clerk."

She agreed. Not yet.

Wondering about the escort they'd receive, she didn't let it sway her. "What are we waiting for, then?" They'd never get anywhere doing nothing.

Arizona hurried with Braden to a waiting taxi. The driver gave them a funny look when Braden told them to take them to Julian Blake. The man knew how to get there. Another oddity. Or not. This was a small island. Everyone knew everyone.

Pulling out Crawford's card, Braden pressed in the number. Shortly thereafter he explained what the clerk had told them, particularly about the hotel manager.

"He said he'd check into it," he told Arizona.

The taxi driver turned onto a narrow dirt road. A sign read Keep Out. Another read Private Property. Arizona shared a long look with Braden. Dare they meet Julian Blake on their own?

"We're just going to talk to him," Braden said. "What could possibly go wrong?"

The taxi bumped over the uneven road. If this was a driveway, it was long. At last, they passed an open, elaborate iron gate. If Julian didn't welcome visitors, would he leave the gate open? Seeing cameras moving on each side of the gate, she understood why it didn't necessarily have to be closed all the time. The security was tight here.

The thick forest of trees opened in a clearing and a stone villa came into view. It was breathtaking. A main section with large windows jutted forward in front. Windows lined two levels on the back portion. Above the entry,

a balcony had tables and chairs. The drapes were closed in whatever room it was.

The taxi stopped in a circular driveway, just in front of wide stone stairs leading to a courtyard entrance.

"Wait for us," Braden said.

One of the double front doors opened and three men emerged. The man in front exuded an aura of power. Average in height, thick brown hair, eyes covered by sunglasses, he wore white pants and a white vest over a long-sleeved pink dress shirt. Showy.

He stepped down the stairs, the two other men following.

Arizona stopped on the flagstone driveway, Braden beside her.

"Mr. Blake?" Braden began.

"What business do you have coming to my home?" he asked in an East Coast accent. He wasn't from here. He was American and must have moved here at some point.

"We apologize for arriving unannounced," Braden said. "But we have a rather urgent matter we'd like to discuss with you." When Julian didn't respond, he explained who they were and why they were here.

"Tatum McCrae, you say?" the man repeated, making a show of ignorance. He shook his head. "I haven't heard of her."

He was lying. He had to be.

"We know she came to see you before she disappeared. How do you know her?" Braden demanded. "Where is she now?"

"I don't know your sister. I don't know anyone named Tatum McCrae. Why have you come here?"

Braden stepped forward with his picture. The two men behind Julian moved in front of him. Braden stopped, extending the picture.

The two men didn't move to take it. And Julian put his hands on each of his henchmen's shoulders, who stepped aside to make room for him. Julian stepped, closer to Braden and Arizona. Removing his sunglasses and holding them in his hand, his dark, fathomless gaze drifted down and up Arizona, and then shifted to meet Braden's indomitable eyes.

But Julian wasn't affected. "You came here for nothing."

Braden continued to stare at the man.

"And unless I tell you it's all right to come to my home, I suggest you stay away. Next time I won't wait to ask questions."

"Where is my sister?" Braden asked again.

"This is the last warning you'll get. Leave now. Never come back."

Another stare down commenced, Julian mocking, Braden calculating.

"Let's go." Arizona had a bad feeling about this.

After a few tugs on his arm, Braden went with her back to the cab, looking back at the villa until it vanished from sight. Dust billowed up from the dirt road. Flowering evergreen trees and a variety of others, perhaps white cedar and mango, gave the illusion of paradise.

When they reached the gate, two Jeeps waited just inside, angled toward the road. Four men stood outside of the vehicles, all of them armed. They each held some sort of automatic weapon, the barrels long and pointed to the ground at the moment. Around their waists, pistols hung.

Fear shot into Arizona as the driver began to slow.

"Don't stop," Braden said.

Arizona could hear the driver breathing and his eyes were round, the green of them stark against his dark skin and the whites of his eyes.

"They must want us to drive through the gate," she said, trying to calm him.

He drove past. The men outside the Jeeps moved as they did, facing their departure. But then they all climbed inside the Jeeps.

The taxicab driver's eyes remained wide as he looked into the rearview mirror.

"Drive faster," Braden said from the backseat.

The driver complied, as eager as them to get away. The dust cloud behind them rose higher.

The cab fishtailed around a turn and raced up a hill. On the other side was Soper's Hole. Cresting the hill, it came into view.

The Jeeps stopped at the top of the hill. Arizona waited for gunfire. None came. She waited for them to chase them again. They didn't.

"They're not following." Why weren't they?

The driver slowed as they reached town. Then he pulled into a gas station and parked.

"Get out," he said.

Braden tried to pay him but he waved his hand. "Get out. You walk from here."

She and Braden did as the driver asked. When the taxi drove away, she said, "Gave him a pretty good scare."

"Julian Blake gave him the scare." He turned to her, each thinking the same thing. Why? Why was Julian Blake someone to fear on this island?

He started walking toward the center of Soper's Hole. She jogged to catch up to him and then walked beside him on the sidewalk. Five minutes later they reached the busy town center. It was clean and beautiful. The street wasn't in very good condition, but cars parked along the side and the sidewalk was dotted with black streetlamps. Big flowerpots were placed between, and multicolored, wooden

benches offered seating along storefronts. People entered into and emerged from shops, walked along the street, talking, smiling, peering into store windows.

Then those that weren't tourists began to take notice of them. At first Arizona thought she was mistaken. Why would they single them out? A man leaning against the enclave of the entrance to a gift shop puffed a cigarette as they passed, his dark eyes following them eerily. Two women sitting at one of two tables on the patio of a café spoke quietly together between glances at them.

A dark blue Cadillac slowed on the street, rolling beside them on the other side of parked cars. The window moved down. Crawford was driving. Why was he here?

"Everything all right?" he asked.

When she and Braden stopped walking, he stopped the car.

"We were just chased off Blake's property," Braden said.

Crawford looked from him to Arizona as though digesting that announcement. "Why don't you both get in the car?"

Braden touched his hand to Arizona's back and opened the back door for her. She climbed in and he got into the front passenger's seat.

Crawford began to drive. "I can appreciate your concern for your sister, Mr. McCrae, but I'm going to have to ask that you leave the investigation to me."

"His goons had guns," Braden retorted.

"The more stormy weather you stir up, the harder it will be for me to do my job."

Braden didn't argue.

"I understand you feel helpless and you need to do something. Time is of the essence. But I assure you, I'm doing everything I can to find Tatum. Tortola is a quiet

community. A safe community. I intend to do my part to keep it that way."

"Are you going to talk to the hotel manager?" Braden asked.

"I just left there. And he explained what I suspected. Most around here like to leave Julian Blake alone. They prefer not to have any contact with the man."

"Why is that?" Arizona asked. "Don't you think that's strange?"

"No one will ever say Julian is a friendly fellow. But that doesn't make him a criminal. He prefers seclusion. Many come to islands like this for that reason."

"But he has armed guards," Arizona argued.

"I have seen no evidence of that. He is good at concealing his activities."

Hearing the detective's frustration, Arizona sighed. "You have to agree that it's strange."

"Oh, I do agree. There's just not much I can do about it right now." Crawford checked the rearview mirror. "Where am I taking you two?"

Braden told him the name of their hotel just as Arizona's cell phone rang. She dug into her purse and retrieved it. Lincoln.

"Lincoln?"

"Hey, Arizona. How are you?"

"Fine, you?"

"Doped up on pain medication, enduring Mom's care at home and working. And I just found something big."

"What? You're supposed to be resting."

"I rest. When I'm awake, I work. You want to hear this or not?"

"What have you got?" Her words made Braden twist in his seat to see her and Crawford glance in his rearview mirror.

"A news report of a missing woman in Tortola. Three months ago. The article said she checked in at the Frenchman's Point Hotel and was never seen again. She has a sister in Oregon. I gave her a call and she had something very interesting to say."

"What was that?"

"The missing woman was having an affair with a man who lives in Tortola. His name is Julian Blake."

Sucking in her breath, she met Braden's eyes, which hardened at her reaction. "We were just chased away by the very same man. Tatum went to see him before she disappeared."

Lincoln cursed.

Had Braden's sister had an affair with him? Both women had disappeared.

Crawford kept looking in his mirror.

"Can we talk to her?" Arizona asked her brother.

"She'll come to you. She's on her way to Tortola now. I gave her your hotel information."

The woman had been looking for her sister just as Braden now was.

"Thanks, Lincoln."

"Glad to help any way I can. Vengeance for my knee."

She ended the call and stared at Braden.

"What?"

She glanced at Crawford. "There was another woman who disappeared three months ago. She was having an affair with Julian." She allowed Braden some time to process that. "She has a sister in Oregon."

"I'm familiar with that case," Crawford said. "If Julian is behind both disappearances, he's covering his tracks well. He checked out when I questioned him."

"Tatum would have told me if she was seeing someone," Braden said.

"Would she have? Julian doesn't seem like a typical boyfriend." Far from it. And Arizona wondered why Crawford hadn't told them about the other missing woman.

Chapter 4

Braden sat with Arizona inside the busy hotel restaurant. The first missing woman's sister had called Arizona's cell number when she'd landed and asked to meet them here. Braden didn't want to put the woman in danger, but he was curious to see if one of the hotel staff would say or do something. The manager, perhaps.

A short, plump woman in her early thirties appeared, her peppered dark hair cut above her ears.

"That looks like the woman in the picture Lincoln sent."

"That's her." Braden lifted his hand.

Charlene Andrews nervously approached. "Mr. McCrae?"

Braden stood and shook her hand. "Thank you for coming all this way."

"I've been looking for Courtney for weeks. I'm glad to help in any way."

"This is Arizona Ivy."

"Yes. Ivy." The woman took her hand in polite greeting and then sat. She made no show over her obvious recognition of the name.

Putting her purse on the floor, she changed her mind and hung it over the back of the chair. She removed the light sweater she wore, letting it drape over the handbag. Sliding the roll of silverware over, she curled her hand around the glass of water on the table. Nervous.

Braden reached over and put his hand over her wrist. "We're very sorry about your sister."

"I can't believe she's still missing." Tears glistened in her eyes.

"Mine is missing, too," Braden said. "We'll find them both."

"Oh." The woman covered her mouth with her hand, stopping herself from crying. When she regained her composure she straightened with a few blinks of her eyes. "The kind gentleman who called me explained about Tatum. I'm sorry, as well, Mr. McCrae."

"Can you tell us what happened to your sister?" Arizona asked.

"She told me that she went on a trip to Tortola to see a man. She met him online. Which I always thought was strange. Courtney isn't the type to do that sort of thing. But she'd been complaining that she wasn't going on many dates and she was ready for a relationship. The fact that she found someone long distance bothered me. But she claimed to like this man very much."

"That's when she went missing," Arizona helped her.

"Yes," Charlene replied with a quiver in her voice.

"Can you tell us anything about him?" Braden asked.

"His name was Julian Blake. My sister said he was a retired high-risk insurance underwriter. She never said anything bad about him. He must have fooled her well."

"Can we have copies of their email correspondence?" Arizona asked.

"Her computer was stolen shortly after she disappeared. The police haven't been able to find anything. My sweet sister." She wiped her eyes. "Our mother died a few years ago and she's all I have left."

"Was anything found in her house? Any evidence at all?"

Charlene shook her head. "She was living with me. Nothing else was out of place. Only her computer was taken from the guest room." She looked from Arizona to him. "She just lost her job and was looking forward to going to the Caribbean. She even thought she might move there. To be with *him*." Her face soured with the injustice. "That evil man. I don't know what he did to my sister. That's the worst part. Not knowing. Is she alive? Is she dead? It's torture not knowing. I want to believe she is alive, but too much time has passed. She'd have called by now. If she could call, she would." Then she looked imploringly at Braden. "Have you learned anything? Did Julian kidnap your sister?"

"She was seen getting into a taxi that took her to his house. It appears she was willing."

"At first. That monster is up to something. He lured my sister, and now he's lured yours." She breathed through her anxiety. "Lord only knows what he's done with them."

Braden saw Arizona slump with empathy. "We'll do everything we can to expose him."

She definitely was a crusader for victims. She may be offering a false promise. Julian was evil, all right. But he was also dangerous.

Arizona watched Charlene leave the restaurant. She wasn't staying here. She had a room in Road Town and

was flying out in the morning. She passed the hotel manager. Only then did Arizona notice him. He'd been watching them.

She glanced at Braden and saw he'd noticed, too.

He stood and she stood with him, trailing him out of the restaurant. The manager saw them, his face going deliberately blank, faked nonchalance and then he strode toward the reception desk. The clerk wasn't there.

"Do you think he's working for Julian?" she asked Braden when they emerged outside.

Charlene had gotten into an unmarked cab.

"I don't know. Let's not take any chances." He flagged a taxi, this one marked.

"Follow that car," he told the driver when they climbed into the backseat.

"This isn't the way to her hotel," Arizona said as they passed the turn.

In the backseat of the car ahead, Charlene began talking to the driver. She then tried the door handle, or searched for one, her hands going over the doorframe and lower. She twisted in the backseat, looking through the rearview mirror with stark eyes and an open mouth to accommodate for what must be frightened breaths.

"What's he doing?" Arizona whispered, eyeing their own driver. He didn't appear to notice anything unusual, or if he had, he kept it to himself.

The car ahead approached Julian's driveway and turned.

Their driver didn't slow.

"Turn!" Arizona shouted.

The driver glanced back at her. "This is Julian Blake's home. We do not go there."

"Turn, damn it!" Braden shouted.

Flustered, the man turned onto Julian's driveway. "We are not to go to this home. I take you to gate and that is all."

"Fine." Why was everyone so afraid of Julian?

Maybe that was a stupid question. Tatum had disappeared and the last time anyone saw her, she was on her way to see him.

"Look."

She followed Braden's point. At Julian's gate, several men stood. One of them was Julian Blake. The unmarked taxi had stopped just before the gate.

Julian noticed the second car approach and didn't seem surprised. In fact, he seemed to have expected this, for Arizona and Braden to follow.

The driver stopped the taxi behind the unmarked one containing Charlene.

None of the men at the gate were armed, or so it appeared. They wore stylish dark suits, contrasting with Julian's pristine white. The man had a thing for white. Did he enjoy how it made him seem pure? A cloak to his inner darkness.

One of the men moved forward to open the rear door of the other car and reached inside. He dragged a struggling Charlene from the backseat.

Arizona climbed out of the cab with Braden. And stood beside him, watching Charlene being manhandled while Julian moved closer.

"What do you think you're doing?" Charlene shrieked at Julian. "What have you done with my sister?"

"Let her go," Braden said.

With a wicked grin, Julian took hold of Charlene and shoved. Braden caught her.

"You're an animal!" Charlene choked out as she regained her balance and stood beside Braden.

Julian kept his gaze on Braden. "Maybe I didn't make myself clear before. I don't like trespassers."

"You forced me here!" Charlene retorted.

"According to whom?" He glanced behind him.

The driver of the unmarked car had gotten out and was now leaning against the closed driver's door, taking cash from one of Julian's henchmen.

Julian leaned to look through the windshield of the taxi she and Braden had ridden in. That driver put up his hands and said through his open window.

"I want no trouble."

In other words, he'd lie if he had to. He'd lie to protect himself and his family. Everyone feared Julian that much. It was appalling.

"We just want our sisters," Charlene said. She'd likely done this before, pleaded with Julian for her sister.

"I don't have your sister. How many times do I have to say it?"

"Liar!" Charlene yelled. "What have you done with her?"

Julian moved his look back to Braden. "Leave this island, or next time I won't be this generous. Next time—" he stepped closer "—I won't let her go."

While Arizona's stomach churned in disgust, Charlene slapped him. Two of the suited men reached into the folds of their jackets and stepped forward.

Julian raised his hand and they stopped, just like in one of her father's movies. Except this was real.

Seeing Braden's fists clenched at his sides, Arizona decided it was time to go. She slid her arm on the inside of his.

"Let's go."

"The voice of reason," Julian taunted.

"We'll be back," Braden said, unafraid. "If you have Tatum and Courtney, I'll find out."

"You won't find her here. If you were smart, you'd look closer to home."

What did he mean by that? The man in the white BMW flashed in Arizona's mind. Did Julian know him? Was Tatum being held somewhere in the States? Were they wasting their time looking here? That couldn't be. Why drag Tatum all the way back to the States?

Julian walked to the driver's window of their taxi and leaned down. "Take them to the airport. If they don't leave, let me know."

"Yes, sir," the driver answered as though he worked for the man.

"We'll be sure and tell the police all about this," Arizona said. Did he think he could get away with anything?

"Go right ahead," he said with confidence. "I will simply tell them you were trespassing." He spread his arms to indicate the people around him. "I have witnesses."

This was ridiculous. The taxi driver would lie for him? Lie to police?

"If you value those close to you, you will not return." To the taxi driver, he repeated, "Make sure they leave the island. If I don't hear from you, I will send someone to your home."

"I'll take them to the airport. You have my word."

"Very good." Julian clapped his hands together, moving back to where he had stood in front of them. "Then we have no issue. We all can go on with our lives and you will leave me to my privacy."

If it weren't for Charlene and the taxi driver, Arizona would refuse to go. She and Braden could stay and continue their search, but innocent lives were at stake.

She looked beyond the gate, wishing they could get inside the villa. There had to be a way.

"Let's go," she said to Braden and Charlene.

She urged Braden back to the taxi. They had Charlene, which was enough for now.

"Have a safe trip home," Julian called, accentuating the word *safe.*

If they stayed, they'd no longer be safe.

Inside the taxi, Charlene sat in the back with Braden, who stewed with anger. He'd kept quiet, but she could feel him brimming on the edge of control.

What Arizona didn't understand about all of this was that if Julian wanted something from Braden, why hadn't he asked for it when he'd had Charlene? Wouldn't he have used Arizona for the same purpose? Unless Julian wasn't linked to the arms deal.

Then why had Tatum gone to see him?

Braden's cell phone rang and he answered, displeasure changing his frown.

"Serena."

Who was Serena? His ex, judging from that look.

"I told you I was going to be out of town for a while." He sighed after a few beats. Arizona could hear the elevated tone of a woman's voice coming from his phone.

"Can't your parents watch him?"

This was about his son. More high-pitched arguing resounded from the phone.

"All right. All right," he cut the voice off. "We'll be there tomorrow night." And then he said as though in answer to her question, "Me and…a friend. But it can only be for one night, Serena. I can't risk any more than that."

Risk? He was afraid of exposing his son to this. Arizona couldn't blame him. If whoever had followed him would try to take Arizona, they'd certainly try to do the same if they knew he had a son.

Chapter 5

It was dinnertime when Arizona and Braden arrived at his house, a single story with one big window beside the garage and two smaller windows to the right. The house was steel blue with white trim; the yard was simple but healthy. A curving front bed contained leafy shrubs and river rock. A mature tree shaded the green grass. There was another car there, a woman standing in the driveway with her arms folded. In a black dress, her blond hair was up in a spiky bun and her red lipstick completed the image. A boy appeared, flying a toy helicopter over the hood of the Mercedes. The woman admonished him and he stilled for two seconds before resuming his play.

Great. Just what she needed. A night with a kid. They'd planned to meet with Lincoln tomorrow to talk strategy. Braden had told him what happened with Charlene and he wasn't keen on allowing Arizona to leave the country again. She was going with or without either his or

Braden's consent. Lincoln must have picked up on that in the course of his conversation with Braden. He hadn't fought her much on the matter. But that was after Braden had assured him.

I'm capable of protecting her, he'd said. And after watching him fight the BMW man, neither she nor Lincoln could doubt it. The engineer could fight. Call her crazy, but the trait didn't fit. Why had he learned to fight so well? Hobby? She'd think he'd rather fiddle with hardware than learn how to become a human weapon. It only made her that much more curious about him. And a little more leery of the feelings that were stirring inside her.

Braden parked on the street, the silver Mercedes sedan taking up too much space in the two-car driveway. The flat line of his mouth and stormy brow revealed his displeasure in seeing the woman. His ex-wife. She was a striking woman. Very beautiful. Tall and curvy, but thin.

"Daddy!" The little boy dropped his helicopter and ran full speed for Braden.

He crouched on the sidewalk to receive the boy, hugging him and lifting as he walked up the driveway.

"I wanna go to the zoo tomorrow."

Braden let the boy down. "That'll have to wait, Aiden."

"Aw. Why?"

The woman eyed Arizona as she came to a stop beside the two. Her gaze traveled down her jean shorts to her sparkly silver sandals, and then back up over her white-and-gray sequined tank top and matching hat.

Finally, she turned coldly to Braden. "You're late."

"I can only have him for the night."

"What? I have plans for the weekend!"

"Any other time, I'd change my plans. But I can't this time."

The woman scoffed, putting her hand on her hip. "Take

him with you, then. I have plans, too. This can't always be about you."

"When was it ever about me?" he challenged. "My sister is missing."

She lowered her hand and her snide expression smoothed. "What?"

He told her what happened in clipped, brief sentences. "I have to try and find her."

"Can't the police do that? Since when do you go off on your own to handle that sort of thing?" She eyed him with new interest.

"Are his things in the car?" Braden ignored her questions and opened the back door of the Mercedes. Leaning down, he lifted a small leather bag.

Facing her, he said, "We'll drop him off in the morning."

The woman slowly glanced at Arizona, unfriendliness gleaming in pretty blue eyes that were darker than hers.

"Why don't I just take him home now, then? You obviously don't have time. And your sister..."

Yes, take him with you, Arizona thought. Now was not the time to entertain a six-year-old. Besides, the idea of spending the evening with a bundle of irrational energy made her stiff.

"I'll keep him for the night. I haven't seen him in two weeks. I'll take one night."

"I wish you would have been that eager for me when we were married." She passed another haughty glance at Arizona. "Is your friend staying? Isn't it inappropriate to bring girls around Aiden? He's only six."

"Arizona, this is Serena. Serena, Arizona Ivy."

Serena went still and stared at Arizona. "Ivy?"

Arizona could have strangled Braden. Did he have to

say her last name? She grew so tired of being recognized all the time.

"Jackson Ivy's daughter?"

"That's me. Jackson Ivy's daughter." She hated being identified through her father. He had little to do with who she really was, other than being her father. Her annoyance came out in her tone and she didn't care.

Serena looked from Braden to her. "How do you know Braden?" She asked as though she thought it was impossible. Another enlightenment that she hadn't expected.

"He and my brother are friends."

"You never told me that."

"Would it have made a difference?"

Catching his meaning, Serena lowered her gaze and then shifted it to Arizona. "It must be fabulous being part of such a famous family. What are you doing with Braden? Surely there's a movie star or two who'd die to have you."

Braden started for the front door. "I'll drop Aiden off at nine."

Aiden grabbed his helicopter and bolted for the door.

Arizona followed, looking back at Serena and seeing her hesitation. Or was it regret? Braden was friends with the son of a famous movie producer. Would that have been enough to keep her happy when they were married? Or had seeing Braden with Jackson Ivy's daughter made her realize that Braden was more desirable than she'd originally thought?

Inside, Aiden yelled and ran around the living room with his helicopter, making gunfire sounds. He zigzagged Arizona's way, raising and lowering the helicopter.

"You're a mountain," he cried exuberantly, flying the bird right in front of her face.

Arizona flinched backward, her entire body stiff. Did the boy even know how annoying that was?

He began making gunfire noises. *"Psh-psh-psh-psh..."*

The helicopter flew past the mountain again, this time crashing into it. Arizona grabbed the helicopter after it poked her arm and made the sound of an explosion as she tossed the toy over his head and onto one of two white-leather sofas.

Braden watched her with amusement she didn't get. Wasn't he going to tell his son to stop invading her space?

Aiden looked up at her, going still. An instant later, he ran over to the helicopter and bent over, shaking his butt at her right before a fart broke free. Then he busted into laughter.

"Pth, pth, pth," he imitated the sound of his fart, laughing some more, looking back at her as though expecting her to find it just as funny.

Alien.

What was wrong with children?

"Take your bag upstairs, Aiden."

Aiden grabbed his helicopter and then his bag, farting twice more on the way up the stairs, laughing and looking back at her again. The stairway was open and led to a landing above the kitchen.

"I'll get dinner ready." Braden passed the door to an office and a bathroom, then walked into a modern living room. The white sofas accented the wood flooring, coffee table and blinds. And the TV stand held the most important piece of furniture: a huge flat screen. The kitchen was open to the living room over a snack bar. He took out three cans of cheese ravioli from the pantry. From the freezer, he took out a box of frozen French bread. Turning on the oven, he found a kettle and began opening the cans of ravioli.

"Don't have any fish? Potatoes? Maybe a salad?" she teased.

"Have you ever tried to get a six-year-old to eat fish?"

"My parents made me eat what they were having."

"And I bet you enjoyed that."

No, she hadn't. "I have a versatile palate as a result." She liked almost any kind of food.

"Aiden likes a variety of food, too, as long as it's not too spicy."

She put the buttery bread onto a cookie sheet while he stirred the ravioli and turned it on low.

With more roaring, Aiden bounded down the stairs and into the kitchen, bumping into Arizona as he flew his helicopter. She moved out of the way and he flew the helicopter by Braden, who leaned down and tickled his son.

Aiden laughed and twisted away, dropping the truck he held in his other hand. Plopping down onto the floor, he rolled the truck in circles, squirming in circles himself while he flew the helicopter.

Arizona felt a tension headache tighten in her head.

"What is it about kids that bothers you?" Braden asked.

She could never answer that question with any certainty. "They're annoying."

"Because you don't relate to them?"

From the floor, Aiden burped and then laughed when they both looked down.

"What's there to relate to?"

He chuckled. "That's not what it's about." He went about getting their dishes ready while she tried to decipher what he meant. If she couldn't relate to kids, how would she ever not find them annoying?

Choosing the chair opposite Aiden, Arizona stirred her bowl of cheese ravioli and the bread soaked with butter on the small plate beside it. Kids could handle these calories. She couldn't.

Across the table, Aiden spooned a saucy noodle into

his mouth. The sauce dripped down his chin and splashed onto the table, missing the bowl by a mile. Oblivious, his next spoonful held one too many noodles. Some fell onto his lap. Still, the boy was oblivious to all of it. He delved into more, ignoring the bread.

She ate what she could of the kid meal, losing her appetite as Aiden's fingers grew more and more gooey and sauce began to dry around his mouth.

The boy saw her watching him and grinned, chewing a mouthful. Then he scooped some more noodles and teased her clumsily, shaking the spoon and then using his finger to create a slingshot. He let go but his tiny fingers didn't make the ravioli fly across the table at her as he'd intended.

He giggled.

So funny. Arizona made a face at him.

"Aiden," Braden chastised.

The boy did his best to appear sheepish, a poor effort.

Arizona suffered through her bowl of ravioli, guarding herself against the playful challenge in Aiden's eyes. Finally the boy finished, and she escaped Aiden by helping Braden clean up.

"Time for a shower," he said to Aiden, who was in the living room now, engrossed in a cartoon.

"Aiden."

Still no response.

"Aiden!"

The boy's head snapped to attention.

"Shower. Now."

"I don't want to take a shower," Aiden whined in protest.

Leaving the kitchen, Braden fought with him until the boy began screaming and crying. Arizona sat on a living room chair, all too happy to leave the horrible task

of bathing to Braden, flipping the channel to a program about hot-air balloons.

A while later she realized the shower was off and she could hear voices upstairs. Standing, she climbed the stairs, not sure what drew her. Maybe it was the tone of Braden's voice. Deep, but full of affection. She heard that without hearing what he'd said.

At an open doorway, she peered into the room. Braden was reading a book to Aiden. They had eaten late. And Aiden's eyelids were drooping. Neither noticed her.

"Daddy?" Aiden asked drowsily.

"Yes?"

"Who is that lady?" His voice as soft and vulnerable, no resemblance to the troublemaker at dinner.

"She's a friend."

"Like Mommy?"

Braden hesitated. "A little different than Mommy."

"She doesn't like helicopters."

"She likes real helicopters."

"My helicopter is real."

Braden chuckled. "Okay, it's real then." He looked up and saw her then. "She's a girl. Girls don't like boys' toys."

Arizona smiled. That depended on what kind of boy toy he was referring to.

He grinned back at her, not missing her thoughts.

"Why don't you live with us anymore?" Aiden's sweet face tipped up as he looked up at Braden. He still hadn't noticed Arizona.

All humor fled Braden. He didn't know how to answer. "It's an adult thing, nothing you need to worry about. All you need to know is that I love you and I'll always be there for you."

The boy reached out his little arms and Braden took him in for a hug.

"I love you, too, Daddy."

Intruding on this private moment, Arizona went back downstairs. But something had taken root in her. Was there anything more pure than a child's love? And to see Braden's reaction to it, to his son saying those words during a hug. His eyes had closed and he'd turned his head to kiss the side of Aiden's head. Love had permeated the room. And her. It pierced her. Unexpectedly.

A sound woke Braden.

He sat straight up on the bed. The room was dark except for the light from his alarm clock. Another noise. Someone was moving around on the lower level.

Had Arizona gotten up?

Throwing the covers off him, he rose from the bed. With his son in the house, he wouldn't take any chances. Not with how strange everything was right now. Putting on a pair of jeans, he left the room. The first door on the left was Aiden's room.

He looked inside. His son slept peacefully.

Across the hall was where he'd put Arizona. The door was closed. He walked down the hall to the stairs. The sounds were coming from his office. Shuffling, as though someone were going through his things. Was he being robbed?

He searched for a weapon. Getting a knife from the kitchen might make too much noise. So would going to his car for his flashlight.

Moving quietly down the stairs, he paused in the living room. The door to his office was open. Whoever was in there was rooting through his desk.

Anger roiled inside him. How dare anyone break into his home? His son was upstairs sleeping. Recalling how Julian had taken Charlene, he clenched his fists.

At his office door he peeked around the corner.

A tall, big man dressed in black worked at unhooking his computer. The man who'd driven the BMW. He paused and looked toward the door.

Braden entered his office just as the man pulled out a gun. What the hell was he after? What was Julian after? Had he gone after Tatum for the same thing? And when she hadn't produced it…?

Diving alongside his desk, he heard two silenced bullets embedding into the drywall. He kept his desk in the middle of the room to break up the space. It was also to allow more room for his son to use the surface, frequently putting his laptop on the opposite side of him. Braden loved those times, when he could look up from his work computer and see Aiden playing a computer game.

Watching black boots stride slowly across the open space under his desk, he crawled along the wood floor toward a sofa in front of a gas fireplace. Taking cover there, he grabbed a decorative poker from a holder. Then he waited for just the right time to spring up.

Swinging the poker with a practiced move, he struck the man's gun hand. The weapon sailed through the air and hit the wall near the door, clattering to the floor.

The man punched him, striking his jaw and sending him off balance. The next contact came from a well-placed kick. Doubling over, he rammed his elbow back into the man's sternum, then turned to attack. This man could fight, but so could Braden.

He froze as the man reached his gun.

"Daddy?"

Braden's heart sank with dread.

The man turned his weapon toward the door just as Arizona appeared in the opening of the doorway and snatched Aiden. Plucking him out of harm's way.

Braden lunged for the man, ramming into him. The man grunted, and then the gun went off as they both fell to the floor, sending the gun clattering to the wood floor. Braden wrestled with the man, who managed to get the upper hand. Underneath him, Braden was about to roll out of the trap when Arizona appeared above them both, a bulky lamp in her hands. She brought it down hard and the base shattered on the man's head.

The man groaned, staggering off Braden on his hands and knees. He was near the gun. As he took hold of it, Braden jumped to his feet. The man aimed behind him as he ran for the French doors that opened to a small patio on the side of his house, one of them open a fraction. That was where he'd broken in.

Braden wrapped Arizona in his arms and tackled her just as the man fired. His first thought after that was his son. When the man vanished through the door, Braden sprang upward and rushed into the living room. Aiden stood ramrod-stiff, eyes big and round.

Kneeling before him, Braden put his hands on the small shoulders that would someday expand into those of a man. He watched the boy's face crumble into a sob. His tiny hands reached for him, which sent both affection and rage through him.

While detectives worked to gather evidence in Braden's office, Arizona sat on one of his white sofas with Aiden, the detective on the other. The boy had sought her out when a detective began to question him. He snuggled next to her, his hands hooked around her arm and his cheek resting on her shoulder. Arizona ordinarily would have moved away from this close contact with a creature she didn't understand. But his fear erased that defense mechanism.

Looking down at him, she saw his eyes drooping.

Sweet. Innocent. At peace now that the danger had gone. She rubbed his arm, with him in the crook of hers and feeling strangely at ease.

When she looked up and saw Braden watching her from where he stood next to the detective, she realized he'd witnessed the tiny smile his son had given her. Something more meaningful than the first time she saw him warmed the exchange.

"Mr. McCrae?"

Arizona turned with Braden to the detective who was trying to regain his attention.

"After Ms. Ivy hit him with the lamp, what happened?"

"He picked up his gun, fired at us and ran out the patio door."

"And you're certain it was the same man who attacked Ms. Ivy?"

"Yes. I'm very certain. It was the same man. He tried to take her."

With a sigh, the detective tapped his notepad with his mechanical pencil. "And he was at your computer, you said."

"Yes," Braden answered.

"What do you think he was after?"

Braden hesitated before shaking his head in defeat.

"Your sister was all the way in Tortola when she went missing. What could that possibly have to do with this?"

Finding the answer to that wasn't something they'd accomplish any time soon. It wasn't anything anyone would accomplish any time soon. That was what frightened Arizona. They needed time, and they didn't have any. They'd delayed their flight back to Tortola. The longer they stayed here, the longer Tatum was in danger. But they couldn't ignore what was happening here, either.

"What could he want from your home computer?" Arizona voiced her question aloud.

Braden hesitated again. "It was my work computer."

His work computer? That changed the dynamics. More and more, Arizona was convinced his job was somehow the connecting factor.

"He was after information," Arizona said.

"No," Braden said, looking over at her sharply.

He was in denial. She sure wished he'd snap out of it.

"Then why try to abduct you?" the detective asked Arizona.

"To force something out of Braden." She looked at him. "You said yourself that he was probably trying to use me against you."

"But you said Tatum was an executive at a freight forwarding company and that their exports didn't include Hamilton components," the detective interjected.

"They didn't. They don't," Braden said with conviction.

Arizona didn't miss it. "Maybe Tatum's kidnappers would like to include them now."

The detective tapped his notepad again, and Braden glowered at her.

The tapping stopped and he looked at Braden. "Your sister planned to go to Tortola and was seen getting into a cab."

"Yes. That's what the hotel manager said."

They were going to have to talk to that man when they returned to Tortola.

"If she intended to be there, then she may have been working with him."

To steal technology? Arizona watched Braden reject that notion. She'd like to do the same. Why would his sister steal from her own brother?

Braden moved around the coffee table, now standing

opposite both her and the detective. “My sister wouldn’t do that. She wouldn’t sell technology to a criminal.”

“Wasn’t she accused of doing just that?”

“Yes, but she’s innocent.”

“Is Julian behind the front company her freight forwarding company shipped arms for?”

Arizona shot a look from the detective to Braden. If Julian had been behind it, he would have said something, wouldn’t he?

“The government didn’t know. The man behind the front company used a false identity. At least, they hadn’t been able to trace the man at the time Tatum was questioned, and she couldn’t tell them anything.”

“Why would she?”

Anger stormed over Braden’s eyes. “Stealing from Hamilton wouldn’t be easy. Even if someone managed to steal my laptop, they wouldn’t be able to access my files. Nothing is stored on the hard drive. It’s all done with access codes to a remote server.”

“Your sister may have gotten them.”

Braden grunted a laugh, a cynical one that was anything but humor. “You don’t know my sister. She didn’t do it.”

The detective didn’t respond. He didn’t have to. His doubt was clear.

“It’s the only explanation, Braden,” Arizona said. “It’s the only thing linking all this craziness to your sister’s disappearance.”

“There has to be something else at play,” he said. “Whatever that is, it’s against her will.”

Not willingly. If only they could figure out what made her unwilling. What had drawn her into a government export violation investigation? What had led to people trying to steal from Braden? And what had led to his sister’s disappearance?

"It's nothing we're going to solve tonight." The detective stood, tucking his notepad away. "Why don't you all try to get some sleep. I'll have a teleconference with the Tortola police in the morning. I'll also talk to Homeland Security to see what kind of help we can get from them. Do you mind if we search Tatum's house?"

Braden shook his head. "She has an apartment in Denver and is selling the one in Atlanta. She was living in Denver when she left for Tortola."

The detective nodded once. "We'll need to search both premises."

"I'll arrange for my parents to let you in. The Realtor in Atlanta will help you there."

"I'll let you know if we find anything. In the meantime, please don't go back to Tortola. Leave the investigation to us."

Arizona looked at Braden. Together they shared the secret that they already had airline tickets.

Chapter 6

Braden could tell Arizona wasn't looking forward to seeing her brother. Since Lincoln had been released from the hospital, he was recovering at home, grumpily, according to her. No doubt, he felt the way Braden did. He wished Arizona could stay here instead of going back to Tortola. Braden wished he could take his son, too. Serena had agreed to stay at her parents', but he'd still worry. He needed to hurry. Go get his sister and get home as fast as possible.

Arizona bounced up the steps to Lincoln's front porch. Her spaghetti-strapped stonewashed denim top had the privilege of holding her breasts, and the peacock-chiffon bodice flowed around her slender shape. Matching peacock earrings dangled from her lobes, her blond hair tucked behind her ears. Another pair of faded jean shorts left her legs bare and she'd decided to torture him again in those red shoes.

"Your son will be fine with his grandparents," she said.

The unexpectedness of it threw him for a second. How had she known he was worried about that?

She stopped at the front door. "They'll go after us. The more distance we put between Aiden and us, the safer he'll be."

Because she believed Julian was behind the arms dealing, and that he was after technology through Braden.

"American Freight shipped arms for the front company, not technology," he pointed out.

"In the end, it's all the same. Weapons technology builds arms." She eyed him funny, as though she read his thoughts. "But I get that she may not have been willing."

He didn't feel like talking about that anymore. "Let's get this done so we can get back to looking for my sister."

"This is a necessary diversion." Facing the door, she gave it a distasteful frown. "But do I have to go in with you?"

"Lincoln has some intel for us. And a place to hide when we get there. We have to go in." And he wasn't leaving her out here. He glanced around the neighborhood. All was quiet, but that could change in a blink. Just like the last time they were here.

She sighed. "I know."

Her friction with her brother was both amusing and telling. Lincoln thought what Braden did; Arizona strived for exactly what she sought so hard to escape. Working in news, she'd still be in the public eye. She'd never remove herself from her Ivy name that way. Better if she did what Lincoln suggested and start up a nonprofit.

She turned the handle without knocking or ringing the bell and entered ahead of him.

The sound of a loud football game blared from the big

TV. Lincoln craned his neck, trying to see who entered, his bandaged knee elevated on a big leather ottoman.

"Arizona?"

She went to him, leaning over to adjust the pillow supporting his knee. "Don't tax yourself, Lincoln."

He grimaced with the movement of his knee, but managed a response to her sarcasm. "I'm not going to lecture you. I hurt too much."

Holding back a grin, Braden walked to the dining room table adjacent to the living room, where he saw satellite images and maps of Julian's property and the properties surrounding it. It was what had brought him and Arizona here. Lincoln was going to help get him inside the villa and search for Tatum, or traces of her.

"Do you have anyone coming over to help you?" Arizona asked her brother.

"Mom tried to send a nurse."

She straightened with her hands on her hips. "And you refused, of course."

Lincoln eyed her indignantly. "Why weren't you answering my calls?"

Arizona picked up a big plastic mug from a side table. "You're out of water." She went into the kitchen, the sink in the island counter facing the living room.

"Why didn't you answer your phone?" Lincoln hollered.

"I was busy with a robber who was looking for technical information on Braden's computer," she answered.

Braden stopped looking at the satellite images of Frenchman's Cay and moved back into the living room. Arizona returned with the mug, refreshed with ice and water, and put it on the table.

"Why didn't you answer my calls?" Lincoln repeated, clearly not believing her.

Remaining leaned over, she moved so that her face was above his. "I didn't want to be lectured."

He held on to her gaze with real concern. "Answer your phone when I call."

Her demeanor softened. "Okay."

The brief exchange showed Braden a lot. They may be at odds when it came to Arizona's stubborn insistence on being a reporter for the rest of her life, but underneath was a well of deep affection, an unbreakable bond. She and Lincoln were close.

He had that with Tatum. They were close in age and hung out before adulthood led them in different directions. He wished he hadn't lost that connection. And he wished he hadn't lost it while he was married to Serena. But that was when he had. He'd spent too much time and energy trying to make his wife happy.

What if he never saw her again? It was taking too long to find her. A pang of fear sliced him. No. He could not allow that. He had to find her.

"Do you have any idea what these people are trying to get from you?" Lincoln asked.

"No." He caught Arizona's look and ignored it.

She went into the kitchen again, this time to inspect Lincoln's refrigerator.

Tatum had run a freight forwarding company that frequently shipped items controlled by government regulations. He worked for a highly technical corporation. Different arms. Same export restrictions. Hamilton didn't export. They sold to the U.S. government. Only. But that didn't mean someone wouldn't try to steal from them.

"There's a file over there with the images and maps," Lincoln said to Braden. "Property lines and utilities. I also have the name of a man who'll have equipment you're going to need."

Although Lincoln didn't push the technology angle, he must be thinking what Arizona thought. "Great. Thanks. Where will we be meeting for the equipment?"

"I'll let you know. Have to be careful." He gripped his leg above the bandage on his leg with another grimace.

Arizona paused in removing things from the refrigerator. "Have you taken your pain medication?"

Lincoln stopped rubbing his leg to look at her. "Yes, Arizona. But it still hurts like holy hell. What are you doing in there?"

"Making you a casserole that will feed you for a few days."

"Cheesy chicken?" His mood brightened.

"None other."

Lincoln looked up at Braden. "She's a great cook."

"Arizona?" He watched her open a can of Campbell's nacho cheese soup and chuckled. She looked as if she could be the star of a chick flick, dressed that way, red lipstick, dangling earrings, all legs.

"Seriously. She can cook."

The smell of slowly cooking chicken wafted into the living room. She added onion to the mixture and returned her attention to the bowl of vegetables and cheese.

"She still hot on the trail for a story?" Lincoln asked.

"I don't think so." She'd been respectful of him in that regard.

Lincoln's brow lifted. "It must be the similarities between Tatum and her fiancé."

Trevor had been kidnapped in the Caribbean and Tatum may have fallen to the same fate. If that were true, she had a deep, compelling reason for wanting to help him. Or maybe it had nothing to do with want. Maybe it was more of a need.

* * *

This time they flew to the airport closest to St. John Island. There was ferry service from Cruz Bay to Road Town, but Braden had chartered a boat. It would be less conspicuous, and he and Arizona could stay mobile, docking at different marinas if necessary. The important thing was to stay off Julian's radar for as long as possible. She walked beside him toward the fifty-foot Hatteras yacht. He was glad to be back on his sister's trail. The sooner he could find her, the sooner he could go home to his son.

The port was busy, with taxis picking up and dropping off tourists and the noise of ferries leaving and arriving. Early evening, there were plenty of people milling about.

Aboard the yacht, Braden began preparing to motor somewhere more secluded. He doubted Julian would learn they'd returned, but he'd err on the side of caution. He saw Arizona go into the wheelhouse and moments later heard the engine start. When he'd suggested they charter a boat, he shouldn't have been surprised when she'd taken over the details and made the arrangements herself. She'd sailed many times before.

He detached them from the pier and she drove the boat out to sea, following the shoreline in search of a place to moor.

Arizona flipped through the satellite stations, not staying on any one long enough to engage. He could feel her boredom.

Abandoning his notebook where he'd been jotting down ideas about his sister's disappearance, he went to her. He took the remote from her and sat beside her as she eyed him indignantly.

She was wearing a navy-blue sundress with two big white stripes across her chest with white sailing shoes and star earrings. Casual but still sexy on her. He found a his-

tory channel and put the remote down, far enough away from her impatient hands.

"Don't you ever have a day where you do nothing?" he asked.

She thought about that a moment. "I don't watch TV."

"I can tell."

Her blue eyes drilled into his, searching for clues to his teasing. He'd rather talk anyway. To her. Despite the inner voice that cautioned him not to, he was compelled to find out more about her. The desire had been there from the start. Seeing her with his son changed things, made it harder to deny what drove him.

"Normally when I'm on a boat like this, I'm with friends, fishing or parasailing or something," she said, as though she felt she had to explain.

Doing something adventurous. Active. She loved to be active just like him. He'd met other women who shared that passion with him, but none to the degree Arizona did. She matched him that way.

And she didn't abhor kids as much as she claimed. He saw it for himself. She cared. When Aiden wasn't jumping all over the place and making noise, he was a lovable kid.

He shouldn't be thinking this way. Not only did he not trust her, he needed more time to get past his divorce. Aiden needed more time, too. He hadn't adjusted yet. He still harbored hope that his parents would get back together.

"Stop looking at me like that."

"Like what?"

"Like you're enjoying the fact that I don't do well with idle moments." Close, but not quite. He was glad she hadn't guessed his true thoughts.

"I don't do well with idle moments, either."

Standing, she wandered over to a table and traced her

finger around the top of a lamp. "Did your ex-wife like the same things you did? Being active? What things did you have in common?"

Apparently, she was as curious about him as he was about her. That could be dangerous. He tried to think of the things he and Serena had in common.

Arizona stopped tracing the lampshade and lowered her arm to her side. "Didn't you have anything in common?"

Wonderful. Now she wouldn't let it go. "We had chemistry."

"Chemistry." She said it flatly. "As in…sex?"

He didn't reply.

She moved back toward the sofa. "You married her just because you had good sex?"

"It wasn't only that." Now it was his turn to stand up. He moved over to the glass door that led to the stern.

It wasn't something he hadn't wondered. Why had he married Serena? Her question on what they had in common still bothered him. Didn't he know? He hadn't thought of it when he met her. The sex had been great, but it wouldn't have been that way if he didn't have feelings for her, would it?

"Wow," Arizona said.

He turned to face her incredulous expression. "It was more than that."

"Was it?"

She'd already met Serena. What more could there be? Serena was materialistic and frequently came across as haughty. Funny, how Arizona came from far more money and behaved with considerably more integrity. Serena had her pegged for another of his kind, the working class. The middle class. And then she'd discovered who Arizona was. He wondered if that bothered her. Her ex-husband hadn't

been good enough for her but he may be good enough for someone like Arizona.

"I'm beginning to understand why you've been divorced twice." She'd stepped closer to him.

"I loved Serena. She was the one who left me." Even to him, he sounded defensive.

"Do you still love her?"

He thought about it for a moment. "No. It didn't take long for me to disconnect." Which is what had told him he hadn't loved her as much as he thought he had.

"Huh." She half nodded, noncommittal.

"Haven't you ever had relationships fail?" he asked. "Haven't you ever been rejected?"

"Well...yeah. Sometimes."

Sometimes?

She began wandering again. Fingering the back of a chair this time.

"You're the one who does the rejecting?"

Stopping, she flashed a glance to him before resuming her wandering. A picture of a beautiful sailboat received her attention next. She looked up at it.

"I wouldn't call it rejecting. Boys broke up with me in high school."

"But not after?" After Trevor. He began to get a bigger sense that not just his recent divorce stood in the way of a relationship with her.

"I haven't been interested in men lately. My family tries to set me up with people every once in a while, but I always end up in tabloids." She scoffed. "In hindsight, I can see why. None of them mattered that much."

She'd loved Trevor that much. No one compared. The last thing he needed was another woman who had expectations he couldn't—and wouldn't—live up to.

"They weren't Trevor?" He finished her sentence.

She pivoted. "They set me up with all the wrong men. Sons of rich men. Some were famous. Others were just overgrown spoiled children."

"Or engineers."

She folded her arms and didn't respond. But he had her thinking.

"They weren't Trevor," he repeated.

"I just wasn't interested in any of them," she snapped. "Can we talk about something else?"

"Sure. How about the real reason you want to be a respected journalist?" She still hadn't faced the root cause of her disinterest in men. She hadn't let go of Trevor.

She took some time assimilating that.

As they stood across the salon from each other, staring, the moment stretched. He looked at the way her breasts plumped above her folded arms. She ran a look down to his jeans. Then their eyes met again. Hers remained offended. His, he was sure, were a lot warmer.

"You think I've turned to journalism because of Trevor?" she asked.

"Yes."

That made her mad. "What is wrong with making a positive change in my job?"

"We were talking about your inability to date men."

Lowering her arms, she walked to him. "I don't have an inability. And this is about more than dating. You and Lincoln both think my ambition is a bandage for Trevor."

He took in the flawless perfection of her skin and the fiery light in her eyes. "All right. Then explain your disinterest in men. It's been four years since Trevor died."

Her head jerked back as though avoiding a slap, and then she did her own absorption of his face, negating his accusation. Disinterest did not describe what was shooting between them right now. Whether she didn't believe in

mistakes or not, it would be one if they started anything up. His divorce, her fiancé's death. Both were baggage they'd have to overcome. While he may want to, it might be too soon. And if Arizona hadn't overcome her fiancé's death after four years, when would she?

"Do you really believe a serious journalism career will give you recognition? Is that really the only reason you're pursuing it?"

"It's not the only reason. There's money and recognition, too."

"Oh, yeah, the recognition. You're not really making a change, though, are you? International news is still news."

"Real news."

"It will keep your name in the press." Jackson Ivy's daughter. Not Arizona Ivy. Jackson Ivy.

That made her fumble for a moment. "Reporting is what I do. It's what I know. I went to college for journalism."

Her unhappy profile and the sound of defeat in her voice put him in check. "Just another observation. You also jump out of planes and scuba dive at night. What's not to love about that?"

It worked to disarm her. Smiling, she opened the glass door and stepped out onto the stern, where a small area opened and two built-in benches offered seating. He followed her to the stern railing.

"I love this," she said. "St. John is one of my favorite places. It's still so wild."

Most of it was a national park. The ocean shimmered in the setting sun. He stood beside her as the burning orb slipped beyond the horizon and cast the sky into marvelous shades of pink and gray. He had to agree. This was one of the best places to be. Sunsets would never be redundant to him. He'd never get tired of seeing them, and he shared that with her. They had so much in common. Was he mis-

taken about that? Had he finally found a woman he had more in common with than sex?

A sudden urge came over him to disarm her. Charm her. Enchant her. But…

Into what?

That last thought stopped him from doing something he was pretty sure he'd regret in the morning.

Arizona was still plagued by everything Braden had said earlier. Trevor did have a lot to do with her disinterest in dating, but not her professional aspirations. Why did he think they were intertwined? Why did Lincoln? It was the idea that her ambitions were nothing more than a tool to occupy the emptiness in her heart that bothered her.

She watched him steer the dinghy to shore, broad shouldered, short dark hair unaffected by the wind. What was it about him that made her care what he thought? And why did his probing trouble her so much? Because he was right?

She would still be in the news if she became a good reporter. But it wasn't the news that she took issue with. It was being Jackson Ivy's adorable daughter, the one who did the silly news. Isn't she cute? If she did serious news, she'd be taken seriously.

Helping to pull the dinghy up onto the beach, she walked with him through the sand along the shore. They were supposed to meet Lincoln's friend here.

The sky was dark now and the beach secluded. Lincoln had helped them choose this cove. There was a campground near here, but no resorts.

A man appeared ahead, moving toward them. Arizona thought he was a local or a tourist and not the man they were meeting.

"Douglas?" Braden said the code word.

The man stopped. "Roger."

The man glanced at Arizona before turning. "This way."

At the edge of a group of palm trees, he stopped next to a long duffel bag. Braden removed a wad of cash that had bulged his front pocket and handed it to the man, who flipped through the hundreds and then nodded. Without a word, he left them there.

Braden hefted the duffel over his shoulder.

"What's in there? Enough to start a rebel war?" she asked as they walked back to the dinghy. Hopefully they wouldn't have to use any of it. Writing about violence she could do. Living it was different.

Watching Braden handle the bag, Arizona was glad her brother had overfilled it. He moved with grace and ease as he put the bag into the dinghy. She enjoyed the show. He turned to her, offering his hand. She gave him hers and he tugged her closer, lifting her by her waist and depositing her into the boat. Her hands still on his shoulders, she looked down into his magnificent green eyes, cloaked in the night. Lingering a little longer, he finally slid his hands off her waist and began to push the boat to deeper water. She sat, entranced, still tingling from his hands.

Back to the boat, she helped him secure the dinghy and then went into the salon with him, where he put the bag down.

Arizona sat across from him with her legs tucked under her. Four pistols, two automatic rifles. Plenty of ammunition. It was like going through an inedible trick-or-treat bag.

"Ever been target practicing?" he asked.

"Yes." She picked up a pistol and selected the corresponding magazine and shoved it into the gun. "Lincoln remembered which gun I used, too."

"I think I can get by with this." Braden held another pistol, testing the feel of it in his hand.

"Target practice?"

"No, a field in the middle of nowhere when I was eighteen." The memory put a smile on his lips.

"Engineer," she teased.

He lowered the gun. "After a friend and I finished shooting beer cans, I took my gun apart and put it back together."

"What is the fascination with that?" And why the hell did she find it so sexy? On him?

"I had to know how it worked."

She tried to douse the appeal of his curious mind and that grin. She'd listened to Trevor for hours as he went on and on about his work, the projects he'd been involved in, the challenges and his joy when he overcame them. But he hadn't enchanted her quite the same. She'd loved his passion but she hadn't really listened to his stories. With Braden, she hung on every word.

Seeing a petite belt with a holster fastened to it, Arizona took it and slipped it around the waist of her jean shorts. Picking up the gun, she stood and slipped the gun into the holster. Slipping it back out, she tested her own handling, careful not to point it at Braden.

Seeing him watch her, she put it into the holster and spread her arms. "Do I look like a wild west girl?" She gave a little wiggle to her hips. She'd have to thank Lincoln for thinking to add the holster.

When Braden didn't respond, she looked up from her new toy. His eyes smoldered with something other than amusement, rising from her hips. He stole her breath as he devoured the sight of her. That trigger-quick attraction was back again. The impact of it rendered her still.

He stood, a slow unfolding of his statuesque body. Then he stepped over to her, his eyes never wavering. She looked up into them, enchanted, enticed, anticipating.

Reaching for her, his fingers worked the belt of her holster. Her breath hitched as heat flushed her. His green eyes held her captive. Releasing the belt, he tossed it onto the duffel bag.

She couldn't tell what he was thinking. Did he not like her wearing a gun? He liked something. He still looked at her, not moving away.

Then he stepped closer. He lifted his hand and cupped the side of her face. Arizona parted her mouth to breathe easier. She tipped her head back and put her hands on his stomach, feeling hard, ribbed muscle under his shirt.

His head came down. His eyes bored into hers.

What was stopping her from letting this night go wherever it led? Neither one of them could predict the future. So, it was soon after his divorce. So, he had a son. None of that mattered right now.

"Are you thinking what I'm thinking?" he asked.

That she was contemplating sleeping with him? "You tell me."

"How about if I just show you?"

She had a need to keep this light. Nothing serious. She could walk away from that. And so could he. "Okay, but I'm warning you…if at any time the geeky engineer comes out in you…"

He grinned, sexy with creases along his mouth. Then his humor fled. He kissed her, just once. Soft. Smooth. Warm. Then he withdrew and she drowned in his eyes again.

She slid her hands over his muscular chest, up over his sinewy shoulders, and pressed her body against his. Angling her head, she urged him for more. His hands moved around to her rear and lower back, holding her where she wanted to be.

An endless kiss later, he lifted his head. She drowned in

the passion in his eyes, soft and burning beneath the external lights. The gentle rock of the boat swayed her with him.

He kissed her again, slow and poignant. Transported to a world of sweet desire, she gave herself over to it, reveling in it, worshipping it. Kissing Braden reunited her with something lost, something she never thought she'd encounter again.

Breaking the kiss, Braden lifted her against him. She wrapped her legs around his hips and he walked with her to the master cabin, where he laid her on the bed.

Before coming down with her, he pulled off his shirt, grabbing the hem and pulling it forward over his head, muscles rippling. Arizona removed her short-sleeved button-up shirt and left the rest as Braden kneeled on the mattress and straddled her. He unclasped her bra, his fingers brushing her skin and fanning chills of delicious anticipation from where he touched to her groin. Laying the cups of her bra aside, he freed her breasts, staring down at them before taking them in his hands. He held one and thumbed the nipple of the other.

He kissed her mouth while he continued to toy with her. Impatient, Arizona reached between them and tugged at the button of his jeans. He left her long enough to remove them, and she removed the rest of her clothes, shrugging out of her bra and kicking out of her shorts.

Then he was on her again, as breathless as her. He kissed her hard, his body pressing her into the mattress. His erection was unmistakable and near what awaited. She tipped her hips, rubbing against him. He groaned and began probing. She was so ready for him that he slid right in. For a moment he went still, fighting for control. Arizona held on to him, her fingers digging into his shoulders, feeling the muscles work as he held himself up on his hands and pulled back for that first thrust.

Arizona arched her body with the singe of lust that numbed her. She heard her own rough breathing, half moans full of pleasure. Braden moved back and forth, agonizingly slow. She lifted her knees and hooked her ankles around him, rocking with him. The sensations catapulted her back in time. This was how it had been with Trevor. Deep and consuming. Full of rightness.

Braden pushed into her harder, his hips meeting hers before withdrawing for another, and another, until skin slapped against skin.

Arizona couldn't get Trevor out of her mind. It removed her from the moment. At first slowly, then with significant impact. Her desire was doused by it. Sex with Trevor had been this way because she'd loved him so intensely. What was this with Braden? Certainly not love. And he was a man who married based on how spectacular the sex was.

This had the makings of some pretty spectacular sex.

But Arizona grew increasingly more despondent. Missing here was the rightness she'd had with Trevor.

Braden was still slamming into her. Now that it meant nothing to her, it lost its pizzazz. The fizz died out like day old soda.

At last he began to notice her lack of participation. His movements slowed. She was still very wet and he slid back and forth easily. The friction solicited enough sparks to make her contemplate changing her mind.

He pushed in once more and went still, looking down at her, studying her, quite perplexed. She was certain this had never happened to him before.

"Something the matter?" he asked.

And it became almost funny. What kept it from slipping to that point was the very real fact that sex with Braden felt similar to what she'd had with Trevor, a man she loved to her core. She didn't love Braden that way.

"I…I can't…"

"You were on your way to," he said.

"Yes, I was…until…until I…"

He waited, cocking his head in his disbelief.

"It reminded me of Trevor," she blurted.

"What did?" He searched her face.

"Not you." Oh, Lord this was awkward. "The…the sex."

He spent a confused moment staring at her some more. "How did it remind you of him?"

Her legs were still open and he was still lodged inside her. "Could you…?" She pointed down where they were still joined.

Even more flummoxed, he rolled off her and sat beside her, looking over at her, expecting answers.

"Just—" she sat up with him, leaning on her hand, not caring that she was still naked "—when we were…it felt similar…and…Trevor popped into my head…and then I couldn't get rid of him. He stayed there while you were…"

Did he understand now?

He gaped at her, appalled. "You were turned off because you were reminded that I'm an engineer? Really?"

"I…" She didn't know what to say.

Braden climbed off the bed, angry now. Injured ego. She let him get dressed and leave the cabin. How could she explain to him that it was more than that? More that entailed meaning, too much of it.

Chapter 7

Unbelievable.

Braden woke the next morning to the crushing memory of Arizona. Everything had gone great until she froze up and it was like making love to a blow-up doll. Not that he'd ever done that before. It was the worst sex he'd ever had in his life. And he felt responsible. He'd failed to give her pleasure.

It was unspeakable. Absurd. How could this happen to him?

Flinging the blankets off him, he got up from the couch and saw Arizona in the galley, fully dressed and making coffee. He was glad somebody could sleep last night.

She turned with a steaming cup and stilled for a second when she saw him, then went to the booth-style galley table and flipped a small notebook shut.

"What are you doing?" Taking notes about his sister? Preparing her story?

"Just journaling." Putting her cup down, she tucked the journal into a backpack purse and then lifted the cup again, sipping. Nonchalant. Sneaky.

"About what?" Bad sex? Would he prefer that or his sister?

"Nothing much." With one hand, she retrieved another cup and poured him some coffee.

He took it from her. "No story, Arizona."

"I know. No story." And then she mumbled, "We should get going."

What had she been journaling about? He believed her that it wasn't his sister. He'd rather not examine any other possibility.

While he released them from the mooring, she went to the fly bridge and started the engine. When he finished, he took over the controls, annoyed as hell. Why had he allowed them to go as far as they had? She'd wiggled her hips with that holster on and he'd been a goner.

She stepped back and out of the way, taking a seat and looking ahead at the sea. He was too angry to talk to her.

"I won't give my father's friend anything I write until you approve it first," she said.

"Why is it so important to you?" More important than respecting his family's privacy.

She didn't respond. They'd already gone over this, and he already knew why.

"It won't bring Trevor back," he said. "And it won't stop people from identifying you through your father, either."

He might as well be talking to a wall. She kept her face averted, staring out to sea. If she'd been rigid before, she was a stone now. There'd be no getting through to her now. She was lost in grief she had never been able to cope with. She'd convinced herself that no man would compare with the one she loved. And why did he care so

much? Hadn't he told himself he needed time? It was too soon for a relationship.

Yeah, but did he have to suffer unfinished sex with Arizona? It was his own damn fault. He was the one who'd come on to her. She was playing around, but he'd been the one to initiate. How could he have foreseen what would happen?

"About last night..."

He held up his hand. "No need to talk about that. It was a mistake." He looked at her purposefully. "And I do believe in them."

She didn't say anything for a while, only sort of pouted at him. "I'm sorry. I shouldn't have let you kiss me. I wasn't ready."

She was apologizing? He couldn't take her mind off of Trevor. She should be ready by now, and he should have been able to get her mind off another man.

"Why is it so hard to let go of him?"

When she didn't respond, he sensed that she couldn't.

She loved him. That was the reason. She knew it; she just couldn't tell him that, not after they had slept together.

"Losing him doesn't mean you have to live the rest of your life alone, pursuing a career that will consume all your time." He should just let this go. But something made him keep pushing. Maybe it was his injured ego. Maybe it was that he actually did care.

"Trevor has nothing to do with why I want to be a reporter."

"Yes, he does." He was more convinced than ever. She'd closed herself off from love so long that she didn't know how to reopen herself to it. "You should follow your heart. You can be just as busy running something like a non-profit organization."

He watched her resist what he said with the shake of

her head, as though no one understood her. Then she grew defiant. "Is that what you did?"

Follow his heart? Was she questioning his choice in becoming an engineer? "Yes."

She registered his certain answer. Her eyes closed slowly with acquiescence. She believed him.

"Then why are you so familiar with guns? And why are you not afraid of dangerous situations? It's like you're ready for battle 24/7."

Had she really picked up on that? Her insight was keen. A flashback to his childhood sneaked up on him. He'd told no one about it but that single event had changed him. And yes, it had made him more aware of the hazards of living. But he wasn't going to talk about that with her. He didn't talk about it with anyone.

"My sister is missing," he said. "I've never been in a situation like this before."

"Are you sure? You sure were ready for it."

Not welcoming where this could lead, he didn't respond. He felt her inspecting him. She did so for several minutes before she turned back to the sea.

It wasn't far to Tortola, and Frenchman's Cay grew bigger as they approached. They sailed past, and he spotted the dock leading to the vacant house. Mooring offshore, they took an inflatable dinghy to shore. The mountainous foothills blocked the view of Julian's villa. If he had guards on the lookout, they wouldn't be able to see the dock.

Securing the boat, he and Arizona started up the slope. There were earthen stairs guiding the way. At the top, he found a rock and broke one of the small windows. Clearing the glass, he crawled into a lower-level bedroom, making sure Arizona got in behind him. The house was large but not as large as Julian's. And it was one level. Making their way from the bedroom where they'd broken in,

they emerged into a huge open space with three couches arranged before a towering wall of windows. Deep blue rugs contrasted with the light-colored tile. Beyond the sitting area was a rectangular glass table with six tall-backed blue-cushioned chairs.

Passing the sitting area, he saw a hallway led to the garage and a bathroom and a closet. The bathroom and the closet separated the hall from the kitchen. There was a kitchen island with a sink. Whoever stood there during meal prep could look up and see the view. At the far end of the kitchen, there was a passageway to the garage and the hall.

After opening the garage door and finding it empty of vehicles, Braden returned to the living room where Arizona stood at the window. He joined her.

The hillside below and ocean beyond shimmered in the sun. And to the left, they had a clear shot of Julian's villa. Lincoln was good. This location was perfect. They had a great view of the back and some of the road leading in. They could watch the comings and goings of Julian and anyone else who had access to his villa, and hopefully learn of a way in.

Putting down the duffel bag, Braden unzipped the top. Arizona knelt beside him, sexy in her jean shorts and glittery I Love NY T-shirt. Her blond hair was pulled back, with some strands loose and hanging along her face. Her hair wasn't short but it wasn't long, either, just enough for a simple but stylish ponytail. Long lashes lowered over smooth skin. Slender nose. Raspberry lips void of lipstick. Everything about her switched on his baser instincts, revving up a masculine response to her feminine simplicity. Even that ponytail. He imagined holding on to it while he…

Her blue eyes shifted and caught him.

She blinked as though startled and then that same smoky response took over. She reacted to him so quickly.

But just as quickly, the thought of having to erase Trevor from her mind cooled him off.

He found the binoculars in the duffel bag and straightened to go back to the window. Nothing stirred over at Julian's villa.

"We have until dark to find a way in," he said. That was a few hours away. Seeing Arizona contemplate the challenge of waiting alone together, he pulled up a chair and propped his feet up on the wide wood frame of the window. Better to watch the inactivity at Julian's villa than her.

Braden tucked ammunition into the pocket of the black flak jacket and eyed Arizona doing the same. She still wore her T-shirt but had changed into jeans and hiking boots. The flak jacket fit her curves well, her gun holster hanging below, resting against her shapely thigh. Entirely too much of a girl to be wearing a gun.

"Maybe you should wait here," he said.

After adjusting her gun holster, she lowered her hands to her side and said, "You have more experience at this sort of thing?"

"I'm going to look for my sister. You don't have to go with me."

"I'll go with you. Four eyes are better than two."

"Not if someone starts shooting at us. Then we have two too many."

She cocked her head. "I want to help you find your sister. And I can shoot a gun just as good as anybody in that house down there."

There was no arguing with her. "I can do this alone."

She angled her head, not as cocky as before. "Can you?"

He headed for the door. He wasn't experienced at this

and neither was she. But they could both shoot a gun. Tatum could be in that villa, being held against her will by a predator. And predators, Braden would not tolerate. If they found Tatum, he'd make sure both women made it out okay.

Outside, he heard Arizona's booted feet crunching over the stony ground. Why he found that adorable, he'd never know. Maybe it was her small feet. Maybe it was the graceful way she moved. Maybe it was everything about her.

He led her into the trees with only stars to light their way. The terrain grew steep.

"Why are you so good with guns?" she asked from behind him.

"I wouldn't say 'good.' I target practice, that's all."

She contemplated that a few steps down the slope. "I can see why you'd be into weapons. You design them. But you seem too…I don't know…ready to use them."

He held a branch aside for her. "We're getting close. Be quiet."

Pausing under the branch he held, she looked up at him, too perceptive. "There's something you aren't telling me."

How could she tell that? "Would you like someone to hear us?"

"We aren't that close." Her astute scrutiny didn't abate. "Did something happen to you?"

Why did she think something had to have happened to him to make him learn how to shoot guns? Lots of people owned guns and shot them. Had she seen something in him? As he looked into her blue eyes that searched and searched the depths of his, he began to think so.

"Yes, my sister disappeared," he snapped. "Am I supposed to stand by and do nothing?" He let the branch drop, forcing her to step out of the way. He resumed his trek toward Julian's villa.

"Something did," she said.

Irritation simmered as he reached a clearing and the back of Julian's villa came into view. The place was well lit by exterior lighting, Braden spotted several cameras mounted to the villa itself. He stuck out his arm when Arizona would have stepped forward. He pointed and she saw the cameras.

He scanned the surroundings. A grouping of trees would provide concealment and get them closer to the villa. There was no fence around the perimeter so that would help.

The villa sat at an angle to them. He could see the west side and the back, which faced southwest. Large windows on the ground level showed promise of revealing something. There was no movement outside.

"How are we going to get in?" Arizona asked. "He's probably got alarms."

"There's a servant's door in the back."

"Really?" She leaned to see around him. "How do you know?"

"I saw someone use it from the other house." She hadn't been looking through her binoculars then. Braden had looked through them all afternoon. It was either that or look at her.

He suffered more of her scrutiny.

"You're really good at this. A natural."

Ignoring her leading tone, he guided her toward the door. Following the trees, Braden stopped, making Arizona do the same. He watched the cameras move.

"Now," Arizona said when the camera closest to them turned away.

He ran with her to the building, flattening his back and looking up. The cameras didn't have a view this close to the building. Another camera did, this one remained sta-

tionary. Braden took out his pistol, fitted with a silencer, and shot the camera. Now they'd be able to enter without being seen.

With any luck, Julian's thugs wouldn't notice for a while. And with more luck, there were no motion detectors in place.

Peering into one of the ground-level windows, he saw nothing unusual inside. Just a large family room. Moving along the building, he approached the servant's door. Just then, the door opened and a servant appeared, taking a trash bag out to a Dumpster in an enclosed area.

He and Arizona froze as he made his way back. The servant didn't see them. Arizona breathed out a heavy sigh.

Braden continued toward the door. Testing the knob, he found it unlocked. As he opened the door just a little, he saw a large commercial-grade kitchen. A chef worked before a countertop, cutting potatoes. He was alone.

When he turned and went into a large refrigerator, Braden led Arizona inside.

Down a hall, they emerged into a sitting room. No one was there. It was silent. Two bookshelves took up each side of the far wall, and a painting of a sailboat hung between, hip-high white paneling connecting them. A white sectional was positioned in the middle, tables and plants scattered around, and to his and Arizona's left was an entertainment center, closed for now.

Arizona followed him to the stairs on the other side of the wall where the entertainment center was. Slowly and quietly they climbed. No sounds came from the main level. Rounding the wall, Braden stepped into a wildly colored living room. Black, red, white, blue and yellow blinded the eye. Across from them, a partial wall divided a grand dining area into two entries. Adjacent to the living room

was the open, octagonal entry with open railings exposing the upper level.

They approached a hallway.

Sounds from a room made him stop. Voices from behind made him look for cover. Arizona took his hand and pulled him into a bedroom.

"I told you to make sure the villa was ready for my father's visit," a voice said. Julian's.

"We have, sir." The other man must be a servant.

"Then why isn't the Land Rover ready? It's a mess and you haven't repaired the air conditioner."

"Horace is taking care of it right now."

"Right now, in the middle of the night?"

The servant's answer was muffled. The two were moving away from the hallway.

Braden went out into the hall, his hand still clasped with Arizona's.

"Let's get out of here," she whispered.

He moved down the hall anyway...Tatum.

The sound of a television grew louder. Arizona's hand gripped his tighter. She was scared.

He debated leaving. But what about Tatum? If she were here...

At the room where the television played, he peered in quickly. No one was there. Had Julian been there before his servant interrupted him with news of the Land Rover? He was sure uptight about his father coming for a visit.

There were two more rooms down this hall and a bathroom, and no sign of Tatum. Braden checked closets and armoires. Nothing. Not even toiletries.

He led Arizona back into the hall. At the top of the stairs, Julian's shouting vibrated.

"I want everything perfect, do you understand? Not a thing out of place!"

A barely audible "Yes, sir," answered.

Just then, a man appeared behind them. Braden hauled Arizona out of harm's way. Before he could turn to defend them both, the man slammed a gun down on his head. Everything went black.

"Braden!" Arizona started to kneel beside his fallen body when the man who'd knocked him unconscious grabbed her from behind.

Steel biceps held her arms to her side and back against a big frame. Julian appeared at the bottom of the stairs. He stared at her with his dark, eerie eyes, registering who she was and then Braden lying unconscious on the floor.

Then those cold, evil eyes lifted. His dark hair was thick and messy and his face was leathery for his age.

"They broke into the villa, sir," the man holding her said.

"Take her to a room upstairs."

The man steered her toward the hall.

Arizona fought. She kicked; she writhed. She used every trick she'd ever learned, all to no avail. The man who forced her up the stairs was practiced. At the door of a room, he shoved her inside. She flew, sprawling onto her hands and knees.

The man jerked at her belt and removed her gun. Then he turned and left the room. By the time she got up and ran to the door, it was locked from the outside.

In one horrifying moment she wondered if this was what had happened to Tatum. Had Julian's men forced her into this room and locked her here until whatever fate had been decided for her had been carried out? She spun around, fighting fear as she searched the room. It was a pretty bedroom. Soft, earthy colors on the queen-sized bed, adorned with pillows. Dainty nightstands matched.

A two-foot-high stand held a giant television. Swooping drapes were pulled back to show off a spectacular view of the mountain and ocean beyond. She was facing the back and could see the house where she and Braden had been all afternoon.

What would happen next?

She didn't have to wait long. The door opened and Julian walked in, two of his armed guards behind him.

Arizona stood her ground. Showing fear would only feed his perversion. She'd wait for the right opportunity and then she'd strike.

"Why is it that I keep receiving unannounced visits from you?" Julian asked.

His bloodshot eyes were small and beady. His seedy, pocked face clashed with his impeccably pressed white shirt. So did his messy, dark brown hair.

"We're trying to find Tatum McCrae."

He swung his arms open, the innocence not working in his favor. Or was he mocking her? "I've told you before. I don't know anyone by that name."

"She took a cab here."

"Did she now? Well, then perhaps it wasn't me she came to see. I have lots of staff."

"Let us search the villa."

Julian stepped closer still, until she could smell his decaying teeth. She drew her head back.

"You broke into my home to do just that," he said. "You are not welcome here."

He exuded a dark confidence that was bolstered by the presence of the two guards, big and dumb, only there to do Julian's bidding.

"Where is Tatum?" And Braden.

Straightening, he ignored her question, clasping his hands behind his back. "When I phone the police, they

will believe me when I tell them a man and a woman broke into my home and threatened me."

She didn't respond. They had broken in.

"Perhaps my message wasn't clear before."

"You mean when you had us chased off your property by armed men?"

"Perhaps you require a stronger message."

"Why do you need armed guards?"

Instead of answering, he nodded to his guards. The two strode farther into the room, approaching her. Julian left the room, closing the door behind him. She didn't hear it lock.

What were these two going to do?

A stronger message…

Arizona backed away, glancing around for some kind of a weapon. One of the men held back while the other advanced; he was balding, wearing a tight black T-shirt and black jeans with big, bulky boots. His pistol was hanging at his side.

She'd had enough self-defense classes to help her, but she had to be careful.

Just then he did something unexpected. He put his gun on the dresser to his right and smiled, his cold eyes never changing. He didn't think he needed a weapon with her. Behind him, the other man still held his.

She didn't think either one of them would kill her. Julian meant for them to deliver a *stronger message.* What would that entail? Rape?

As he neared, Arizona bided her time, then at the right moment, she ducked and rolled him over her shoulder. The element of surprise worked. She lunged out of his reach and faced the second man. He had long scraggly black hair and gray eyes. Creepy eyes. No empathy.

He aimed the gun at her head. She still wore the flak

jacket. He didn't fire. He moved with her, facing her off. She allowed him to get close. When he raised his gun to knock her head, she blocked his wrist with her forearm. As the gun toppled to the floor, she stabbed his eyes with her fingers. He yelled and stumbled backward. The man on the floor was getting to his feet.

Arizona ran for the door. Sure enough, it was unlocked. She ran out and slammed it shut behind her, driving a dead bolt home into the doorframe just as the doorknob began to turn. One of the men inside rattled the door.

Arizona didn't wait. She ran down the hall.

At the end, she found an open stairway, narrower than the main one. The servant's passage. She descended.

Where was Braden?

At a landing in the stairs, a woman appeared through the wall. It was a camouflaged door.

"This way," she whispered.

Who was she? Arizona didn't hesitate or waste time asking. She flew through the door, and the woman shut it. The room she found herself in was small with a kitchenette area. The woman's living quarters.

"Thank you," Arizona said.

The woman approached, taking her hands in hers, urgently imploring her with her eyes. "You must leave this place and stay away."

"Where is Tatum McCrae?" Arizona demanded.

"I didn't know." The woman appeared agitated. "I swear, I didn't know."

"Didn't know what?"

The sound of footsteps pounded on the servants' stairs.

"Find him!" a man's voice growled.

"You must leave. Now." The woman steered her toward another door. "He is waiting for you outside this door."

"Who?"

The woman opened the door and Braden stood there, hands leaning on the doorframe above his head. When he saw her he visibly sagged with relief, lowering his arms and looking at the woman.

"Thank you," he said.

"Do not come back."

Braden took her hand and pulled her down the hallway. "How did you get away? Did that maid help you?"

"Shh!"

"Did she?"

"No. Come on!"

He'd fought his way free and then intersected the maid. His prowess with self-defense was out of the ordinary. But she didn't have time to think on that now. Neither of them had guns anymore and they had to get out of here.

Back in the rec room, he pulled her after him, toward the broken window. When they reached it, he pushed her through first and then followed. She raced behind him for the trees. Just as they passed the first few trunks, she heard voices shouting. Braden let go of her hand.

"Run!"

She was already running as fast as she could. The slope steepened and it grew taxing to keep up the pace while climbing.

"I see them!"

Arizona cursed. She tripped over a rock and tumbled, slamming into the trunk of a tree.

Braden hauled her back up.

The first man was on them. Arizona used her feet to kick his chest while Braden blocked a punch from another. The man she fought sailed backward, running right into the second man. There didn't appear to be more of them.

Braden grabbed her hand and ran with her through the trees again. Cresting the hill, they ran down the other side.

Leaves and branches smacked her and she swatted more out of her way. Then the vegetation cleared. They were now on the earthen stairs. This would take them to the beach. Braden took her hand again as they flew down the stairs, then finally they made it to the sandy beach. She helped him move the dinghy out into the water and then jumped in while he started the small motor.

Gunfire erupted.

"Get down!" Braden shouted.

But there was no protection in an inflatable dinghy. Braden pushed it full throttle. Bullets shot into the water just out of reach. The yacht was far enough out to escape the gunfire. Leaving the dinghy in the water, they climbed aboard and Braden started the engine.

Arizona watched more men join the two who'd chased them through the trees on the beach. They stood in a line, weapons at their sides, admitting defeat.

They docked at Soper's Hole Marina late at night. Braden had taken precautionary measures and had a slip reserved already. A backup plan. He sure was good at this. It only kept her curiosity stirred as to why. There had to be more to it than his employment with a weapons manufacturer. She was especially certain of that after seeing the way he avoided conversation about it.

Helping him tie the boat, Arizona kept looking out to sea and checking the lit dock. At this hour of the night, very little stirred.

"Are we safe here?"

"As safe as we are anywhere."

How comforting. Following him into the salon, she put fear aside and gave in to curiosity that wouldn't leave her alone. "Were you ever in the military?"

"No." He peered out the salon doors, searching the dark

marina. He had a sharp eye. A practiced eye. Watchdog. Warrior. This man fell prey to no other living creature.

He turned during her thoughts. She was staring at him. And even when his eyes met hers, she couldn't stop. The way he made her feel last night still hovered in her heart. Not since Trevor had she felt anything similar. She'd always avoided men who reminded her of what she'd lost. Last night proved why. She'd never experienced that with any other man, the deep desire, the makings of love. The intensity had overwhelmed her, and the result had manifested itself in the form of bad sex.

"Still reminding you of Trevor?" He moved deeper into the salon, preparing the sofa for sleep. He'd stand guard out here through the night.

How many times could she apologize? Yet, an apology wasn't what he wanted. "I should have known to stay away from you." It wasn't as though he hadn't had ample warning. He knew she avoided engineers. "Don't take it personally."

"Me?"

Did he think she was? Or was he surprised she'd said that, and was not taking it personally? But he was. His ego showed it.

"Men are so sensitive about sex. They have to be the best a woman has ever had. God forbid if they ever run across one that spoils the illusion."

Too late she realized how that sounded.

"Thank you for pointing out that I wasn't the best you've had."

"I didn't say that."

Pausing as he dropped a pillow onto the sofa, he eyed her skeptically.

"I can't control the way I feel," she said. He, on the other hand, had to be in constant control. She saw it in his acute

awareness of all that surrounded him, maybe even in the way he gauged love on how good the sex was. He'd married twice because of that.

"You can control how much Trevor influences you're feeling."

"The same way sex influences you?"

"Sex is important to any relationship."

It had been with Trevor. It could be with Braden. If she let it….

Chapter 8

Lincoln hobbled on his crutch to the kitchen, rinsing off his plate. Everything was harder without the use of his leg. The bullet had torn through his muscle and the doctor said he'd have weeks of physical therapy once the wound healed. He was already doing some now. He had his manager covering for him at his martial arts studio, but he worried about getting back up to speed in time. Healing may take a while, longer than he could afford.

And bounty hunting. He'd be out of commission there, too.

He hoped Arizona was doing all right. Arranging all those weapons had been a stretch for him. But he'd rather have an armed Arizona than a vulnerable one. Besides, she knew how to shoot. And she had Braden.

Movement out his window caught his attention. A truck backed into the driveway of the house next door.

He lived in an older section of Denver. Most of the

homes on this street had been renovated. His was the most recent to see improvements. The one next door hadn't yet. Its exterior wasn't in bad shape. Most of it was redbrick. The trim was cracked and the paint peeling. The front porch was stone. The yard gave away the lack of care. Weeds, overgrown shrubs, a patchy lawn and a falling-down fence all told the tale. He hadn't been inside but he'd bet the cost of his pricey renovation that it was in disrepair.

A woman climbed out of the cab of the moving truck, a white Lab right after her. The dog bounded around the truck, into his yard and back to its owner, who, Lincoln saw, was about as hot as they came. In a pink tank top with faded jean shorts, her legs went on for a mile down to green flip-flops. Her curly red hair was up in a ponytail, poking out from the back of a pink baseball hat.

Did he have a new neighbor?

She opened the back of the truck and slid out a ramp. Just when he was going to go out front and offer to help, he remembered his shot leg.

Her Lab ran up the ramp and ran back down, tongue flopping with her ears. The dog was a girl.

After the second trip, he decided he had to do something. Hobbling out the front door, he made it to his driveway when he saw another car drive up to the redhead's house.

The Lab saw him and bounded over with a deep bark. Lincoln tried to crouch and the Lab jumped onto him, her front paws on his thighs. The dog licked his face as he pet her.

"What's your name?" Seeing a tag hanging from her collar, he read, "Madeline. Who would name you Madeline?"

She was a beautiful creature, all white except for a reddish tint that was deepest on her ears and eyebrows and

faintly down her back and tail. Her stomach and paws were pure white. Trim and streamlined, she had the makings of a great hunter. The energy, too. She could hardly stay still.

Bounding away, Madeline ran back to the van, sniffing until she stopped and perked her ears to the newcomer.

A man climbed out of a black Jetta, the car too small for his frame.

Lincoln winced as he straightened, pain shooting up his leg as he maneuvered the crutch under his arm. He headed back for the front door.

"I thought I told you not to come here."

Hearing the woman's voice, Lincoln stopped.

The muffled response from the man was unintelligible from here.

"How did you find me?"

They were inside the truck.

"It's not like you left the city."

Had his neighbor moved to get away from the man?

Lincoln saw Madeline, agitated and pacing at the base of the ramp. She put her paws on the ramp and growled.

Dogs were an excellent judge of character. Maybe this man hadn't come to help her unpack.

"Just go." The woman marched down the ramp carrying a box. The man followed, carrying another.

Madeline kept out of the way, trotting after her owner into the garage.

Lincoln moved to the edge of his driveway.

"It's a nice house. I can help you fix it up."

"Are you crazy? Leave. Now."

Madeline growled again.

"Shut that thing up," the man shouted.

"She never liked you. I should have paid more attention to that."

"You're going to piss me off."

"Get the hell out of my house!"

The sound of a fist hitting flesh preceded a surprised gasp from the woman.

"Bastard!"

Hearing the woman begin to wrestle with the man, Lincoln crutched his way into the garage. The door leading into the house was open.

Madeline was just inside, her front paws lifting off the kitchen floor with each agitated bark. Then the dog lunged for something out of Lincoln's sight.

"Ouch! Stupid dog!"

Had Madeline bitten the man? Lincoln reached the open garage door in time to see the man try to kick the dog. But she dodged out of the way and rounded for his other leg, clamping down for another chomp.

Way to go, Madeline.

The redhead was climbing to her feet, using the kitchen counter to stand. She turned, holding her jaw.

The jerk had hit her hard enough to knock her on the floor. Rage boiled up in him. He didn't care how much his leg hurt. Entering the house, he spotted the man trying to kick Madeline again, but the dog was far too agile for his slow swing. Lincoln used his crutch as a weapon, lifting it just as the man saw him. He jabbed the man's temple, sending his head backward.

With startled eyes, the man stumbled and crashed against a pantry door and then landed on his hands and knees. Lincoln limped over to him, using the crutch to thump him on the head again, making sure some of his teeth sliced the soft tissue of his mouth.

The man yelled. "What the…"

Lincoln kept pummeling his face. "You like hitting women?"

The man tried to grab the crutch. Lincoln put weight

on his good leg and kicked the man's arm, swiping it away from the crutch, ignoring the pain in his injured leg.

"Huh?" Lincoln goaded, pounding the man with his crutch. "You like that?"

"Stop!" the woman shouted.

Madeline barked wildly but didn't attack. Smart dog. He liked Madeline. He and Madeline were going to be good friends.

"Stop it!" the woman grabbed Lincoln's arm.

He stopped hitting the man on the floor. His face was bloody. So was the rubber end of Lincoln's crutch.

The man on the floor glared up at him with a mixture of alarm and anger. "Who the hell are you?"

Lincoln turned to the woman. "Are you all right?"

"Get out."

Not the show of gratitude he'd expected. "What?"

"Get out." She pointed to the garage door.

"Your boyfriend hit you."

"And that is none of your business. I don't even know you."

"I'm your neighbor. I was going to offer to help you unload your truck when I heard this piece of work." He indicated the man on the floor.

She eyed his crutch. How had he planned on helping her with that? He could hear her thinking.

"I'm not accustomed to limitations," he said.

She continued to stare at him, his charm falling flat. "I don't care who you are. You don't just barge into somebody's house and start beating people up."

The man rose to his feet, taller than Lincoln by about an inch. Madeline growled, baring her pearly white teeth. Nice-looking fangs. Good girl.

Her eyes shifted to him and he received an acknowledging blink.

Lincoln chuckled. "Cute dog."

The man's fist began to swing for him. He was going to punch him? Lincoln easily blocked the attempt, letting the crutch fall and driving his own fist into the man's throat. Just hard enough to let him know he was no match for Lincoln.

The man choked and struggled for breath.

"What are you doing?" The woman ran to the horrible man, pawing and mewling to see if he was okay. It made Lincoln sick.

He bent to pick up his crutch, petting Madeline's head when the dog came to him. "Good girl. You watch your mama."

Standing up, he saw the woman and the man eyeing him with appall. Okay, maybe he'd misjudged this.

"Sorry. I thought you needed help," he said to the woman.

"Go away and never come back," she stormed.

Some women liked men who knocked them around, he guessed. Weird. He crutched into the garage and over to his house. Inside, he went to his kitchen window. Nothing stirred next door. But moments later, the man helped the woman unload the truck.

Lincoln gave up, mystified over why any woman would scold the help of someone who'd only defended her, and then welcome an abusive man into her home. Let him help her unload her moving truck.

After heating up a frozen dinner, Lincoln went to sit on his back patio, enjoying a glass of wine with his painkiller and the cool, starlit night.

Beating up that guy had hurt his leg.

A sound from next door disturbed his peace. He liked it better when he had no neighbor.

Soft laughter filtered over the fence. That and bubbles.

She had a damn hot tub. Was she in there with that jerk? Not hearing any other voices, he realized she was talking on a cell phone. Girl talk. She sounded nicer than he'd experienced in person.

Lincoln stood and took his wine inside.

After watching a movie and cleaning the kitchen, he went up to bed. It took some time getting up the stairs. His room was on the same side as his new neighbor.

Not getting why he was drawn there, he went to the window to see how much of a view he had of the inside of her house. Quite a bit. Did she have every light on in her house?

The truck was still parked in the driveway and he couldn't see if the jerk's Jetta was still in the street. The blinds in the upper level room were open. They were open in every room. Or were there any window coverings at all?

There must not be. Otherwise, why not shut them? Unless she welcomed Peeping Toms.

Just as the thought came, she appeared in the upper-level window. He could see her clearly. Wearing a short nightie, she sauntered to the window and stood there looking at him.

He couldn't move. She was so beautiful and he was being a reprobate by continuing to watch, but she was too much of a vision to turn away.

Flipping him off, she turned and lifted the nightie over her head, tossing it to the floor with attitude. Her naked butt swayed as she went to the bed and climbed in.

Beautiful but bitchy. And what was the deal with that guy? Why had she allowed him to hit her? Why was she mad at him for defending her?

Chapter 9

Braden took Arizona down to the most public place in Soper's Hole the next morning. A café with a busy patio, a real tourist attraction. They'd be safe here.

She sat across from him, still looking around like a scared cat. Scared but ready to strike. He couldn't deny how much he liked that about her. He refused to be a victim, too. He just couldn't talk about why. He was, however, amazed that she'd zeroed in on that about him. No one else ever had, not even his parents.

Instead of watching the street as he'd planned, he watched her. She was doing the watching for both of them. She probably would rather do that than look at him. All morning she'd barely said anything to him. She had probably made up her mind there was nothing between them after their night together, thinking of Trevor instead of him while he was inside her. Those few sparks they'd had in the beginning were a fluke.

Damn. Why couldn't he stop thinking that way? Sex wasn't everything. He of all people should know that. He'd had two failed marriages that had been based on sex. Arizona was giving him a complex.

At another table, two couples talked. One of the women held a baby, a little girl who'd begun to fuss. The woman tried to soothe the baby while the other woman smiled her adoration.

The baby quieted and drifted off to sleep.

"Aww, that's so cute," the other woman said.

The two men got into a conversation that had nothing to do with babies.

Braden noticed how Arizona watched. She was completely absorbed in the baby. Then she noticed him and shook herself out of her trance.

"What's cute about that?" she asked.

Aiden hadn't been cute to him when he was born, either. But once the skin stopped being so red and chapped and his young blue eyes looked up at him, his whole world changed.

"It's different when they're your own," he said.

"Yeah, but look at that woman. She doesn't have any kids and she's making a fool of herself over there."

"Maybe she didn't bring her kids on vacation."

Arizona took that in and continued to study the scene, baffled and struggling to understand.

"When they're your own, they're part of you, body and soul." She turned to him as he tried to give her some insight. "You see the similarities, both physically and behaviorally. And you have a huge responsibility for that tiny life. They depend on you for everything. They learn from you." He glanced over at the now-sleeping child. "It's their innocence, and knowing that someday they're going to grow up just like you did. You want them to have every

advantage in life, to be the best they can be. Better than you." Looking back at Arizona, who listened intently, he finished. "But most amazing is the love you feel for the miracle you created. There's nothing to compare to it. It's the best feeling in the world." He didn't have to pretend how powerful the bond was between him and his son.

"That sounds like a fairy tale," she said. "I don't see how I would ever feel that way. All I know is that I don't want to have a helpless baby to look after. I don't want to be responsible for bringing any child into this world."

At least she'd called it a fairy tale. She didn't have a completely frozen heart. Why was she so blocked off to the concept of babies?

She truly didn't want to have kids. Her career was more important. There were some women out there who made those decisions. Maybe it was for the best. Maybe women like Arizona weren't meant to be mothers.

He thought of Aiden and his future. If he ever remarried, he'd make sure the woman accepted him as though he were her own. Not being able to satisfy Arizona in bed lost some of its importance just then. Aiden was his top priority. He was better off without a woman than with one who didn't want kids.

Arizona turned from the patio as a couple on bicycles pedaled by. Her dreamy look revealed her wish to be doing something like that, something fun and with a hint of adventure. Disconcerting, how he'd like to do the same. Get on a bike and ride the island. Just think of all the great places they'd experience.

"Excuse me?"

Braden turned with Arizona to see a woman standing at their table. It was the maid from Julian's house, the one who'd helped them escape. She glanced around anxiously.

"You," Arizona breathed.

"I don't have much time." She dug into her purse.

"Sit down," Braden said. "What's your name?"

The woman sat, glancing hurriedly around as though afraid to be seen. "Patty Williams." Her fingers trembled as she lifted out a small velvet bag. "This belonged to her."

She handed the bag to Braden.

"To Tatum?" He had to confirm.

She nodded.

With foreboding circling his core, he opened the bag and pulled out a necklace with a familiar emerald pendant. His parents had given her this for her last birthday.

"Yes."

He drilled Patty with an expectant look. An explanation was necessary right now.

"She was there," Arizona breathed.

"I never saw her." She looked imploringly at Braden, begging for him to understand. "Julian asked me to take a box of clothes to donate, and the necklace was among the items. Since he was giving them away, I didn't see the harm. He invites many women there who leave things behind. It wasn't the first time I've donated for him. I only kept the necklace."

"What things did you donate? Tell me about them."

"There wasn't a lot. Just a few outfits. Nothing personal like cosmetics or other toiletries. There were different sizes, too, so not all of them came from the same woman." She looked imploringly at Braden. "Until you came searching for your sister, I suspected nothing."

"Have you told the police about this?" Arizona asked.

"I didn't know who she was until yesterday when I heard Julian talking. You broke into the house and I heard him tell his guards to catch you both and lock you in rooms until he figured out what to do with you before his father

arrived. He said he couldn't allow it getting out that your sister had been there."

"Is she still there?" Arizona asked.

"Julian is afraid of his father?" Braden asked.

"I didn't know she was ever there," she said to Arizona. "I just heard him talking, that's all." Then she turned to Braden. "Julian seemed as though he was afraid his father would find out…about your sister, and…whatever he's done with her."

Braden lowered his head as a wave of dread sank him down. If he'd killed her…

He'd donated her things. Didn't she need them anymore?

Arizona reached over and rubbed his back.

"I'm so sorry," the maid said.

Julian had given all her possessions away. They'd be dispersed among the homeless or poor and no one would ever be able to trace them back to Tatum. The police wouldn't be able to prove they'd come from Julian's villa.

Except for the maid. She could prove Tatum was there.

"We'll take you to the police now." Arizona looked at Braden. "We have to tell Crawford. He should question her."

He agreed wholeheartedly and was happy her thinking was right in line with his.

"No!" The woman stood abruptly, waving her hands in negation. "I cannot go to the police."

"Why not?" Arizona stood with her. "A woman may have been kidnapped. Possibly killed. You know something."

"And I've told you. Please do not tell the police I came to you. I don't know what Julian will do if he ever finds out I talked to you. I returned what isn't mine. That's all." The woman turned to go.

"Wait." Braden rose and Arizona followed the woman onto the sidewalk.

Braden gently took hold of her arm and stopped her. "Please."

"I've told you all I can. Probably more than I should have." She tugged to be free, round eyes frantically searching around her for anyone who might see.

"You said Julian invites many women to his villa."

"Yes."

"Can you tell us who they are?"

She shook her head. "I never learned their names. He takes them to his suite and they're gone by morning."

Gone by morning. What the hell was going on?

"What about his father? What can you tell us about him?" Braden asked. He was desperate for information.

"Carlos Ramirez isn't Julian's real father. He raised him from a child. I don't know what happened to Julian's mother. One of the cooks said she left him. Carlos is not very fond of Julian but he's never turned him away."

Did Carlos know what Julian was doing while he was away? "Neither am I."

"What does Carlos do for a living?" Arizona asked.

"He inherited money from his mother. From what I have heard, he travels a lot and is rarely home."

"And Julian?"

"He is supposedly a retired insurance underwriter, but there are many suspicious meetings that take place at the villa."

"What kind of meetings?" Braden asked.

The maid searched around again, agitated. "Please. I must be going. If I am seen here…"

"What kind of meetings?" he demanded.

"I—I do not know. Men come to the villa and they meet in the basement behind closed doors. There is a meeting

room down there. None of the staff knows what goes on in there."

Braden didn't remember seeing a meeting room when they'd gone to the villa.

"Some say his meetings are with friends, doing favors for money, that kind of thing," the maid continued.

"Black-market favors?" Arizona asked.

"Carlos does not support Julian other than to tolerate him living in the villa." She looked both ways on the street. "Please..."

Braden stepped back from her. "Thank you for coming. And for returning Tatum's necklace. It means a lot."

The woman smiled tentatively. "Take care. I wish you the best in finding your sister."

She crossed the street and walked down the sidewalk to the corner, where she disappeared.

"What now?" Arizona asked.

"Crawford."

"Exactly what I was thinking."

Arizona sat beside Braden in Detective Crawford's office. Yellow walls and blue chairs added cheer to the doom and gloom of everyday police work.

"This definitely confirms Tatum was there." Crawford looked up from examining the necklace. "I suppose I should thank you." He held up the emerald. "This is the best lead we've had so far. I'll get my men on it."

Arizona relaxed against the chair. Instead of allowing his ego to rule the day, he'd set it aside and accepted the help. Maybe he'd get somewhere in the investigation now.

"And I'll go question the maid myself. Discreetly, of course. It would probably be best if the two of you stayed away."

Braden nodded once.

Arizona agreed they shouldn't be the ones questioning the maid. "What about all the other women he brought to his house?" If they could find one or two of them, maybe they could shed some light.

"There've been no other open missing person reports. Tatum and Courtney Andrews are the only two."

And both were connected to Julian Blake. How long had he been getting away with this? The injustice of it ate away at her composure. She'd love to see him caught.

"What about murders?" Braden asked. "Do you have anything unsolved?"

Arizona was impressed with his thinking.

Crawford took affront. "Tortola isn't a hub for crime. We pride ourselves at maintaining a safe, tranquil island where travelers can find pristine beaches."

In other words, no? The detective's patience was wearing thin. He had two tourists doing his job for him. He appeared to appreciate the lead of the necklace, but he should have been the one to find it.

Leaning back against his chair, elbow on the arm, he rubbed his chin beneath a poker face, not answering Braden's question.

"Do you?" she pressed.

"I'll look into it."

It was all they'd get. Why? Had his ego overpowered the day after all? Or was he stalling for other reasons?

"We'll try to stay out of your way from now on," Braden said. Then he stood. "Let's go."

Arizona followed him out the door. When they were outside, she couldn't keep her thoughts to herself anymore. "There are murders, aren't there?"

"That's what we're going to find out."

She was glad he had the same intentions as her. Crawford hadn't thought to check into the unsolved murders.

He hadn't thought to check into a possible connection to Julian. Was it island life that made him so lax or something else?

A short walk down the street brought them to the local library. A white stone building with colorful flowers blooming in the landscaped front, it was old and beautiful. Opening one of two heavy, worn wooden doors, they entered.

A reception area branched off into rooms of books. Beneath florescent lighting, Arizona followed Braden into the reference section. There were two dated computers and shelves of nonfiction books.

She took one computer and he took the other. After navigating her way through the library's archives, she found files of old newspapers.

"Here." She showed Braden where to go.

She began searching through newspapers. A murder would make headlines on this island. They were sporadic and not in sequential order.

"I still don't see why Tatum would have come here," she commented as she skimmed headlines. "It obviously wasn't for vacation. She had a reason." And that reason involved Julian. "That woman's missing computer, the break-in at your house. You're an engineer for Hamilton, and your sister worked for a freight forwarder caught doing unauthorized exports."

"Keep looking," Braden answered.

He took it sorely whenever she brought that up.

"What if this is all a result of arms dealing?"

He said nothing. Probably because she only voiced what he didn't want to believe, that his sister had been involved in something illegal even though she'd denied it.

"Julian is a high-risk insurance underwriter and supposedly retired. He'd have connections to companies like

Hamilton. Maybe even exporters like the company that fired Tatum." If Julian discovered Tatum had a brother and where he worked and what he did there, he may have targeted Braden next.

"Tatum wouldn't have done business with anyone like Julian."

"What if she didn't have a choice?" Julian targeted women. That contradicted her theory that he'd gone after Braden.

Braden looked at her, pausing what he was doing. He'd already considered the possibility. But what could have happened to make her claim she was being blamed for something she didn't do?

A few minutes passed before Braden went still again, this time an article capturing his attention.

"A woman's body was found on a beach," he said.

She got up and went over to him, leaning over to read the article with him.

Mina Paoli was strangled before she was left on the beach in Lower Belmond Bay. She had on a swimsuit.

"She was a local," Arizona said, staring at a photo of a young woman, dark skin and beaded hair. She was pretty.

"And worked in a pub serving drinks," Braden added. "Kind of blows your technology angle."

"So it would appear." She went back to reading the article. Mina's parents owned the pub where she worked. Maybe they could go there when they finished.

Something disturbed her about the article. "She was missing for several weeks before she was murdered." And she was murdered six months ago.

Arizona resumed searching through the files. An hour later she came across another article. "This woman was from South America."

Braden leaned around the desk wall that separated the

computers and read some of the article. "Roselda Alvarado. Client manager for an information-technology company."

No arms there. How odd. Where was the link between these women and whatever had made that man come after Braden? Or was there even a link?

"Missing for three weeks before she was found dead a year ago," Arizona pointed out. If these murders were linked, the killer waited to kill his victims. And the women were from all over the world. America, South America and local.

"We're closing in five minutes."

She turned with Braden to the librarian who'd come to stand at the opposite end of their table.

"We're just about finished." Arizona quickly skimmed the rest of the articles dating back to coincide the length of time Julian had lived on Frenchman's Cay.

"Time to go." Braden waited for her to get up from her chair and then followed her outside.

It was dark now.

"The Long Beach Pub is just up the street," Arizona said.

"I was thinking the same thing."

The pub was a short walk down Waterfront Drive. Wood buildings lined the road with diagonal parking that butted up to the structures, leaving little room for walking. She and Braden walked in the street and came upon the pub, painted turquoise with bright yellow trim around the windows and a single white door. A patio overhung above the entry, boasting only three or four tables.

Braden held the door and Arizona entered. Two casement windows in the front and a patio door on the side would do a fair job of allowing in light during the day. Wood tables filled the open room, three of them occupied among muted conversation and the occasional clank

of dishes from the kitchen. Island music played through ceiling speakers, a subtle crackling adding to the laid-back charm of the place.

A young woman appeared from an open doorway in the back, giving enough of a glimpse of the kitchen to reveal its cramped space. "Would there be two now?"

"We're looking for Ingrid and Carlin. Is this their restaurant?" Braden said.

"Ingrid is always here. She runs the place more than Carlin." The woman beamed. "Who's asking for her?"

"We're here to talk to her about Mina."

Her big, toothy smile vanished. "Wait here." She made her way back to the kitchen.

A moment later, a heavy black woman with beaded hair held in a net appeared. Her skin was light brown and her eyes a magnificent green. Her daughter's beauty was reflected in her.

"Are you police?" The woman asked, eyeing them up and down skeptically.

"No," Braden said. "My sister is missing and we think your daughter's murder may be related somehow."

The woman stopped before them, pain still fresh in her eyes. "What do you know about my daughter?" She finished wiping her hands on her apron.

"Only that she was murdered and her killer is still free," Braden said. "My sister's last known whereabouts was Julian Blake's villa."

Arizona saw how he waited for the woman's reaction. There was only confusion.

"I do not know a Julian Blake."

"Can you tell us about your daughter?" Arizona asked as gently as she could. "People she knew? Places she went?"

Tears glistened in her eyes. But she nodded and ges-

tured toward a table along the wall, far enough away from the three occupied tables.

Arizona sat beside Braden, the woman taking up half of the seat across from them. Putting her purse beside her, Arizona took out her notepad and a pen, aware of Braden's glance. This wasn't just for her story, if she ever wrote one. She'd have everything written down so they could piece together what happened to his sister and find her.

The woman had difficulty finding her voice. Grief ravaged her. "I was having a hard time with her," she began. "She was going off with a bad crowd. Staying out late." She shook her head. "We close at eleven here and she'd go out after that."

"Did she wait tables?" Arizona asked.

The woman nodded.

"Where did she go the night she went missing?" Braden asked.

"She never told me where she was going. She'd just come home when the sun was rising."

"Who was she with?"

"I already told the police. The boy she was seeing was on a trip to the United States. My daughter was with other friends until about midnight. She had a bicycle and her friends told police she left the house where they were partying on it. Her bike was found on the side of the road with a flat tire."

She'd stopped in the middle of the night to fix her tire and had been kidnapped before she'd finished. Arizona hid her shudder as she imagined the girl's terror.

"We couldn't find her." The woman began to sob.

Arizona reached across the table and covered the woman's hand with hers. It hadn't been very long since her daughter's body was found. And her kidnapping appeared random. It lent a note of credibility to Crawford. Random

acts of violence were difficult to solve. Whoever had taken Mina may not have known her. Which made sense if the other kidnappings were related. All were from different countries. Random.

Outside, Braden walked close to Arizona, encouraged and also worried. Encouraged because if Tatum had been abducted by the same man who'd taken Mina, the chances were good that she was still alive. The murders occurred weeks after the abductions. He refrained from letting too much hope buoy his mood, however. What if he couldn't find her in time? And what if the murders weren't related?

A parked car caught his eye. It was running and he could make out the shape of a person inside. No, two. Men. Too bulky to be women.

Sliding his hand around Arizona's waist, he pulled her in the opposite direction as he watched the car pull out into the street behind two other cars. The street was fairly busy with activity, but he couldn't rule out a drive-by shooting.

He searched for somewhere to go. Back to the pub?

The car neared, moving slow and holding up traffic. Next to them, it pulled off to the side of the road.

"Keep walking."

Cars streamed past the car even as it inched along, drawing up beside them. The tinted window began to roll down, revealing a dark-skinned man he'd never seen before.

Spotting a taxi, Braden lifted his hand to flag it to the side. It pulled over behind the car and stopped for them.

Steering Arizona, he went to the taxi and opened the back door for her.

"Frenchman's Point Hotel," he told the driver, seeing the outline of two men in the car ahead looking back through the tinted glass.

"Who is that?" Arizona asked as the taxi drove out into the street. The window was down and let in cooling, seaside air.

"No one I want to meet."

"How did they know we were here?" The breeze ruffled Arizona's thick, blond hair.

That was a great question. Had they been followed to the police station? He hadn't noticed. He'd looked, though. Maybe Julian had someone watching them all the time. Or were the men in the car on the side of the law? Had Crawford sent some detectives to follow them? This should be his investigation. Maybe he was trying to make it so.

The car didn't follow them.

Facing forward again, he realized his arm was along the back of the taxi and Arizona was sitting close. So close that her hips and breasts were in contact with him. They'd been in such a hurry to escape the other car that they'd paid no attention to bumping body parts.

She looked up and he was locked in the instant blaze of their confounding attraction. What was it about her? Even lousy sex didn't douse the energy.

It hadn't been lousy for him. And part of him was tempted to take on the challenge and obliterate her fiancé from her head, right along with her stigma of engineers.

Back at the hotel, Arizona headed for the restaurant. She hoped Braden didn't follow, that he'd go up to their room and give her some time alone for a while. She could use a reprieve from his frequent glances, as though he were contemplating something. Ready to pick a fight. Or drop the pretense of distance they'd erected ever since sleeping together.

He followed.

Instead of staying, she decided to get something to

go and take it up to their room. Braden ordered what he wanted and they sat at the bar to wait. She ordered an island drink. He ordered whiskey.

When the bartender deposited his short glass in front of him, she eyed him, full of incredulity.

He sipped while he met her gaze with grievance leftover from bad sex. Watching him down the glass belligerently, she smiled and took a big sip of her drink.

He grunted his cynical humor. "Weak."

What was he after, a drinking war? She lifted her glass and sucked on the straw, rolling her eyes as she drank to see his crooked, mocking grin.

It took her longer to drain her glass.

He raised two fingers to the bartender, who brought two more without a flicker of judgment.

He drank his glass.

"I'm not drinking this like a shot," she told him. "If you want to get sloppy, you go right ahead. Just remember you might kill brain cells you need for your job."

One of his eyebrows lifted. "I know lots of engineers who drink."

"I haven't met any."

"Didn't Trevor drink?"

Derision rolled off his tongue, lingering especially long on Trevor's name. Arizona took in his injured ego and marveled for a moment. His ego was fine in all other areas other than his sexual encounter with her.

"Not accustomed to being with a woman who doesn't respond as expected, huh?" She had to rib him.

"I can make you respond."

Oh, that made her tingle. Maybe she shouldn't provoke him. "What makes you so sure?"

"I'm not Trevor."

No, definitely not. Trevor had been sophisticated and

conforming to society. He'd been smart. Handsome, too. Braden was all those things except conformed. He paved his own way in life. And his handsomeness had a rugged edge to it. Rock-hard abs. Muscular shoulders and chest. Rigid jaw, and stubble. He was smart, but he was also a freethinker. He didn't treat people as though they were beneath him. He didn't hold people above him. He was just Braden McCrae, happy with who he was and what he had in life. Enviable. Except for his hang-up on performance in bed.

"Why is sex so important to men?" she blurted.

He grinned. "It feels good?"

"Aside from that. Why is it so important?"

He stared at her, trying to figure out what she was fishing for. "It feels good."

Laughing, she pivoted on her chair to face him. "Come on. Be serious."

"I am serious."

He was serious. Was it that simple? It didn't explain his ego. "I think you have complexes about women because they're trickier to please than men."

"Are we talking about our disaster in bed?"

Of course they were, but she wasn't going to acknowledge that. "Do you have to feel like you've performed admirably?"

"I'd be an ass if I said no. What man doesn't want to please the woman he's making love with?"

She loved it that he said *with* instead of *to.* "So it's about pleasing women?"

"And feeling good."

"So what if you don't make a woman feel good? What if you're the only one feeling that way?"

"You really want me to answer that?"

"Yes."

"It doesn't feel good when the woman I'm with isn't responding the way I am. It tells me she's not that into me. At that point, I'd rather not be naked with her."

She leaned forward, putting her face close to his. "Are you saying it's a turn off?" He hadn't been turned off with her.

"Not always. Only with women I know I can't please."

Did he know he could please her? He had until thoughts of Trevor had interfered. The bartender dropped a bag of food in front of them.

Saved by the interruption, Arizona wrote their room number on the receipt and stood. She was uncomfortable with the way she felt right now.

He walked with her out of the restaurant, carrying the food, eyeing her triumphantly. He knew it meant something to her that she was among the women he wanted to please. And she'd like him to. The idea of taking that pleasure to the next level tantalized her. Procreation. Isn't that what it was ultimately all about? How would it feel to procreate with him?

At the elevator, she stopped, frozen with what had just gone through her brain. Procreation meant babies. Kids. Screaming. Crying. Irrational tantrums. Clumsiness and messes.

What was it about Braden that had her entertaining even the slightest possibility of having babies with him? It was rash. Her father often told her she was impulsive. She didn't think before she jumped. She had no patience. No fear. She landed on her feet no matter what came in the wake of her decisions. The idea of being that intimate with Braden enticed her that much. Enough to make her jump.

"I could please you if you let me."

While Arizona gaped at him, the elevator doors opened and two couples stumbled out, laughing in drunken humor.

Arizona was barely aware. She followed Braden into the elevator. He leaned against the opposite wall, wholly confident, hands hooked in his front pockets, ankles crossed. Waiting. Smugly.

"I wouldn't be so sure about that, *engineer*." She kept her tone teasing, while temptation intensified.

"I could remove him from your mind." He pushed off the elevator wall and stepped toward her. "I could make you forget him so that the only thing in your mind and body was me. I'd be all that was inside of you."

His low, deep voice was cocky with confidence. Though it was his ego talking, he stroked a warming reaction from her. He could obliterate Trevor and the stigma she'd created because of his death. And he'd use sex to do it. Sex was what made him propose to both of his ex-wives.

"Has it ever crossed your mind that maybe you should step away from sex when you're trying to seduce a woman?"

That only fueled his grin. "Afraid I'll do it?"

Afraid he'd bring her to orgasm without so much as a flicker of a thought for Trevor interfering? Yes, she was a little afraid of that. And as the idea took root in her, she was more afraid than she'd anticipated. More than she'd ever acknowledge, not with him.

"It's what you need."

Mind-altering sex? "Who doesn't?"

"You can make light of it. I understand you lost someone you loved."

"I did love him. That's what made having sex with you so different." She loved Trevor. She didn't love him. What she didn't say was that it had the beginnings of what she'd had with Trevor.

He reached over and pressed their floor button, setting the elevator into motion. She'd been so immersed in

him that she hadn't noticed neither of them had pressed the button.

"I'm impulsive about most things, just not that."

"You're afraid." He sounded amazed.

She could jump out of planes and go on a spontaneous night scuba dive but she couldn't risk her heart for love. Is that what he was saying?

"The worst that could happen is we have a brief affair. The best is you'd have a faithful man and a six-year-old boy."

He didn't mean they'd have a future, he only meant to force her to face what he interpreted as fear of what sex with him might bring.

The elevator doors slid open and she stepped out ahead of him.

He caught up with long strides, leaning his head toward hers as he walked beside her. "Sleep with me again. I dare you."

"No."

"It's not that I'm an engineer that bothers you, Arizona."

"No, it's your first two marriages." That wasn't it, not completely, but she wanted him to stop. "You know what they say about people who can't stay married."

She jabbed the card key into the door.

"No, what do *they* say?" he asked, anger lacing his tone.

"Damaged goods." She pushed open the door and entered.

The door closed behind him. He said nothing.

She turned and saw him standing with his arms at his sides, eyes full of lively energy. But there was more. Her cutting words had hurt him. He wasn't going to engage with her. Doing so would mean he'd stooped to her low level.

"I'm sorry." She hadn't meant to hurt him. "Really,

I…" How could she explain? There was no excuse for her behavior.

"It's all right." His eyes cooled and calmed. "It's obvious you're being defensive. And why is that? You can't let go of Trevor. I get that. What I can't figure out is if it's out of guilt or love."

"Guilt?"

"Hasn't your brother explained it enough for you?"

She felt guilty for not being able to save Trevor. She felt obligated to devote the rest of her life to helping victims. To try and make up for her failure.

Braden moved toward her. Defeated, she stood still as he leaned down and kissed her. Only once.

That was all it took. One touch, and her heart tripped into excited beats and her skin prickled with delicious anticipation.

He kissed her again, fanning flames that wouldn't stop flickering. He didn't touch her anywhere else. Only where his mouth pressed to hers. Sweetly. Proving a point, but a gentle one. He wouldn't take it any further. Just far enough to make her see what he meant.

She'd cut him down and he responded with this. Passion. Love. Not the marrying kind of love. New love. The potential for it. And that is what they had going between them.

He could make her forget Trevor.

With the slant of his mouth, he kissed her more fully, caressing, melding. Then he lifted his head, breathless and burning.

As sweet as this was, she could not let him win that easily. "You're going to have to do better than that."

"I got as far as I wanted tonight."

He was so sure he'd have her flat on her back again, so into him that no one else would matter. Instinct warned her to allow that to happen. There may not be anything wrong

with him for divorcing twice, but he was right about one thing. Feeling too much for him scared her. Not just because of the way she lost Trevor. She didn't think he was ready. He had a son he loved more than anyone and an ex-wife he was still raw over.

Would she be able to hold back if he seduced her the way he intended? Did she even want to?

Chapter 10

Braden's cell phone rang, waking him up. Arizona was sprawled on the other bed, covers askew. It took him a moment to move for the phone. Long, bare legs, smooth and tan, peeked out from the covers. Contrasting with the sexiness of that were her twisted nightgown, open mouth and hair sticking out at radical angles.

He stood and went to the table where he'd left his phone the night before.

"Braden."

"It's Sampson, Braden."

His boss was calling him?

"I know you took a few days off to look for your sister, but I'm going to need you to come in today if at all possible, tomorrow if not."

He needed him to go in to work? Today? "Is something wrong?" Something had to be. He'd left everything in good order before he'd taken personal time off. There were no

components in Test, no anomalies. He refused to give in to the foreboding he felt that this was related to Tatum's disappearance. But what else could it be?

"We had a break-in last night. Someone used your badge."

"My..." He hadn't thought to check for it the night the stranger had tried to burglarize him. Breaking into a secure facility like Hamilton became a lot easier with a badge.

"I'm in Tortola. I'll get there as soon as I can."

"If you don't make it tomorrow, I'll start the termination process with HR."

He'd fire him? Something serious must have happened. What had the burglar taken?

Ending the call, he disconnected and turned. Arizona sat up on the bed with tired but curious eyes.

"Someone broke into Hamilton Corporation using my badge," he said.

Her eyes became instantly more alert. The technology theory was back on.

"My boss wouldn't tell me what, if anything, was taken."

She flung the covers off her. Someone was trying to steal information from him. His job was on the line. First his sister, and now him. He had to at least consider the possibility his sister had somehow drawn him into her trouble, but he couldn't believe she'd done it wittingly.

"Oh, my God. What is Julian after?"

"We don't know if it's Julian who's behind this."

"Come on, Braden, it has to be him."

He looked away as she dressed. "It might be. I'm not saying it isn't. I'm just saying there could be another explanation." One that kept his sister innocent.

"Your sister was caught shipping arms illegally. She went to see Julian and now she's missing. Someone broke

into your house and tried to steal your computer, and then your work. It can't be a coincidence."

"My sister didn't ship arms. If she went to see Julian it was for a different reason, probably the same reason Courtney had for seeing him."

Arizona said nothing, just finished getting ready to leave. He couldn't even tell her to stay here.

"You're forgetting the kind of weapons Hamilton manufactures," he said, annoyed that he cared what she thought.

"Which makes this a lot more serious than it would be if Julian was siphoning arms off the United States. High-tech weapons are different than your average, everyday gun."

He had to find his sister. Only she could expose what all of this meant by telling them why she went missing. But he didn't have that yet. He might never have it. He'd go back to Hamilton and save his job and with any luck, be one step closer to solving this mystery.

Arizona could tell Braden would rather not have her with him. On the way here, he'd told her twice that she could wait in the lobby. And he was edgy, if not annoyed. He walked into Hamilton Corporation with a grim set to his mouth, brow low. Dressed similarly to the way he'd looked when she'd met him, there was no disguising his sex appeal. His navy-blue slacks fit him well and the tan, long-sleeved dress shirt creased where his biceps tapered in from their bulges. She could work here herself in her knee-length, red bubble dress accented with a silver chain that hung to her belly button, and tan four-inch sandals.

"Braden," one of three security guards behind a circular desk greeted. The desk was positioned in the middle of an open lobby, brightly lit by a huge skylight overhead. The entrance jutted out from the main building, which towered roughly thirty stories above the ground.

"Mr. Sampson is expecting you." He picked up a phone and announced their arrival. Then he turned to one of the guards. "Take them to Sampson's office."

"She's waiting here," Braden said.

The guard gave Arizona a visitor badge. "Actually, he wants to talk to both of you."

Really? How much did Braden's boss know about Tatum's disappearance? When the police responded to the Hamilton break-in, had they discussed the incident with the man in the BMW and the break-in at Braden's house? And what would Braden's boss do if she refused to talk to him? He wasn't the police. Maybe he thought he was important enough to tell her what to do even though she didn't work for him.

Taking the visitor badge, she followed Braden to a secure elevator. He entered a code in a keypad on the wall and the doors opened. Stepping inside, she saw him press the sixteenth-floor button.

"How many floors are engineering?" she asked.

"Almost all of them. Corporate is on the top two."

"Foreign land for you."

Only then did he catch on to her teasing. A grin poked the corners of his mouth. "You love it and you know it."

"We'll see about corporate. Engineering…?" She eyed him suggestively.

"I wasn't talking about corporate."

The elevator felt warmer than it did when she'd first entered. Braden was more relaxed now, too.

On the sixteenth floor, they left the elevator and passed one set of double glass doors, behind which was a bustling office center. The next suite over, Braden opened one of the doors. A receptionist led them to the last of a row of offices along the west wall, standing aside to allow them entry. A man with round glasses stood from behind his

desk, several feet from the door. His back was to a window that offered a view of the mountains. The perks of sacrificing your life to a corporation.

He came around the desk and offered his hand to Arizona. "Harry Sampson."

"Arizona Ivy."

He resembled *Iron Man*'s Tony Stark, with a stomach and glasses. Average height, dark hair showing hints of gray. Expensive suit.

"I've watched some of your father's movies. He's quite accomplished."

Of course, a man like him would recognize Jackson Ivy that way. Even though Harry Sampson probably made far less than her father, he was a businessman. Accomplishments that earned revenue drove him. "Is that why you asked to see me along with Braden?"

"I'd rather that was the reason. Please. Have a seat." He turned less cordial eyes to Braden, not noticing her deliberate choice to use the word *asked.*

Arizona sat on one of two chairs facing the desk. Braden was slower to do the same. He was edgy again.

Sampson sat on his chair again, folding his hands on the surface of the desk, primmer than Stark, too. Soft. Not at all what she'd expect from a weapons executive.

"Are the police in Tortola any closer to finding your sister?" he asked Braden.

"No."

He seemed to have expected that answer. Arizona had the distinct impression that he was setting them up for something. A corporate shark circling for the kill.

He leaned back against his chair with a sigh. "The police explained to me what happened to her. The unauthorized exports. Her disappearance shortly thereafter. Do you consider it a coincidence that the exports involved arms?"

"She was wrongly accused."

"Someone used her computer." Sampson nodded as though he had it all figured out. "There's no evidence to prove she facilitated the deal, but the police in Tortola say the last time she was seen she went willingly into a cab."

Arizona could feel the hot steam rolling off Braden. "Are you trying to suggest she disappeared intentionally?"

"It might be convenient for her to do so right now."

"My sister is innocent."

"Hmm." He halfheartedly nodded, noncommittal and dubious. "Or she's very good at covering her tracks."

"You're talking about my sister."

With a bold lack of respect, Arizona noted silently. This guy was a jerk. Braden must really love his work or he wouldn't put up with him. And no wonder he divorced his wife. How could she want him to become this? He was sexy the way he was. Sampson was not sexy. He was all ego sitting behind his big desk with a big view behind him in a big office of a big corporation.

"Why are you involved in this?" Sampson asked her.

"Didn't the police tell you?"

"They said you were nearly abducted and your brother was shot during the attack. The man who made the attempt could be trying to reach Braden for technology."

"Well, there you go."

"Is that what happened? Do you think someone was trying to use you to force Braden to hand over technology?"

"What do you think happened?" she challenged, still not understanding why he wanted to talk to her.

He turned to Braden. "I think your sister is working with an arms dealer."

Braden stood up. "Time to go."

Was he really going to talk to his boss that way? She remained seated.

"And that arms dealer stole your badge," Sampson finished.

Braden didn't respond. He must be reeling with the implications. His sister was the only possible link.

"Why didn't you report it?" Sampson asked.

"I didn't know it was stolen."

"No? No one is threatening you for information? You wouldn't give them what they asked for to save your sister?"

The man was incorrigible. He actually would hold it against Braden for doing something like that. He'd rather Braden protect Hamilton's information than his own sister's life."

"Do you know what was almost stolen?" he asked.

"Almost?" Arizona challenged. "So nothing was stolen."

He ignored her as he continued to laser in a power stare at Braden. "Someone used your badge to access the building and then attempted to crack our network. We had our IT experts here at Hamilton do some investigating and they discovered a couple of disturbing things. The hacker tried to get to some backup files, and he focused on the Intrepid project."

Standing to her left just behind her chair, Braden remained still.

"Whoever broke in was after our laser target designator design," Sampson continued. "And you've been working that project for almost a year now."

What were laser target designators?

"I didn't give anyone my badge," Braden said. "My house was broken into."

"Did the man get away?" she asked.

"Another engineer working late caught him. He ran and got out of the building before security could do anything."

Arizona could see his disgruntlement over what he must regard as incompetence on the security guards' behalf.

"He got nothing?" Braden asked.

"Not this time. Our IT people did look into the activity on your user account and found some files that were saved to a flash drive. Right around the time your sister was resigning. Any idea on where those files went?"

A shockwave hit her. Tatum must have stolen information. Corporations had ways of tracking everything employees did on their computers, and they'd just exposed the truth.

"I didn't save anything to a flash drive," Braden said. He didn't believe for a minute that Tatum could do it. "I save everything to the network."

If he kept nothing on his laptop, then how had the files been loaded to a flash drive? "Was your house broken into before now?"

"No."

Sampson studied Braden's face for several seconds, deciding whether to believe him. "I suggest you don't go anywhere while the police look into this. And I have to warn you, I'm getting pressure to fire you over this."

"My badge was stolen. I didn't give it away."

"You didn't report it missing."

"I didn't know it was stolen until you called me."

"That isn't a very good explanation. It suggests you're careless and don't care much about Hamilton's security protocols. It makes people around here start to ask why."

"It's time to go, Braden." Now Arizona stood with him and then looked at Sampson. "We'll find his sister, and we'll find who's behind all of this."

"I'd rather you left it up to the authorities. One more slip up and I won't have a choice. I'll have to get rid of one of my best engineers."

"Give us a few days," Braden said.

Sampson answered with a reluctant nod.

Braden took her hand and guided her out of the office. In the elevator he punched the wall with a curse. "What the hell?"

Putting her hand on his back, she rubbed. "We'll find her. I'm sure there's some kind of explanation." Such as she stole files from him and something had gone wrong with her arms dealer.

"What are we going to do?" he asked.

His uncertainty had to be unfamiliar to him. This all seemed to be spiraling out of control. Would they be able to get ahead of it before it ruined them both?

"Go to your sister's."

He shot her the rebellious look that she expected, but at least he didn't protest. Maybe they'd find something, something everyone else had missed.

Braden entered his sister's new apartment, a downtown loft with a view of Denver. She'd rented it a few months ago so she'd have a place to stay when she came to visit him and their parents. She'd given him a key.

He'd already been here once and found nothing to indicate her whereabouts. The police had searched it, too, along with her house in Atlanta. Nothing had turned up. Did that mean she was innocent or had they missed some stolen files on her computer? He still refused to believe she'd do something like that. Why? She had everything going for her. She didn't need money.

Heading straight through the airy and bright kitchen and living room, he went to her office. Her computer was still there. He looked around the neat and tidy room. Only a few things were out of place from family and police searches.

If she was the immoral thief his boss had made her out

to be, wouldn't whoever she was working with have stolen her computer? Her apartment building had tight security. That was one of the reasons she'd chosen this place. She was a single woman.

Charlene's sister's computer had been stolen. His computer had nearly been stolen. But not Tatum's.

He booted her computer. He wasn't looking for clues to her whereabouts. He was looking for files.

Arizona put her hand on his shoulder. Glancing up at her, he saw her empathy and realized he'd hesitated with his hand on the mouse.

Disgruntled, he opened the browser and read the folder names. One was called Braden.

Could she be more obvious?

Growing angrier by the second, he opened the folder. A list of files appeared. Seeing the types, he didn't need to open them to know what they were.

Clicking hard, he closed the folder and put his elbows on the desk to rub his face with both hands, reeling with what he could no longer deny.

Tatum had stolen files from him. Memory raced back in time to two weeks ago, the last time she'd been at his house. Had she gone into his office? He'd had to deal with Aiden, who'd behaved like a tired six-year-old that night. She could have. Somehow she must have gotten his remote login to Hamilton's network. Had she watched him log in and he hadn't noticed? He wouldn't have thought anything of it. She was his sister. Someone he should be able to trust.

Fast-backward to three months ago. Tatum, asking him questions about his latest project. He'd told her about the laser designators. She'd asked a lot of questions he couldn't answer. It was classified.

Someone else must have told her what to look for. What files to find. Copy. Steal.

"She must have wanted you to find this."

Lowering his hands, he looked up and back at Arizona.

"The folder is named Braden," she said.

"Or she wasn't worried I would." Or didn't care. Or hadn't thought to hide it.

Neither of those options made sense. His sister wasn't stupid. Then why name the folder Braden?

He opened the folder again, looking at the files more carefully. There were some missing. She hadn't gathered them all. Had she known? She was a smart woman but she was no engineer. Key algorithms were missing from the folder. He searched other folders. Nowhere were the algorithms stored.

Why hadn't she copied them?

Was it ignorance or something else? Feeling hope soar out of control, he stopped it short. His sister had stolen the files. So she hadn't known the algorithms were important. The kind of technology she'd dabbled in was way out of her realm. Cutting edge. She was a freight forwarder, not a rocket scientist.

Hearing Arizona shuffling around in Tatum's bedroom, he stood and went there. She'd left him alone in the office. She knew what it did to him to finally accept his sister's betrayal.

She bent over and looked under the queen-sized white, ruffled bed. Her fantastic butt was prone and offered some relief to the weight of his disappointment.

"What are you looking for?"

She straightened. "A motive."

Yes, he'd like to know what made his sister steal from him, too. He looked around and caught sight of her safe in the walk-in closet.

Reaching into his jeans' pocket, he pulled out his wallet and berated himself for allowing denial to cloud his think-

ing. He found the piece of folded paper his sister had given him the night she'd given him a key to her new apartment. He went to the safe and spun the dial. The combination opened the safe door.

Inside was a single piece of paper. A copy of a birth certificate. And the name matched that of Charlene Andrew's sister, Courtney.

"What is that?"

He handed the birth certificate to Arizona, who frowned as she read the name. "The father's name is blank."

Leaning closer, he saw that the entry was, indeed blank. He moved his eyes and met hers.

"What was she doing with this?" Arizona voiced his own musings.

Tatum had wanted him to find all of this. She may have even rented this apartment to make it easy for him. Then why steal the files? Because she had stolen them. Nothing could absolve her of that. How could she have betrayed him like that? She had to have known it could cost him his job. What would make her do it? No matter how much trouble she had gotten herself in, she should have known she could tell him. But she hadn't. That made her appear guilty. It made her appear she was up to no good. No, not appear. She had been up to no good. There was no denying that now.

She'd stolen highly sensitive files from her own brother and given them to people who were coming after him for the missing algorithms. She'd gone willingly into a cab that had taken her to Julian, as though she'd planned all along to deliberately vanish.

What did the birth certificate mean? Where did it fit in with all of this?

Chapter 11

"Have you found her?"

His mother's frantic tone and the look of utter despair slammed him. She was expecting him to tell her Tatum was dead.

"No."

Relief drained away her apprehension, although she still gripped the arm of the kitchen chair too tightly. His father sat beside her, composed as always. Arizona was to Braden's left. He was grateful she hadn't bombarded him with questions she must have.

He explained what happened at work and his near termination. "Arizona and I just came from Tatum's apartment, and I found the files on her computer."

His mother drew a startled breath.

Seeing her so upset was wrenching. It was the reason he wanted to talk to his parents in person. They needed it that way.

"There has to be some mistake," his dad said.

"I wish there was." In his peripheral vision, he saw Arizona turn to look at him and felt her sympathy. That was why she'd been so quiet.

Arizona put the birth certificate on the table and pushed it toward them. His mother lifted it and his father leaned to see it with her.

His father was the first to look up. "What is this?"

"Arizona and I discovered this woman disappeared shortly before Tatum." He told them about all the women, and their meeting with Charlene Andrews.

"Why did Tatum have this woman's birth certificate?" his father asked, tapping the paper with his forefinger.

"We were hoping you'd know something about that."

"Why would we?" his mother asked.

"Did Tatum talk about her at all?" He looked from his mother to his father.

"No," his father answered while his mother shook her head numbly. His father stared down at the certificate.

"Arizona and I are flying back to Oregon to talk to Charlene again," Braden said. "We told her about the certificate and she wants us to meet her." He didn't explain that she'd sounded apprehensive on the phone when she'd asked to see the certificate.

"You said Courtney was still missing," his mother said. Tears formed in her eyes. "Does her sister think she's dead?"

Braden didn't reply. He couldn't. Charlene did think her sister was dead.

"I'll find Tatum," Braden declared. And for his mother's sake, he prayed she was still alive.

His father rubbed her back as she sniffed a few times.

Braden reached across the table and put his hand over his mother's. "I'll find her."

She offered a shaky smile.

Standing, he went around the table and bent to kiss her cheek. She patted his hand.

"I'm so proud of you," she said. "If anyone can help Tatum, it will be you."

Leaving her in the kitchen, he led Arizona to the door, where his father shook his hand. The grim set of his eyes could be from his mother's pain or the discovery that other women had gone missing. Braden hadn't told them about the murders. That would only upset them further. Until he found Tatum, dead or alive, he'd only tell them what they needed to know.

"Call me as soon as you know anything more," his father said.

"Of course."

Arizona preceded him out the door. His dad stood in the doorway until Braden backed the SUV out of the driveway. Normally stoic, his crumbling strength disconcerted Braden. And made him more determined than ever to unravel Tatum's mystery.

Mindful of Braden's mood, Arizona left him alone and didn't share all the thoughts running through her head as Braden drove their rental to a stop in front of Charlene's house. It was small and white with an enclosed porch in front and a one-car detached garage set back on a badly cracked driveway.

Tatum's computer hadn't been stolen. Security was tight at her apartment, but would that have kept a professional out? Maybe her computer had already been searched and nothing was found—nothing new anyway. Tatum may have passed along what she had, but something was missing. The algorithm files.

Tatum wouldn't know what went into the design of a

weapons system the way Braden did. Of course, she could have missed something. That was the piece Braden wasn't ready to discuss. His sister had stolen files from him. From Hamilton Corporation.

But where was the connection to Charlene's sister? Arizona was inclined to believe that was the link. Tatum may not have exported arms illegally, but somehow she'd been drawn into the scandal.

Arizona stepped up to the porch, opening the screen door. Old, weathered wicker furniture and overgrown plants cluttered the small space. Braden rang the bell.

The door creaked open and Charlene appeared, her short, plump frame tented in a pale yellow floral dress. A free-size style. Her hair was uncombed but it was so short that it didn't matter all that much. She had great skin, smooth and even-toned, making her appear like an overweight twenty-year-old rather than the early thirties she most likely was.

"Come in." She let them inside.

Arizona stepped into a cramped kitchen, the sink full of dishes and counters covered with fruit and appliances and more dishes. It smelled in here.

Charlene took them into her living room, more orderly than what Arizona had seen so far. A long couch was across one wall, family pictures on the wall above. A small TV was on a stand filled with movies. An *NCIS* episode played. The drapes over the only window were closed, leaving it dark and dank.

"Do you have the birth certificate?" Charlene asked.

Arizona slipped the copy out of an outer pouch in her purse and handed it to her. Charlene looked up from the paper.

"Your sister had this at her house?" she asked Braden, who nodded.

"We think Tatum and Courtney may have known each other," Arizona said.

"Courtney never talked about her. But she must have contacted her for a reason." The furtive fluttering of her eyes gave away her hesitance.

"What reason would she have?"

Charlene sighed. "You'd both better come and sit down." She led them to her kitchen and sat at the table.

Arizona didn't feel like sitting, but she did, Braden beside her on one of the wooden chairs.

Charlene handed the birth certificate back to Arizona, who took it and put it back into her purse.

"Courtney was looking for her biological father before she disappeared. I had no idea your sister had her birth certificate, or I'd have mentioned it to you sooner."

The father's name was left blank on the certificate. Arizona saw Braden's lowering brow. Had Courtney thought his father was also hers?

"Our mother was married briefly to my father. After the divorce, she had an affair with a man and gave birth to Courtney, my half sister. Our mother died two years ago, which prompted Courtney to start searching for her father. Our mother never spoke of him, but the last time she saw him she lived in Denver. The hospital where she was born was no help. She was in the process of looking for our mother's neighbor during that time. They were friends who drifted apart once we moved, but Mother talked of her every once in a while." Charlene humphed incredulously. "Courtney must have found her."

And the neighbor must have remembered Braden's father. Courtney's mother must have told her.

"Does he know?" she asked Braden.

"He never told any of us," He turned to Charlene. "How old is Courtney?"

"I'm thirty-five and my sister is thirty-two." Courtney's mother must not have intended for anyone to know who the father of her child was. Otherwise, she wouldn't have left the name blank on the birth certificate.

"Your mother was protecting him," Arizona said to Charlene. This was going to make a great article!

Then she saw Braden's tortured eyes and checked herself.

"I would have never dreamed this was connected to my sister's disappearance," Charlene said. "Surely it can't be a coincidence."

Was Courtney somehow responsible for Tatum's disappearance? And her own? "Tatum may have gone looking for Courtney and got herself into trouble."

She hadn't told anyone because she'd taken the files from Braden. Why? To try and save Courtney? A perfect stranger who could break up her parents' marriage? There had to be more.

"Do you mind if we look through her things?" Braden asked.

"No. Not at all. Most of her belongings are in storage. I haven't had the heart to go through anything. I keep hoping…"

She led them to the guest room. Arizona entered. A frilly, lavender-and-green floral comforter drew the eye, matching an equally dated valance. Braden went to the small wood desk under the window and began searching.

Arizona moved to a tall dresser. On top was a stack of bills and receipts. She flipped through them all, slowing when she noticed the receipts were from Atlanta, Georgia.

"Braden."

He stopped what he was doing to join her at the dresser. Charlene appeared on her other side.

"Wasn't Tatum's job in Atlanta?"

He took the receipts from her. "Yes." He stared down at a receipt. "This coffee shop is on the same street as the freight forwarder."

Arizona looked up at him. He met her thoughtful introspection.

"If she knew how to find my dad, why would she go to Atlanta? Why single out Tatum?"

Charlene's befuddled glance offered no insight, so Arizona turned back to Braden. "Maybe she wanted to test the waters first. She must have known your dad was married at the time she was born."

"And when she got there, she was caught in Tatum's arms dealing scandal?" Arizona nodded.

Braden looked down at the receipt again. "The timestamp on this is before Tatum's resignation."

"Right before." Arizona again met Braden's eyes as they each filtered through the possibilities.

"Are you saying my sister was involved in an arms deal? What arms deal? My sister wouldn't do anything like that. She was a normal person. With a normal job. And a normal curiosity about her biological father."

"We're not saying she did anything willingly," Arizona carefully said.

"She always was the one who asked too many questions," Charlene said anxiously.

"Anything's possible at this point," Braden tucked the receipts into his back pocket and looked at Arizona. "You ready for a trip to Atlanta?"

"Why not?" She was accustomed to a lot of travel, but not to track down a criminal who may have done something with Courtney and Braden's sister.

He kept up a light facade about going to Atlanta, but she could feel his angst. Tatum had stolen weapons information from him. He could no longer believe in her inno-

cence. Not one hundred percent. She didn't doubt he still meant to find her. She was his sister and he loved her. But there was more at stake than that. His job and the safety of everyone around him was, too.

His cell phone rang and he answered.

"Where are you?" He started moving for the front door. "What?"

Something had happened. Hearing a high-pitched voice coming from the phone, she had a sick feeling that it was related to Serena…and his son.

"Stay there. Don't go anywhere." The frantic voice continued. "I'm on my way back to Denver right now. Just stay where you are, Serena."

Hours later, Braden finally reached Serena's parents' house. Parking on the stone driveway, he ran toward the wide stone stairway leading to the double front entry. One of the doors opened and Aiden burst out, Serena in the doorway. Near the first step, he scooped up his son and held him against his chest, relief so great it nearly brought him to his knees.

He didn't know what he'd do if anything were to happen to Aiden. Closing his eyes, he kissed his son's cheek and forehead. "You okay, buddy?"

"A man was looking at us in his car," his child's voice said. "It scared Mommy."

Braden smoothed his brown hair and soft skin, reassured that his son was indeed all right.

Serena approached. "What's going on, Braden? Why are you traveling all over the place and why is a strange man spying on us?"

Adjusting his hold on Aiden, he noticed Arizona watching him and it had little to do with the conversation. She was absorbed in his reunion with his son, as though this

kind of love were foreign to her, but fascinating. It worked to lighten his mood. She was such an oddball when it came to children. She didn't even know her own affinity. Arizona was a lot like a child, still discovering the world around her.

"Braden? Does this have something to do with your sister?"

He turned, realizing not only Serena and her parents had seen his affection, so had Arizona, who'd averted her gaze as though cornered.

"I can't explain everything now," he said. "We're trying to find her."

"Braden, you tell me what's going on right this instant. Our son could be in danger because of you!"

There she went again, blaming instead of trying to resolve. "Did the man try to contact you?"

"No. I called the police."

"What was he driving?"

"A white BMW."

Braden exchanged a glance with Arizona. The same man who'd tailed him and who'd tried to abduct Arizona.

"Mommy's new friend came over," Aiden interjected. "He scared the man away."

Mommy's new friend?

"The police said they'd patrol the neighborhood. My father has some friends in the force," Serena said.

"I take it your new friend is a man?" Braden said.

Her chin went up and she shot a hesitant glance at Arizona. "He's a chief accounting officer."

Of course she'd focus on that. "An accountant scared him off?"

"He's big," Aiden said, his little arm looped around his shoulders. "But not fun like you, Daddy."

Braden kissed his son. "I'm sure he's not that bad." He put his son down and ruffled his hair.

When he straightened, he saw a man step out of the house, Serena's father behind him.

"What's happening, Braden?" Serena asked again.

"I don't know," he relented. "It might have something to do with Tatum's resignation."

"From the freight forwarding company? What does that have to do with you?"

Exactly what he'd like to know.

"We're working on that," Arizona said.

Serena eyed her uncertainly while Braden scanned the house and surroundings. This was a gated community and he already knew the house was alarmed. Serena's boyfriend and her father stood on the front step, waiting. "Is he going to stay here?"

Again, Serena stared at Arizona. Was she reluctant to answer, or was she curious as to why Arizona was helping him find his sister? The idea was probably foreign to her. Serena was anything but adventurous. Adventurous to her was going to a health club for a workout. Nothing outdoors.

"Yes," Serena finally answered. "He's staying in a guest room…with Aiden here."

The way she said that suggested she'd already slept with the man. At least she wouldn't while Aiden was in the same house. He waited for pain to grip him with the idea of another man sleeping with her. He felt nothing.

Would he get over her this fast? He never truly loved her from the start. He'd thought the sex had been a good-enough indicator. But he'd neglected to take into account the woman as a whole.

"Will you be safe here?"

After a moment of consideration, she nodded. He wondered if she'd expected him to be jealous.

"What are you going to do?" she asked.

"Find Tatum. Just promise me you'll watch Aiden until I come back. Don't let him out of your sight."

"I promise."

"Can I go with you, Daddy?"

Braden knelt to his son's level, love mushrooming inside him. "Not this time. I'll be back soon and we'll have a fun weekend together, okay?"

"The zoo?" Aiden bounced up and down.

"Sure. Whatever you want to do."

"Yay!" More bouncing.

He stood up. "Make sure your father keeps the alarm set and don't go anywhere alone. I'll call you to check in." He turned, slipping an arm around Arizona's waist.

"Wait. Braden."

He stopped and looked back, seeing her gaze pass from the way he held Arizona to his face. "Thanks for coming by."

"I'll talk to you soon."

Seeing him with Arizona made her question her thinking, that was for sure. He hoped it helped her make better choices from now on, for Aiden's sake. He no longer loved Serena, probably never truly did, but one thing was for sure: he would never make the same mistake again. Good relationships had to be about more than sex. He wished he could eliminate Arizona from that analogy. If they had a relationship brewing, he could say with complete certainty that it wasn't based on sex. That made him want to make good on his promise to give her good sex and also made him want to run the other way.

Chapter 12

As soon as Braden asked to talk to Tatum's ex-boss, Arizona watched word travel around the open area of cubes behind the reception desk. The receptionist returned with a woman in tow. She was tall and skinny, with hair up in a tight, plain-girl ponytail and eyeglasses small and rectangular. She was dressed in a brown knit vest that Arizona envied, but there was nothing to envy about the brown blouse, brown knit skirt and brown pumps. Those were too prim and boring for her.

"Hi, I'm Rebecca Owens," the woman said as the receptionist made her way back to the front. "The human resources director. You're here to ask about Tatum McCrae?"

"She's my sister, and she's gone missing," Braden said.

Rebecca angled her tight-haired head. "Missing?"

There had been nothing in the news yet, so it wasn't surprising she didn't know.

Braden glanced at the open room of cubicles. A woman

leaned around the edge of her cubicle wall to stare and two men walked by, taking notice of what Braden had said.

"Follow me." The director led them to her office, one of six that surrounded the open area.

She closed the door behind them and then moved farther into the office, facing them with folded arms beside a desk. "What can I do for you?"

"We were hoping you could tell us something about Tatum," Braden said. "Who she may have been talking to before she resigned. Any strange behavior."

A long moment passed as the woman contemplated how to reply. "No. Nothing like that. She behaved rather normally. No one suspected a thing."

"Nothing that would indicate she was being coerced, or working with someone?"

Rebecca's mouth pinched with the hint of cynicism. "I understand she's your sister, Mr. McCrae, but the only reason she isn't in jail right now is we couldn't prove she was working with an arms dealer when the shipment went through."

"What makes you think she did the shipment?" Arizona asked.

"The paperwork was done on her computer."

"She wasn't in town during that time," Braden filled her in. "An arms manufacturer authorized a front company to take responsibility for the export from the United States and designated American Freight Forwarding Services to handle the shipment. Someone picked up the shipment and used Tatum's credentials to run the paperwork."

"Without a license," Rebecca added, quite offended. "The arms manufacturer had a written agreement from the front company stating they'd take responsibility for the shipment. That makes American Freight Forwarding

Services the exporter, and responsible for the routed shipment."

"The front company took responsibility for any license requirements?" Arizona asked.

"Yes. And in this case, there were some. It hasn't been ruled out that we'll be charged with a violation. Immigration and Customs Enforcement is looking for the man behind the front company. We can only hope they find him. Export violations cost companies millions in addition to debarment of export authorizations."

No wonder Rebecca, and probably many others, was so uptight over the incident. She was probably fearing for her job.

"Who else could have done the shipment?" Arizona asked.

"We've done our own internal investigation. It wasn't anyone else working here." She thought Tatum should be held responsible, not the company.

"Did Tatum ever bring in or mention a woman named Courtney Andrews?" Braden asked.

Rebecca thought a moment. "No. Who is she?"

He showed her a picture that Charlene had given them.

Rebecca shook her head. "What does she have to do with any of this?"

"Thanks for your time."

Not expecting the meeting to end so abruptly, Arizona reluctantly followed him to the door.

"If you know something that could help this investigation…" Rebecca said.

Braden opened the door, ignoring her, a deliberate shun. The woman was convinced his sister committed a crime. Why would he help her?

"You should at least talk to the ICE agents," Rebecca said before they left the office.

Arizona glanced back to see her leaning with her hands on the desk, face grim and disapproving.

"She's going to call the Immigration and Customs agents," Arizona said when they stepped outside.

"Let her. Maybe the agents will help find the arms dealer. I'm sure they're more capable than we are. Or Rebecca."

His main concern was Tatum. He felt confident the ICE agents were doing their job in looking for the dealer. They were not, however, looking for Tatum.

"Excuse me?" A woman's voice called from behind them.

Arizona turned with him in the parking lot. A twenty-something woman with fine, long blond hair glanced around and approached, looking behind her toward the building. She was shorter than Arizona and rail thin.

"I'm Sophie Reynolds. I'm a friend of Tatum's. I heard you say she's missing."

"You worked with her?" Braden asked.

"Are you her brother?" she asked instead of answering.

"Braden McCrae. This is Arizona Ivy, a—a friend of mine."

Sophie looked at her. "You knew Tatum?"

"No…" Braden's stutter over how to introduce her had her befuddled. How did he see them? A couple? They weren't really friends. They'd only just met. "I'm helping Braden."

That drew a perplexed expression from Sophie, as if she were thinking how a woman could be of help to a strapping man like Braden.

"Rebecca Owens couldn't tell us much about Tatum's last days at work," Braden effectively directed the focus.

"She wouldn't." Again, she glanced behind her at the building. "Tatum asked me not to talk to anyone unless

something happened to her. I—I mean, I told the feds the truth, but she said this had nothing to do with that."

Braden went as still as Arizona. "What did she ask you not to talk about?" they said at the same time.

The woman dug into her purse. "I've kept this on me since she left for the Virgin Islands." She procured a key. "She opened a safe-deposit box at First Atlanta Bank."

Why hadn't she given this to Braden? She'd moved to Denver. She was going to sell her house in Atlanta. Why do this? Realizing she was staring at Braden, Arizona asked Sophie, "Did she say why?"

"No. She said it was personal."

Personal. It must have something to do with the birth certificate. But if it was personal, would it be related to her disappearance? It seemed so, otherwise, why lock something up with instructions to keep it secret unless something happened to her?

Only Braden was allowed into the area containing the safe-deposit boxes. Tatum had left explicit restrictions. An odd mix of dread and anticipation accompanied him as he opened the drawer. The bank representative had left him alone, an illusion since the big safe door was open and he stood just inside of it. Arizona was just beyond, watching with her hands clasped in front of her. It was so uncharacteristic of her to appear mild and meek, when she was a firecracker. Hollywood might run through her veins but the true core of her was real.

He loved it.

Letting out a breath, he slid open the drawer. Only a single folded piece of paper was inside. A letter. Not even in an envelope.

He took it out and closed the door. Then he left the vault, joining Arizona in the lobby.

"What is it?" she asked.

He kept walking toward the exit. Outside, he stopped behind their rental. Unfolding the paper, he read the letter to himself.

I hope it's Braden who's reading this letter. If not, however, Mom, Dad, please know that I wished to bring this to you in person.

There's no easy way to say it. Courtney Andrews is my half sister.

Braden could read no more. Nothing could have prepared him for this, the confirmation of what he'd already wondered.

Having read along with him, Arizona snatched the page from him.

"It all began innocently," she read aloud.

How did she know he couldn't read it himself, not objectively anyway? His sister had stolen sensitive files from him and now she'd kept this from him. His father had had an affair.

"I don't know how she found me," Arizona continued to read. She read as if she were in front of one of her father's cameras, oblivious to them. "She said she found her father's name among her mother's things after her mother died. She must have researched the rest of us and chose to approach me because I was a woman.

"She told me she didn't want to break up our parents' marriage and that her mother hadn't wanted that, either. She wasn't sure how to approach our father, but her ultimate goal was to meet him. She was born just under a year after Mom and Dad were married, so the affair must have taken place just before that. I suppose if there's any comfort in this, it's that. Dad wasn't married when he had the affair. Courtney swears her mother didn't continue to see him after he was married. She said her mother was

hurt that he chose our mother over her, but she wanted to do the right thing."

Arizona glanced up at Braden, checking on him before continuing.

"I didn't give her any credence at first. But then I began to see she was for real. She wanted to find her real father. She didn't want anyone hurt in the process. Our first few meetings were to get to know each other, and then to decide how—or if—telling Dad was the right thing to do. Mom would have to be told, too. Courtney was cognizant of that."

Arizona stopped. Braden reluctantly looked at her, pain ripping through him. This would kill his mother. Especially now, when her only daughter was missing.

"Around this time, things began to shake up at work," Arizona resumed reading. "After I resigned, I began to look for her. I'd tried calling her a few times, but she never answered her cell. I went to her apartment. She rented one after she found me. There was a copy of an itinerary there. She'd recently gone to the Virgin Islands and booked a room at the Frenchman's Point Hotel."

Arizona stopped reading to look at him again.

"Julian," he murmured.

Had Courtney been the one to steal the laser target designator files? Was she really their half sister or was this some kind of elaborate scheme? And how did Julian tie in with the arms deal? Was he the man behind the front company?

"If you're reading this, it means I'm in trouble, and probably so is Courtney." Arizona finished.

There was nothing in there about the files she stole. Tatum had only revealed Courtney. It made her appear guilty. Or was she trying to protect Courtney? She'd obviously formed a close enough bond with her, otherwise,

why would she travel to the Caribbean to find her? Or had Courtney taken all the money and Tatum went after her for it?

The sound of youthful laughter drew his gaze across the street. Over the top of the rental, he saw a mall parking lot full of carnival rides. People's feet dangled from a Ferris wheel, and a roller coaster roared down a track, kids and teenagers screaming, some with their hands up in the air.

"I wish we could go there right now," Arizona said.

He shot a look to her. She wanted to go to a carnival? "Why?"

She shrugged. "It would be fun. Impulsive. Free of stress."

She *was* impulsive. Adventurous. A kid at heart. It touched him in a way he'd rather not explore too much. It resembled too much the way he'd taken her night diving.

His cell rang. Seeing it was Serena, he answered.

"Braden?" She sounded breathless and afraid.

Aiden. "Serena. Are you and Aiden all right?"

"Y-Yes. But someone tried to take Aiden."

"What?" Braden walked to the driver's door.

"W-we were getting into our car when a man grabbed Aiden and tried to take him from me." She began crying. "He tried to pry him away from me. I held on a-and Aiden kicked him. If it wouldn't have been for Marcus, he may have succeeded. Oh, Braden. I'm so scared. What are we going to do?"

For once, she said "we." She must be really scared. "Call the police."

"I did. They just left. They're going to step up the patrols, but I'm not sure that's going to be enough. That man is determined. You have to do something, Braden. You have to make him stop. If he takes Aiden…" She cried harder.

"Don't worry. I'll make sure Aiden is safe. I promise." There was nothing in the world he meant more. He'd die for his son. "We're on our way."

Serena sniffled and subdued her crying. "We?"

He disconnected. Now wasn't the time to argue about his relationship with Arizona. It was bad enough that he was starting to call it one. He had to get to Aiden. His son meant everything to him. Nothing else in the world mattered.

What could he do to keep him safe?

It was a question that had plagued him ever since the break-in. He couldn't take him along in the search for Tatum. And he couldn't stop searching for her to stay with his son. But his near abduction unleashed the animal in him. Long-buried fears and insecurities surfaced. That must have been how his son had felt when he'd nearly been taken. Braden bristled with the idea. Nobody did that to his son and got away with it.

Where would his son be safe until he found and stopped those responsible?

Chapter 13

Arizona watched Braden tuck his son in at his parents' house. They'd stay the night here and then tomorrow, she guessed, they'd return yet again to Tortola. Seeing him with Aiden gave her pause. He was worried. Twice now someone had gone after his son, clearly to use him as leverage. Most likely for the missing algorithm files. When stopping him had failed, they'd sought out his weakness. Aiden.

Braden was not a man to tolerate anyone going after his weaknesses. In fact, he seemed highly in tune with protecting that. On guard and never vulnerable. But now his son and his sister were tearing him in two. He had to leave his son behind to find his sister. What if he lost his son in doing so?

Arizona had an idea to help.

Leaving the bedside after staring down at Aiden for several seconds, Braden joined her in the doorway, glancing back again. The love he had for his son awed her.

Downstairs in his parents' four-bedroom suburbia home that faced a lush golf course, Arizona wondered if she should find another room. Braden planned to tell his parents about Courtney. Arizona had questioned him on it. Was he sure? Maybe it could wait. But he'd insisted this was the way his family operated. They discussed things in person. It's what Tatum would have done as soon as Courtney was ready.

"Should I…" Arizona pointed to the backyard where a multilevel redwood deck promised a view of golfers and a barbeque.

"No. Stay with me."

Reading the softness of his eyes, she understood. Her presence would help him. This was going to be hard on his mother. But she also suspected he wondered if his father had known. Tatum's letter said Courtney wasn't ready to meet him, but how much did his father know?

"If you want to leave him here, you can," his dad said.

"Thanks."

Would Aiden be safe here? Arizona doubted it. If he hadn't been safe with Serena's parents, he wouldn't be safe here.

"Actually, I was going to suggest we take him to my parents' house in Evergreen," Arizona said.

Braden swung a look to her.

"It's got a ten-foot-high perimeter stone fence with cameras and motion detectors. A big iron gate with security guards. It's where we go for family reunions. It's tight for a reason." So they could have privacy from the press.

Still, Braden stared at her. She couldn't tell if he agreed it was a good idea, if he was appreciative or if he hated it altogether. He could be extremely impassive sometimes.

"I'll call my mother," she said hesitantly.

After a moment, Braden slumped a little. In relief? Re-

lenting to good logic? She wasn't sure. But then he nodded. "Thanks, Arizona."

He'd noticed her awareness of his heightened protectiveness for his son. Appreciative won out. It made her feel good.

Then he faced his parents and pulled out the letter he'd folded and put into his back pocket.

First he handed it to his dad. His dad read the letter, growing increasingly tense as he did. When he finished, he sat down on a chair in the open living room and slowly looked across the coffee table at his wife, who immediately picked up on the change in him.

"What? What is it? Is Tatum...?" Tears welled in her pretty green eyes that looked forty instead of fifty-something.

"Did you know?" Braden asked his dad.

It took the man some time to recover. Then he looked up at his son. "Yes."

Anger slid over Braden, his brow growing ominous and his hands fisting at his sides.

"Knew what?" Braden's mother walked over to her husband and reached for the letter.

His father let her take it, slowly lifting his gaze to watch her read.

The tears that had begun out of anxiety for her daughter now rolled down her cheeks from something else entirely. Braden's dad rose and went to her. She backed away, dropping the letter onto the cushion of a chair and then looking at her husband as the hurt deepened and deepened. She sucked in a gulp of air.

"You knew?" she breathed. "All these years..."

"Please...Marlana, I..." He lost words.

What could he say, really? Arizona's heart wrenched for him and for Marlana, who stood on the brink of sobbing.

"And that birth certificate…the father's name was left blank. You knew then, didn't you? And you said nothing. Until now, when you have no choice…when you're finally caught."

"I…" Braden's father tried again. "I did what I thought was best for all of us."

"Best?" Marlana's shaken voice made Arizona stop looking at her.

"I met her before I knew you. We dated a few times and then she moved away when she went to college. I didn't see her for years. Until a few months before you and I married. I loved you, Marlana. Never doubt that. But seeing her again…after the way it ended with us. It wasn't finished yet. I had to finish it."

"You had to see if you loved her still?"

Braden's father's throat cleared as he struggled with his rocky emotions. "Yes. And it quickly became clear to me that you were the one I loved. I've loved you ever since. Please…please believe me. I wouldn't have married you if I had any doubt. I swear it."

"Wh-when…"

When had the other woman gone to him and told him?

Braden went to his mother, who leaned against him as she continued to regard her husband as though she'd never met him.

"Not for a long time. Courtney was five by then."

A single sob escaped Marlana's fight for composure and strength. She was a woman who rarely lost either, Arizona surmised.

"She didn't want to break us up. She only came to me because she thought I should know. I told her before I married you that I didn't love her. I told her that it was you I loved and I was going to marry you. She was hurt and

upset, but she understood and wished me well. She didn't know at that time that she was pregnant."

"You slept with another woman while you were with me!" Marlana pushed away from Braden to step toward her husband. "How long before we were married did you tell her?"

His head lowered.

"How long?" Marlana demanded.

Slowly he lifted his head. "The week before."

"One week." It came on a whisper, a ragged whisper full of pain. "Is that the last time you slept with her?"

Reluctantly, he nodded.

"You slept with her the same night you told her you loved me and not her?"

"She confronted me about you. She told me I had to make a choice. She did me a favor. I chose you, and I've never regretted it."

"Oh…" Marlana covered her mouth as shaken sobs pushed past her resistance.

Braden went to her side again. And this time she turned against him, burying her face and crying from deep inside.

Arizona wished she wasn't there right now. She felt like an intruder.

"I've been faithful to you ever since. Marlana…" He moved to her and put his hand on her sobbing back. "I had to be sure. Can you ever understand that? If I hadn't met you, she's the woman I would have married. I had to be sure."

Marlana used Braden's chest to support her as she turned to face her husband. Keeping a hand on her son's muscular shoulder, she bore a teary, hurt gaze at her husband.

"Is there anything else you haven't told me?"

"I opened a trust fund for Courtney. I've made depos-

its to it over the years, so she could go to college and have advantages her mother couldn't give her."

"Did you speak to her mother often?"

Braden's dad shook his head. "Only when I set the fund up. After that, I didn't have to talk to her. She preferred it that way. She respected my decision. She wasn't a bad person, Marlana. She wouldn't have had an affair with me even if that's what I wanted. She did what she thought was right. We both did."

"Where is she now?"

He looked at Braden for an answer. He didn't know she was dead.

"She died," Braden said. "Two years ago."

"How?" his father asked in defeat.

Braden shook his head. He didn't know.

"And Courtney…?"

"We think she's with Tatum."

Both women had disappeared. Both women could be dead. He may not ever see either of them again. He lowered his head and pinched the bridge of his nose. "I'm so sorry." Then he dropped his hand and looked at his wife. "I'm sorry, Marlana. I never meant to hurt you. I love you."

"You should stay somewhere else for a while." Marlana turned to Braden and then Arizona. "Make yourselves at home. I'm sorry you had to witness this." With that, she left the room, climbing the stairs, each step full of dejection and making her petite frame seem heavier than it was.

"Did Courtney have any contact with you at all?" Braden asked his dad.

"No. None."

"You know nothing about her and Tatum's disappearance?"

"No. I promise you, I'm telling the truth. When I saw

that birth certificate, it was the first contact I've ever had with Courtney or her mother since I opened the trust fund."

Braden studied him for a long time. "How could you stay away?"

"There wasn't a day that went by when I didn't think of her. It wasn't easy. I wanted to be there for her. I wanted her to be part of my family. But that wouldn't have been fair to Marlana. Or you and Tatum."

"We would have adjusted."

Had Courtney been his child, Braden would have brought her into his family. The magnitude of that gave Arizona shivers. And it spoke loudly of his love for Aiden. He couldn't imagine turning his back on any child of his. He loved his child that much. And he would have loved a child born to another woman just as much.

"Mom would have adjusted," Braden continued.

"I did what I thought was best at the time," his dad responded meagerly. "That doesn't mean I didn't regret a decision I made when I was too young to know better. But after time goes by, there comes a point when it's too late to change anything."

"It's never too late," Arizona said, bringing both men's attention to her. "You can have a relationship with Courtney." If she was ever found. If either she or Tatum was ever found…alive.

Leaving his mother had been difficult. She had a sister who was flying in from Oregon. That helped. And he'd have stayed until his aunt arrived, but time was of the essence, and he had to make sure Aiden was safe. He still had his reservations about leaving him with Arizona's parents. He didn't even know them. And all the security in the world meant nothing if it wasn't better than the expertise of his enemies. Guards could be lazy. Electrical systems

could be breached. He had to spend at least a little while there so he felt better about leaving his son there. A family reunion was weird, but in this case it'd work out in his favor. He'd know by morning if he could leave Aiden there.

Braden drove his SUV through the gate after a guard recognized Arizona and gave them the go-ahead. The fact that he checked Braden's identification was a good sign. There were three more guards inside the gate. All of them wore flak jackets and had rifles hanging on their backs and pistols in holsters at their hips. In the rearview mirror, he saw the ten-foot, black iron gate swing closed and the guards resumed their vigil in front of it.

"My father only hires the best," Arizona said. "Ex-military types."

He sent her a wry look. She'd picked up on his skepticism.

There were a lot of trees on the property, obscuring the perimeter fence. Did the guards patrol it? Reaching a circular stone driveway with a grand water fountain in the middle, he stopped in front of the sprawling mansion. Security cameras were mounted to the impressive roofline.

"Nice," he said.

"This is a quarter of the size of their home in California."

This one had to be around twenty-thousand square feet. Who needed that much room? The home resembled a castle. Made of stone, two giant turrets towered over each side of the structure. Copper gutters along a modern roofline and giant windows were only a few of many indicators of the money it must have cost to build this.

"Wow!" Aiden exclaimed from the backseat.

Braden caught Arizona's flinch. She must have forgotten he was in the car. He'd just woken up when they were driving through the gate and was now growing more alert.

"Does Harry Potter live here?"

"No, but I'm sure you'll find plenty of movies here."

"My aunt will be here with her three kids. One of them is about Aiden's age. There's a playground in the back. And a pool. Miniature golf. Inside there's a game room and a general playroom. You name it."

"Wow! A game room!"

"Yeah. Plenty of room to fly your helicopter."

Without running into anyone, namely her—Braden could hear her thinking.

A valet opened the door for her. Braden let himself out. The house was bigger up close than it appeared from a distance.

"A fraction of the size, huh?"

"Just ignore it." Arizona stepped up the twenty-foot stone staircase to a circular landing surrounded by beds of flowers. Up narrower stairs, they reached the front door, where a doorman was waiting.

"Welcome, Ms. Ivy."

"Thanks, Berto."

"We have you in the west suite."

"Perfect. My favorite."

"Of course, Ms. Ivy."

She looked around the ridiculously large entry. There was a library to the left and a parlor to the right that must serve as a waiting room for guests. The entry was closed off to the rest of the house, but a panel of about six doors was open straight ahead.

Aiden bounded in, carrying his helicopter, flying it beside him.

"Everyone should be here by now."

He looked over at her. "Everyone?"

She bit her lower lip and wore contriteness poorly. "I should have warned you. My mother arranged a reunion.

She does that every chance she gets. The minute I called to say I was bringing you and Aiden, she gathered everyone available to meet here. Her existence is nothing but social events and home decorating."

He took in the grandeur again, his son making helicopter noises and his running feet echoing in the bright, cavernous room. "She decorated this?"

"It's one of her favorite pastimes."

Rich people were funny that way, he supposed. When you didn't have to have a career, you had to find something to do with all your time.

"She designed and decorated all of my parents' homes."

"How many are there?"

Aiden bumped into Arizona and resumed his flight around the room.

"Five?" She screwed up her nose and dodged another collision with Aiden, shooting the boy an annoyed look. "Maybe six."

"All here in the U.S.?"

"England, Switzerland and I think they just bought one in Hawaii. The others are in California, here, and North Carolina. My mother loves the Outer Banks."

This was a side of Arizona he hadn't seen before. She answered his questions factually, as though impressing him were the least of her motives.

"And you think you can top this?" He caught his son and whirled him around. He laughed the way he loved to hear him do and his feet lifted off the ground.

Setting him down deliberately in front of Arizona, he let go. Aiden stumbled and bumped into her again.

He smothered a laugh as she lifted her hands as though the boy were contagious.

"Not top it. Just…get away from it for once." She eyed Aiden as he flew through one of the open six doors.

That was an interesting thing to say. She viewed all of this as part of her association with the great Jackson Ivy. The money didn't matter. She could live without it.

"Now you know why I want my own identity," she said as he regarded her.

She couldn't be more wrong. That wasn't what he was thinking at all. She already had her own identity. Even after being raised rich and pampered, she was a survivor. She made her own way in life. She didn't need money to feel good about herself the way Serena did. She wanted to escape it. And, he supposed, to feel normal. Being this rich must have set her apart from other kids growing up. She'd fought it her entire life. And as a result, she was strong. Independent. Secure.

"What?" She cocked her head. "Why are you looking at me like that?"

He grinned. "You'll never be able to escape this."

"What? I don't need to escape anything."

While he sent her a dubious look, they entered a great room that was surprisingly not dissimilar to those found in suburbia, except this room was bigger.

"They're all downstairs. There's a bar and a kitchen and a walk-out to the pool."

"Everyone's here already?"

"Everyone who could make it."

"On such short notice?" They'd stayed only one night with his mother.

"Spontaneous is our middle name." She smiled at him.

Not hearing anything to indicate a crowd had gathered, he followed her down a wide and curving stairway. Reaching another big room, he took hold of Aiden's hand when the boy would have run to investigate display cases of art. They walked down a hallway, passing one double

door open to a Winston Churchill–like room until, finally, he heard voices.

At the end of the hall, the ceiling arched and opened into a rec room. The bar rivaled any he'd seen in upscale restaurants, with a mirrored wall, polished dark wood and bottles filling glass shelves. Music played at a low volume. Nothing stuffy, just soft rock.

"There she is." A woman slightly older than his mother approached with arms spread. She wore jeans and a long-sleeved silky green shirt. Her blond hair was in a bob and she had Arizona's blue eyes. She was a casual version of his mother, which he found most intriguing.

Arizona hugged her. "Hi, Mom."

"It's so good to see you. Lincoln said you're after some sort of story. A missing person?"

"Braden's sister. I'm helping to find her." She glanced back at him. "That's all. No story."

He didn't believe her. Nice try, though.

"Well—" she patted Braden's cheek "—you make yourself right at home and don't you worry one bit about your son. We'll take good care of him. You concentrate on finding your sister."

"Thank you." He needed to see for himself that Aiden would be safe here. And so far he wasn't sure yet.

"Jackson and I will help in any way we can."

"Thank you." Even if they could send a team of special forces in to save his sister, he wouldn't expect them to. They could help in other ways, and he was grateful for that, especially since her offer seemed genuine. Serena's parents often offered their assistance but they rarely meant it. He felt Arizona's mother was the opposite. She didn't say anything she didn't mean.

Lincoln hobbled over on crutches, blond hair messy and blue eyes smiling, although Braden thought there was

something haunting about them, or something that haunted him. He'd seen it that day he went to his house for help, that first day he'd met Arizona, hidden behind a contagious personality.

"You made it," Arizona said, hugging him.

"Brandie picked me up." He leaned back with a playful look. "My new neighbor saw her and I don't think she knew she was my sister. I think she was jealous."

"You want to make your new neighbor jealous?"

"She's pretty hot. But she's also not very friendly and her boyfriend is abusive." He told her about the woman and her boyfriend who'd hit her.

"She sounds more like a hot mess to me."

Lincoln chuckled. "I can always count on you for the truth."

"Hey, Arizona." Brandie approached. Her sister was a five-foot-eight-ish slender woman with light red hair and green eyes. Striking in beauty.

"Brandie, this is Braden. Brandie is an antiques collector."

"I just ran across a pair of shoes worn by a cowboy who was hung for shooting two railroad officers."

"Fascinating, Brandie," Lincoln said, shaking his head.

"She's always telling stories," Arizona explained.

Brandie crouched to Aiden's level, where he clung to Braden's leg. Bashful initially, but he'd warm up. He'd already been eyeing a room off this one, where lights blinked and games dinged and exploded.

"Would you like to go play in the game room?" she asked.

Aiden looked up at him.

"Go ahead. Have fun."

Shyly, Aiden gave Brandie his hand and she led him off.

"Brandie should have kids of her own," Arizona said.

"If only she'd get over her last relationship," Lincoln said, and then turned to Braden. "But enough on that. Someone came after your son?"

Braden nodded, helpless fury clenching his insides. No one went after his own and got away with it. "Luckily they were sloppy."

"Was it the same man who attacked Arizona?"

"We think so." Recalling they hadn't told him about their trip to Atlanta, he said, "We also discovered I have a half sister who contacted Tatum and went to Tortola. That was why Tatum went there. She was going after Courtney."

"What?"

He explained everything about the arms shipment.

"So, this all has something to do with the arms shipment." Lincoln gazed off at the floor a distance away, thinking it over. Then he met Braden's eyes again. "But if Tatum isn't guilty, then why did she steal your files?"

He thought his sister may have been working with Courtney.

Braden couldn't answer that, and it made him mad.

"How did the arms dealer know to contact your sister or this Courtney woman?"

"He must have known one of them," Arizona answered. Braden was glad she did. He didn't like talking about his sister as though she were some sleazy criminal.

"I know a guy who works with the ICE. I'll see if I can find out where they are in the hunt for the dealer."

"How do you know someone with ICE?" Arizona asked while Braden's mood lightened.

"I knew there was a reason you were the first person I thought of when all of this started," he said.

"Don't be too appreciative yet. He may not be able to tell me anything."

He'd take anything at this point. He had to protect his son. And save his sisters—two of them now.

Arizona hooked her arm with Braden's. "Come on. I'll introduce you to everyone."

He met Jonas, a self-proclaimed singer who had no record label yet. He was overly muscular in Braden's mind, too muscular for his five-foot-eleven frame. Riana was an interior decorator, and unlike her mother, made money doing it. Arizona's aunt was here. She lived in Denver and had two kids, one ten, the other seven. That was who Aiden was playing with in the game room. Clever to have that right off the adult playroom. As long as things didn't get carried away. He didn't see anyone drinking, though. Just smelled something smoking outside.

"Macon, Autumn and Savanna couldn't make it," Arizona's mother said, having followed them from person to person.

Arizona searched around the room. "Where's Dad?"

"He's getting the horses ready. He wants to get to know Braden." She wiggled her eyebrows at her daughter. "Check out the new boyfriend. He's handsome."

"Mom," Arizona protested, rolling embarrassed eyes his way.

Braden wandered to the open glass doors, the smell drawing him as much as the need to get away from Arizona's mother and her ideas about them as a couple. It had a strange effect on him. Appealing. Too much so.

A team of white-clad cooks prepared the barbeque. Of course they wouldn't have to do the work themselves. Braden would rather do the work. Most of the fun in barbequing was preparing the food. He watched the men talk and smile as they grilled and made potato salad beneath white scarves clinging to a log frame and flowing in a slight breeze, blocking enough of the sun. It wasn't a hot day.

He walked to the edge of the patio, looking toward the perimeter. If a man could get over the ten-foot stone fence, he could easily make it to the house unseen. He was seriously considering taking Aiden with him when a man appeared at his side.

"You must be Arizona's new man."

Braden turned to see a russet-haired man stand beside him. He must have come up the stairs near the cooks. He wore a fisherman's hat and dark blue jeans with a long-sleeved, light blue denim shirt. Not *GQ,* just comfortable. His pale green eyes smiled from behind John Lennon style glasses, going well with his near-red, curly hair, which was more of a brown color with a few strands of gray that were barely visible. He was tall and lanky.

"Braden McCrae." He shook the man's hand. "Arizona is a friend."

"Jackson Ivy. Any progress finding your sister?"

"A little."

"Lincoln has every resource available to him helping out. I made sure of it."

"That's very kind of you. He has come up with some vital information for us."

"I wish there was more we could do."

"Watching my son is enough." And keeping him safe. Braden looked toward the perimeter again. He hadn't seen any guards inside the house, only at the gate.

"Let's go for a ride. There's some things I want to show you. And I'd also like to talk to you about Arizona."

Braden went with him down the stairs, past the delectably smelling smoker and grills. A stable hand held two horses by the reins.

"Do you ride much?"

"I've ridden before."

Jackson climbed atop a big black stallion, leaving an equally big chestnut for him.

Braden reined his horse away from the deck, across the lawn and past an outdoor swimming pool with tables and umbrellas mimicking a seaside resort. He guided Jackson where he wished to go.

"Lincoln tells me Arizona is trying to make her way into serious news corresponding."

"She's said as much."

"And she means to do this with you?" Jackson glanced over at him. "It strikes me as odd. Lincoln, too. Her going off to the Virgin Islands to help you search for your missing sister."

And now his half sister, as well. Braden reined his horse more to the left, hoping to catch sight of the perimeter fence soon.

"Ever since her fiancé died, she's been going through a change," Jackson continued. "She doesn't know which direction she's going, although you better not tell her that. If it isn't her idea, she can be the most stubborn woman you ever met."

Braden breathed a short, wry laugh.

"You've noticed?" Jackson chuckled. "Arizona may be my youngest, but she's got plenty of fire in her."

"I'd rather she didn't do a story on my sister. She's been through enough…assuming I find her alive."

Jackson rode facing straight ahead for a bit. "She'll make a lousy news correspondent."

Grinning, Braden studied Jackson's profile. Love and worry combined in the lines around his eyes and mouth.

"She doesn't want to be like you," he said.

Jackson grunted ruefully. "She hates being Jackson Ivy's daughter. Or she claims to. But if you really know my daughter, Braden, you'll see it's all a smokescreen. She

has herself convinced she needs an identity that's separate from me, when in truth, her identity is firmly in place and she's perfectly content with it."

"I've noticed that about her." He reined his horse around a tree.

Jackson did the same on the opposite side.

"It sure didn't take you long," he said when they rejoined on the other side.

And her father was reading too much into that. "It's obvious she's still having trouble dealing with her fiancé's death."

"She blames herself. As if she could have done more."

Braden nodded. That fell in line with all he'd gathered about her. "Once she lets her fiancé's death go, she'll be back on track." He just hoped that happened before she exposed a story on his sister.

"She's helping you because she's driven to help anyone in trouble. And the fact that your sister went missing in the Virgin Islands is uncanny. It's as though she's trying to relive that time, to get it right this time."

Braden hadn't thought of it that way before. "I suppose you're right."

"Of course I am. She's tooted her horn about becoming a news correspondent ever since her fiancé died. But has she done anything about it? No. Not until now."

Not until she felt compelled to help him find his sister, who disappeared near where her fiancé had been abducted and killed. "Well, I sure hope we find my sister alive, then."

Jackson fell silent for a moment. Then he said something he didn't see coming.

"You're good for her."

"I just want to find my sister."

"I don't mean because of that. Arizona would have

found an outlet to her grief sooner or later. You understand her, and she needs that."

If he was entertaining the possibility of something more developing, Braden couldn't tell. Encountering a rebound relationship with her was seeming less and less of a threat, but long term, he didn't trust his track record. He seriously needed more time, to take a good look at his mistakes and make sure he never made them again. The third time had to be a charm, and if a third time never came to him, that was okay. He had Aiden. That was enough.

Up ahead, Braden saw the fence and was glad to have something other than Arizona to concentrate on. It was an impressive structure, and included barbed wire along the top. He guided his horse so that they followed the stone barrier. A little way down, he saw a camera.

"So this is where you were taking us," Jackson said.

He'd noticed Braden had a specific route in mind when they'd set out and hadn't said anything. "You're very perceptive." And kind.

"Your son is safer here than anywhere else you could take him." Jackson chuckled deeply. "The press can be worse than criminals when it comes to finding ways to invade your privacy. They'll do anything to get a snapshot of us here. We can't always be in the public's eye."

"I understand."

"But you needed to see for yourself."

Braden met his look apologetically.

"I'd do the same." He pointed to the fence. "That stone can withstand a fair amount of explosives. There are surveillance cameras every thirty feet or so, and a control center on the top floor of the house in one of the turrets, which has windows all around and is high enough to see most the property. I have guards working 24/7 when we're

on site, both at the gate and in the control center. You don't see them in the house because that's the way I want it."

Braden smiled his appreciation.

"The caterers all have top secret security clearances. My wife jokes that I think I'm the president of the United States. My response to her is I'm just the president of my family, and I'll go to any lengths to keep them safe and the press off their backs when we all need some time alone. This mansion is open to everyone in the family. There's usually someone here at any given time of the year. My wife's sister was here when Arizona called about your son. It worked out well."

For such a rich, influential man, he was sure down to earth. Like his wife. He felt at home here, and he was no longer worried about his son. Tomorrow, he and Arizona could get moving again.

The buffet table was set up and full of food by the time Braden came back from his ride with her dad. Seeing the two smiling and talking as if they'd been friends for years gave Arizona a funny feeling. Her dad liked him. What had they talked about? Her, of course, but what had her father said, and what had Braden said?

Her dad liked him….

She couldn't look away from them together. And she struggled with why her dad's approval meant anything at all.

Crying erupted from the game room.

Arizona turned to see Aiden on the floor, facedown. She stood frozen, not knowing what to do. She glanced to her right. Her mother looked at her expectantly, as though waiting for her to do something. Why didn't she come help her? Meanwhile, her sister chatted away, not noticing the disturbance or their mother's distraction.

Arizona turned away from her mother to see Brandie sitting beside Lincoln, whose leg was propped on a coffee table. They took no notice of Aiden, either.

Jonas and Riana were outside at the buffet table and her dad and Braden had stopped to talk to them.

Aiden's crying continued. Did everyone expect her to go to him? She couldn't just leave him.

One of the other kids in the playroom knelt beside him.

Good, maybe that would be enough.

"I want my mommy!" Aiden wailed.

Oh, hell. Arizona went to him. She knelt beside him.

"He tripped," the boy of ten said.

"Sit up, Aiden." Arizona touched his shoulder, seeing his face contorted with a world's worth of agony, sweet innocent green eyes lifting to hers, a mirror of Braden's. Braden's son. A living, breathing miniature version. Something inside her moved. "Show me where you hurt."

Aiden sat on his rump, his tears subsiding some as he grew distracted pointing to his knee.

"Let's have a look." She lifted his pant leg to expose his knee. Luckily the pants were big. His knee was a little red but not bleeding. "Oh, look at that. I think you're going to live."

His teary eyes registered no comprehension.

"I want my mommy," he said, this time without wailing, but equally tragic.

Arizona had to smother a smile. "Well, she isn't here right now. How about I get your dad?"

"He'll just tell me to man up."

She snorted a laugh. "Sounds like good advice."

He pouted at her.

"You aren't bleeding. If you were, I'd be a lot more concerned. Does it still hurt?"

He nodded.

"Really? As bad as it did when you fell?"

After a bit of consternation, he shook his head.

She messed up the hair on top of his head. "See? You're already manning up."

His little mouth turned up with instant animation that left her marveling over how quickly children found humor in things. His six-year-old laughter lightened her heart further. She had no idea she could have this effect on kids. He was relating to her.

Wow.

"Not so bad, huh?" Braden's masculine voice sent shivers of warm awareness firing through her.

"Daddy!" Aiden sprang up and plowed into his dad, who lifted him for a hug.

Arizona stood. "Pretend you didn't just see that."

"Oh, but I did." He winked. "Dinner's ready."

Good. She was famished. And she needed distance from the confusing way she'd felt with Aiden. A kid had never touched her so much.

Braden turned with his son. "They have mac 'n' cheese with hot dogs."

"Yum!" Aiden exclaimed.

"And French fries if you pick out the onion and peppers."

"Ew."

Braden chuckled. "Just kidding. There's regular fries. And dessert."

"Yay!"

Arizona followed them. Not so bad…

What was happening to her? Who was this woman who'd softened for a child? And not just natural adoration that anyone might feel. This packed a punch. Arrowed straight to her heart. Braden's eyes…

Braden put Aiden down and made him hold a plate. The

boy watched him, eyes looking way, way up at his tall, handsome dad, expecting him to fill the plate with food. Her hands trembled ever so slightly as she held her plate and loaded it with salad.

She dug her hand into a bowl of cheeseburger flavored chips to keep her hands occupied. When she dumped them onto her plate, she saw Aiden watching. Dreamy eyes went back to the bowl of chips and then he poked his dad's arm. Braden was talking to her dad again, laughing at something he said. Damn it.

Aiden poked again, to no avail.

"You want some of these?" she asked.

"Yes. Yes. Yes." He jumped up and down with each exuberant word.

She put a handful onto his plate and was rewarded with a big, toothy smile.

"Honey, when you get older, you're going to knock all the girls off their high heels with that smile."

He laughed hard—the way only a young child could when they had no idea what you meant. The only thing they understood was that you were trying to be funny.

It triggered a smile of her own. He was a cute kid. No getting around it. The kid was a total gem.

"I like you," he beamed up at her.

Shock bolted through her, stunning her into stillness and stopping her breath for a second.

"Kids do like honesty."

She whipped her head to her right, only then seeing that her mother stood there, making it worse by saying, "I always knew you'd come around."

"Stop, Mother. I'm terrible with kids." The movie *Matilda* came to mind as she moved down the table with everyone else. Maybe she should take up shot put and throw darts.

"That's not what I saw."

"Mom..." She sent her a warning look, nervously glancing at Braden, who watched with growing affection.

His gaze ran down her body, covering every inch of her in the halter-style blue-striped summer dress with a wide, red belt and red shoes.

"You underestimate yourself," her mother insisted.

"Azona." Aiden poked her.

She looked down in time to see his finger pointing to a chafer of French fries. The caterers were gods.

"You like crispy fries?" None of her siblings had liked them growing up. Just mushy fries. Ew.

"Yes, yes, yes." More jumping.

Her sentiments, exactly. Using the utensil to deposit a giant portion onto his plate, she cautioned, "Don't forget the ketchup."

Then she put a giant portion onto her own plate. Fruit and vegetables tomorrow. She munched on a fry.

"I think I just figured out your problem with kids."

Pausing in the act of licking her finger, she looked at him. "What is it?"

Sliding his arm around her, Braden drew her against him, each holding a plate to their side.

"You're a kid yourself," he told her fondly.

"I'm a..." What did he mean?

While she ruminated over that, he kissed her. Brief but potent. She slowly opened her eyes to see his full of satisfaction.

Claps were subtle around them.

"Daddy!" Aiden complained.

Never one to blush, Arizona was out of sorts to feel her hot cheeks. Now was not the time for him to challenge her with seduction. His earlier confidence that he could make her respond seemed off now. In front of her family? His

playfulness suggested he'd intended that, but now his eyes told a different story. The kiss hadn't been planned or intentional. He'd been compelled to do it.

"Doesn't like kids but she likes Braden's," Brandie teased.

"She likes Braden," Riana said.

"And he likes her."

Escaping Braden's arm, Arizona moved away from the crowd and headed toward a long table meticulously decorated with fresh flowers and linen. How would she get through this night with all the confusion racing around in her head? She was teetering on the edge of something big, something life altering. It was happening too fast, hurtling her out of control. Even diving out of planes she was in control. This felt like falling without a parachute.

Chapter 14

Sometime after two, Braden decided to give sleep a try once more. Leaving the game controller on the ottoman, he flipped off the giant television that was mounted to the wall. He'd wandered through the mansion and found this entertainment room near the family room where they'd all gathered earlier. Ever since he'd foolishly kissed Arizona, he'd been kicking himself.

Did he really want to prove to her that he could make her respond to him? Make her forget Trevor? Fill her with thoughts of only him? Something inside him must. He wished he didn't feel so uncertain about her, about allowing this to go further.

And then there was part of him that wanted to explore. Was it merely her rejection? Could he even call it that? He hadn't been able to bring her to orgasm. What man wouldn't be marred by that?

Making his way back upstairs, he saw lights on in the library. They hadn't been on when he'd come down.

Stopping in the open doorway, he saw Arizona sitting at a computer. Dark wood bookshelves lined three walls. The wall ahead of him was full of windows. Sitting areas and three desks allowed for serious research or just plain curiosity. A person could get lost in here for hours. As Arizona had obviously done. Still in the summer dress she'd had on all day, she must not have gone to bed yet. The lights had been on when he'd passed the library earlier, but he hadn't seen her.

She looked up and saw him, her hands going still on the keyboard.

Typing?

Anger swirled and tightened his chest. She was writing her story. Is this how she did it? Sneaking around in the middle of the night?

"Hey," she said, clicking the computer mouse. "Couldn't sleep, either, huh?"

"How's the story coming?"

She froze in the act of standing. "I wasn't writing about Tatum."

Then why had she closed everything? "What were you doing?"

"Nothing. Chatting in a blog. I couldn't sleep." She moved away from the computer.

"Arizona..."

She passed him in the doorway. "I wasn't writing about Tatum, Braden. Why are you so uptight about that?" She spun to face him in the hall. "I can see why you'd want to protect your sister's privacy, but with you it's almost overboard.

"You didn't see how much it hurt Tatum to be driven out of a job she loved and have her name dragged through the mud."

"And now she's missing. What's wrong with getting the word out?"

He couldn't tell if she'd given up trying to get the story or if she was waiting for him to give in. "People still think of her as the one who enabled an illegal arms deal." Didn't she see? His sister would suffer even more if a story was released and it broadcasted her false accusations all over the country or the world.

"We might be able to find her faster. There will be more resources working with us."

"Speculation. You can't predict what would happen."

"Okay." She folded her arms. "I get it, Braden. I wasn't writing an article. I was..." She looked away.

"You were what?"

Tapping her foot, she was full of consternation and didn't answer. Finally, she dropped her arms and pivoted, storming toward...wherever. It could be anywhere in this gargantuan house.

He trailed her.

She made her way downstairs, through the rec room and out the back door. Not stopping there, she walked out into the yard until she came to a playground.

At the swings, she sat and began swinging. Seeing him, her eyes pouted over his insistence to keep bothering her.

Taking the swing to her right, he rocked his feet to get him moving a bit, but didn't try to keep up with her. Clearly she was being a kid again, swinging as hard and high as she could. This new side to her explained a lot about her issue with kids. She was the youngest of eight. She thought she couldn't relate to them, when in fact, she related too much. He had to withhold a warm chuckle.

"What were you looking for?" he asked on one of her downward swings.

"Go away," she answered on the next.

"Just tell me."

Another swing, two. She eyed him with each pass. On the verge of spilling what was on her mind—in a big way.

"Sex?" He couldn't resist.

"No!"

"Hamburger-flavored potato chips?"

That won a tiny smile from her. "No. But close."

She leaned back as she swung down. He waited.

Her swings slowed. "It was a…mom site."

He stopped rocking his feet.

She stopped kicking off the ground and her swings slowed some more. He allowed her a moment of reflection. She must need the time, which told him she was confused.

About Aiden. Of course. And her ability to relate to him.

"You are a natural," he said. "You may not feel that way, but you are. And Aiden *does* like you."

She stomped her feet onto the ground, digging in and billowing up a mini cloud of dust as she stopped herself from swinging and just sat beside him. He loved how she'd come out here to vent. On a swing. Kid at heart.

So was he…

Realizing he must be wearing a stupid grin, he decided to lighten the mood.

"Why were you named Arizona?"

She smiled again. She was on to him and his tactics. "Are you picking up where you left off at the buffet table?"

"No." God, no. Was he?

She started to swing again, only this time it was mellow, smooth, low swings. "My mother said it was because I was an unexpected ray of sunshine, but the last four of us were unexpected. I think it was because she gave birth to me during an unusually hot summer."

They gazed at each other, a timeless thing that had noth-

ing to do with the topic. He sensed her responding, too. Whatever had unsettled her was gone, resolved. Whether she knew it or not.

She sighed and her eyes grew sultry. Then she got up from the swing and moved in front of his. Grasping the chains on each side of his head, she leaned over him, blue eyes more than meeting his challenge of seducing her. She was taking control of it. He found it intoxicating. Proof that he hadn't been wrong. He could have her. Satisfy her.

As though interpreting his thoughts, she straddled him, slipping one, then the other of her long, slender legs on each side of his inside the swing. Her boldness was different than any other woman he'd been with. Some he'd been with took initiative, but Arizona had a way about her. It was in her eyes. In the way she moved.

She proved it when she put her hands on each side of his face and kissed him. He swung them a little, beginning to wonder if his thinking was all wrong. His divorce was still fresh, but this felt so right.

"You're ruining my seduction ploy," he said, a way of diverting his thoughts.

"We started out fine before, too."

Bold, brash. Sexy. And disturbing. He'd felt right with the first two women he'd married.

Arizona kissed him again, her eyes still glowing in the darkness.

To hell with it.

Moving one hand to the back of her head, he deepened the kiss. She reciprocated in the sweetest way. Running his hands up from his hold on her waist and lower back, he stopped their swinging and cupped her breasts.

She broke free of his mouth and gripped the chain ropes of the swing, watching his hands over the silky material of her dress. There was no easy access to her bare skin.

Holding her rear, he stood from the swing and carried her toward the house. Inside, he continued on, with her wrapped around him, kissing his mouth. It stirred his blood but didn't deter him from his purpose. Taking her to bed was a temptation he could barely deny, but he wanted her so hot for him that her fire couldn't be doused.

At the library door, he entered and set her down just inside. She kept kissing him. He kissed her back, taking over and delving deeper, teasing her.

Then he stopped. "Don't stay up too late."

Startled, she only stared at him at first. "What?" She glanced around, dawning coming slowly.

Then she zeroed in on him. "You…"

"You won't be able to resist me next time." He pecked her lips once more and, grinning, turned and left her standing there.

She couldn't believe he'd done it. Arizona finished getting ready and left her room. Since waking up this morning she'd berated herself for starting anything with Braden. She couldn't even blame him for leaving her cold in the library. What had possessed her to climb on top of him?

Him, of course. She couldn't resist him. But as soon as he'd teased her and the ramifications of what she'd done had sunk in, she'd felt empty. And thoughts of Trevor had begun. She hadn't slept at all last night.

Why she'd climbed on top of him was easy to answer. Like it or not, seeing him with her father had touched a warm place in her that hadn't been touched in a long time. Her dad might be rich and famous, but he was just a dad to her. She'd grown up with his wisdom and practical discipline. He loved their mother, and she loved him. Never had there been a time when she'd thought of her family

as a tabloid story. It wasn't until she'd grown up that she'd begun to feel that way.

Seeing Braden with her father had definitely altered something in her.

That was the disturbing part. Because with that came the loss she'd suffered with Trevor. She'd felt exactly the same way with him. Trevor and her dad had gotten along well. Her dad had supported his proposal to his little girl.

Morosely, she made her way down to the informal dining room. They rarely used the formal dining room here.

This room was a reflection of her family. Full of color and spunk, there was a fully stocked bar, and framed posters of their favorite animated films lined the walls. Through a panel of windows and double glass doors was a balcony. The kitchen was open to the room, although most of the time they had a kitchen staff do all the work. Jackson Ivy liked to smell the food as it was being prepared, and he wanted to be able to see the culinary delights being created. Family was important to him, but the press never splattered that all over their rags.

Talking and laughter was already filtering through the halls by the time she approached the dining area. She'd dragged on the time, dreading having to face Braden.

Her mother's boisterous laughter was the first thing to greet her as she entered, her father leaning down to kiss her briefly, his dark red hair always looking tousled with its natural curl. Lincoln sat with his leg on another chair. Her aunt sat at one end of the table, trying to keep her kids from whining about being hungry when the smells from the kitchen were so fantastic. A giant TV played a morning news show at a loud volume.

Braden sat with Brandie, the two smiling along with Lincoln at whatever had made her mother laugh. Then Braden saw her and his smile changed. Faded? No, just

changed. His eyes communicated intimacy before he caught it and nothing more could be seen in them. Aiden must still be sleeping. He'd had a big day yesterday.

Jonas entered, patting her back once. "You guys sure are noisy. I heard you all the way up on the north side."

Riana passed him and Arizona. "He's lying. I woke him up."

"When are you going to get a real job?" Brandie said from beside Braden.

"I have one."

"You call that band a job? You don't even have a record label."

"I will, and I'll do it without Dad's help. Unlike you." He strode over to the snack bar where a platter of fruit and scones sat.

Riana stood beside Arizona. "Dad helped her open her store and now she's the black sheep among us."

"She must be doing something right because she's making money."

"I'm not knocking it. She's the only one who did it that way. I took out a loan for my business."

"Dad's friend is going to read a sample of mine." She wasn't getting money from him but he'd called in a favor for her.

"That's not the same. You're doing all the work yourself."

"So is Brandie."

Everyone had an identity crisis in this family. She saw Riana register the same and then wander off, going to the coffee carafes.

Arizona moved closer to the table, feeling Braden watching her.

The news program broke to a picture of Tatum. Last night, her father had told her a reporter had contacted him

shortly after she and Braden had left American Freight, trying to get information about her relationship with Braden. He'd waited for a moment when Braden wasn't beside her. He hadn't given the reporter an inch. While her father couldn't avoid the press, he never threw her to them, either. He had, however contacted Michael Benson to let him know what Arizona was doing and the attention it had attracted. Benson had been enthusiastic about an exclusive once Tatum was found. That was part of the reason she couldn't sleep last night. Doing the article excited her, but she couldn't ignore the way Braden felt about it. That had led to thoughts of his son. Which was more important to her? The story or Braden and his son?

Tatum was already in the news, just as Arizona had predicted. This was the moment she'd been waiting for, the moment when she'd be free to do her story without turning Braden against her. But it still felt wrong.

Braden stared at the TV screen as a reporter interviewed Sophie Reynolds, the woman who'd led Braden to the letter from Tatum.

"It didn't dawn on me who Braden was with until after he left with her," Sophie said.

"What was she doing with him?" the reporter asked.

"I don't know. Helping him, it looked like. Or maybe they're seeing each other."

Braden's cold eyes slid to her.

He couldn't possibly blame her for Sophie talking to the press. After several potent seconds, he stood up and walked toward the exit of the dining room, brushing past her without a word.

She went after him, her family uncharacteristically silent. In the front entry, she found him at their bags. The servants had brought them down for them.

Lifting his, he faced her. “If Aiden is safe here, so are you.”

She stopped. “What?”

“You don’t have to go with me.” He lifted his eyes to take in the grandeur. “You never did.”

“I want to go with you.”

“What for? A story?” He shook his head. “I told you, no story.”

“And I told you, it would get into the news anyway.”

“Only because I was a fool and let you go along. I should have known your father would protect you.”

“What about Aiden?” She didn’t mean to throw that in his face, but he wasn’t being fair. “If I hadn’t been involved, what then?”

Anger stormed his eyes and he lifted his luggage.

She grabbed his arm before he could walk away. “It isn’t my fault Sophie talked.”

“It isn’t that, Arizona. The media is on to you now. They’ll follow us.”

“No. We can get to Tortola without them knowing. My father can help us.”

“I can do that without you.”

“I want to help.”

He walked to the door.

“Braden…I need this.” The outburst came from deep inside her. It was a raw need. Something she hadn’t confronted until now. Trevor’s death was the cause, and she was afraid helping Braden would heal her. Just as Lincoln had said. It had never been just the story, but what motivated her went much deeper than she’d allowed herself to acknowledge.

Tears bloomed in her eyes.

She’d helped victims before, but nothing compared to this. Tatum was missing, possibly kidnapped or murdered.

Arizona clung to the hope that she was alive. She clung to the hope that she could help Braden save her. And if they couldn't save her, would Arizona ever be able to let go of Trevor?

Lincoln put his arm around her, propped on one crutch. Only then did she notice he'd joined them, along with everyone else except her aunt and the kids. Her parents stood behind Lincoln, her mother's hand on her dad's arm, anxious with concern, her dad a silent observer. Brandie and Raina were behind them, in the interior doorway of the entry, both in dresses, Raina leaning against the door frame, Brandie with her arms folded, curious as any sister would be over the drama taking place.

"What about the story, Arizona?" Braden asked.

It was an exclusive. It could change her life. And it had nothing to do with Trevor. Did it?

"You don't have to be different from Dad, A," Lincoln said.

He'd always been on Braden's side. And it wasn't the first time he'd harangued her. But what if Trevor was playing a role in her decisions? Lincoln said she jumped in to help victims because of that tragedy. And he thought she went on adventures to blot out the pain.

"You have changed," her dad said, moving to Lincoln's side. "What's wrong with being like me? When did you start thinking you needed to be different? If I didn't know better—" he glanced at Lincoln "—thanks to your brother who loves you very much, I'd wonder if you weren't proud to be an Ivy, that you'd rather be part of another family. Is that what you want?"

Contrition twisted her core into melting humility. Her father could be hard-hitting and this time was no exception. He'd arrowed straight to the truth and hadn't spared her feelings. "No."

A memory of how the press had found her even though her father had done everything he could to protect her, that first time was burned in her mind forever. The crazed look in the reporter's eyes. He'd do anything for a story. He hadn't cared about her.

She looked at Braden, appalled that she'd even considered doing that to him.

"It's okay," he murmured, dropping his luggage and coming to her. He took her hand and pulled her from Lincoln's arms and into his. "I'll take you to Tortola, and I'll make sure you don't get hurt." He looked up and to Lincoln's side at her father.

Arizona didn't see whether her father gave his nonverbal consent, she was too warm and reassured and comforted in Braden's arms.

Chapter 15

True to Jackson Ivy's word, he got them to Tortola undetected. Now they were on the way to see the maid who'd helped them escape Julian. Braden felt a definite shift in Arizona and he was having trouble reconciling how he felt about it. She'd crossed a milestone regarding her dead fiancé. What it meant for him, he was reluctant to entertain.

"We have to find a way to get inside Julian's house," Arizona said, walking beside him along a street, reading a map and checking the address they'd found on the maid. She was in a pair of overall shorts, big jewelry and rhinestone-covered sandals, showing off those legs again.

He forced his attention back to the task at hand. The last time they'd tried to get in Julian's villa it hadn't worked very well. But it was the only way they'd find out if Tatum was there. Getting in was the challenge. The maid had helped them before, maybe they could convince her to help them again. If she could look around for them. Check out the meeting room she'd mentioned…

"Here." Arizona stopped. "There it is."

A tiny, weathered bungalow sat close between others almost identical, but each painted different colors. They stepped up to the front door and knocked. There was no bell.

No one answered. Braden knocked again, checking around the quiet neighborhood. No one drove by. No one was outside.

"Maybe she's at work," Arizona said.

Could be. But if she was there, they wouldn't be able to get close enough to talk to her. He peered into the front window. It looked like a chair was tipped over in the kitchen.

Instinct triggered his wariness. This didn't feel right. What if she'd been seen meeting them at the café?

He tried the knob. It was locked.

"What are you doing?"

Checking the neighborhood again, he left the dilapidated front porch and made his way to the back.

Arizona trotted to catch up. "Braden."

He stopped short at the back door, which he saw was cracked open about an inch. Turning, he put his hands on her shoulders. "Stay out here."

She looked from the cracked-open door to his face and nodded, understanding what had him on high alert all of the sudden.

Sliding the door open, He entered the kitchen and immediately covered his mouth and nose. It smelled awful in here. Lying on the floor in front of the stove was Patty Williams, and a pool of blood had dried beneath her.

Remorse ran through him in a shockwave. She must have been murdered shortly after she'd met him and Arizona. And no one had missed her, least of all Julian.

Taking out his phone, he called Crawford. He'd said he

was going to question her. Had he been able to? He left the house, closing the door all the way.

Arizona stood just outside, arms folded, eyes round with apprehension. "Is she dead?"

"Crawford. It's Braden McCrae," he said into the phone, keeping his eyes on Arizona. "We just left Patty William's house. She's been murdered."

Arizona covered her mouth with her hand while Crawford's silence revealed his surprise.

"A few days ago, too. She was probably killed the same day she came to see Arizona and me."

"I've been trying to contact her. I stopped by her house and then went to see Julian. He told me she'd taken a few days off for vacation."

"And you didn't think you needed to check to make sure he wasn't lying?"

"Mr. McCrae…"

"Why didn't you check inside her house?" It hadn't taken Braden much to discover Patty murdered.

"I rang her bell and knocked."

But hadn't looked in the windows. He wasn't trying very hard to solve Tatum and Courtney's cases. He was deliberately lax.

"She's dead because she gave us proof that Tatum went to Julian's villa," Braden said. "Did you question him about the necklace?"

"Of course I did. And he denied it. Did you expect him to tell the truth?"

At his snapping tone, Braden teetered between believing him and not.

"What about the hotel manager? He has to know something."

"If he does, he isn't talking."

Braden had an idea on how to make him talk. "We'll take the investigation from here."

"You'll do nothing more than impede our efforts," the detective answered. "You're not a policeman, Mr. McCrae."

Was he glad about that? "I don't need to be to find my sister." And if she was dead, and Julian was responsible, he just might take it to a more dangerous level.

He disconnected.

"What are we going to do now?" Arizona asked, obviously ill over the realization that Patty was dead.

Putting his hand on her back, he steered her away from the bungalow and then took her hand as they headed back toward town, ever watchful of anyone suspicious. With Patty gone, they had no one else to turn to.

When they reached town, he saw the clerk from the hotel sitting on the patio of the café he and Arizona had frequented. When she saw them, she reached into her purse for some cash and dropped it on the table as she stood. Was she running or had she been waiting for them?

"Is that..."

Braden nodded. "Yes."

The clerk emerged from the café, looking one way and then the other before approaching them. She'd been waiting.

"I heard you were back on the island," she said. "Keep walking."

They walked up the street.

"One of Julian's maids is missing." Her scared eyes searched for anyone watching. "I haven't been on the island long. I came over from St. Maarten because my boyfriend lived here. But we broke up and I miss my family. I am going back. I quit my job at the hotel and I am taking the ferry this afternoon." She turned to face them and they all

stopped on the sidewalk. “If you had not shown up today I would have left all of this behind me and not looked back. But I am glad you did.” She searched around her again.

Braden did, too, and saw no one taking notice of them.

The girl bit her lip and looked at the shops across the street awhile, before turning to them again. “There was a woman from South America who came here alone. A tourist. She stayed at the Frenchman’s Point Hotel.”

Braden went still, excitement pumping through him.

“She went to Julian’s villa and disappeared after that. And then…” Torment ravaged her, her breathing erratic. “She was killed.”

“We read about her,” Arizona said. “You saw her go to Julian’s?”

The clerk shook her head. “She told me that’s where she was going. Sometimes tourists talk to me. She had been there several days and had begun telling me of her trip. She was happy to have met a man.” Tears billowed in her eyes and one spilled over. “My manager…” she sobbed.

“It’s okay, you can tell us,” Arizona said.

“He told me never to speak of the women.”

Braden shared a look with Arizona, who turned to the clerk.

“Why?”

More tears spilled over. “I do not know, but he threatened grave consequences if I did. I took a chance telling you about your sister.”

Braden took hold of her arm and started looking for a taxi. “Come on. We’ll take you to the ferry and make sure you get on.”

She sniffled and wiped her dark face. “Thank you.”

Arizona trailed behind them.

“What else can you tell us? What grave consequences was your manager referring to?”

"Nothing he would do. He was taking money from Julian Blake in exchange for his silence. Most of the women who go to the villa…they don't return. Julian uses the hotel for his feeding ground. With all the tourists coming and going, he has got a steady flow. Some are reported, others…"

"We know of four women. My sister, her friend, the South American woman and a local woman."

"There have been at least two others."

"Oh, my God," Arizona breathed from behind them. "And you never went to the police?"

The clerk twisted to see her. "I could not. I was not afraid of my manager. Julian, however. He is not a man for someone of my station to cross. I have no one here, and the police seem to turn a blind eye on matters of concern with him."

Now Braden looked back at her.

"Crawford is in on it?" she spoke her question aloud.

"In on it or taking money like my manager."

"Or afraid to do anything." Braden paid extra vigilance to his surroundings. Seeing a taxi, he raised his hand. He'd be damned if another woman would be killed in their search for Tatum and Courtney. What still confounded him was the lack of connection to stolen technology.

"What is Julian doing with the women?" Arizona asked as the taxi pulled to a stop along the street.

"I do not know. Torturing and killing them. Julian Blake is a sick man. I cannot wait to get off this island and never return."

Braden opened the back door, scanning the street and shops. Assured they hadn't been seen, he climbed in after the women. He and Arizona would take her to the ferry and wait with her until she was on it and safely away.

* * *

After the ferry disappeared on the horizon, Arizona and Braden took a taxi back to their rental, which they'd parked in town. After that, they drove to Frenchman's Point Hotel. Arizona was increasingly frightened that this would not end well.

Braden was hell-bent on paying a visit to the hotel manager. They raced to a stop at the hotel.

"You can wait out here if you want," he said.

She'd never seen him this zealous. The fire in his eyes was from more than desire to rescue his sister. This came from a piece of his past he refused to talk about.

She climbed out of the silver Hyundai Terracan.

Inside the lobby, people milled about, entering the elevator, checking in or out at the reception desk, which was less one clerk. The manager struggled to keep up. But his eyes shifted and caught sight of Braden's approach.

Arizona doubted he saw her. One look at Braden and he had to be afraid.

He quickly finished with the guest, who smiled and left. The manager moved along the desk to the opening at the end, where he emerged to meet them.

"Where is my sister?" Braden demanded.

"We've already had this discussion."

"That was before I found out you were taking money from Julian."

Braden waited while the import of that registered. Arizona saw the man swallow. "I don't know who you've been talking to, but I don't take money from Julian."

"Oh, I think you do." He stepped closer.

The manager stepped back. "You don't understand."

"Don't I?" Braden kept stepping closer until the manager could back up no more; the wall was at his back beside the entrance to the rear of the counter.

"Who were you talking to? That idiotic clerk of mine? I'm glad she's gone. She was a nuisance."

Reaching up, Braden fisted both sides of the man's suit jacket. Pulling him forward, he shoved him back against the wall. Hard.

"Where is my sister?"

"I don't have any idea."

Such rage tightened Braden's features, she wondered if he'd explode. "Braden?"

The manager's eyes slid to hers in trepidation.

"Tell me now."

"I swear, I don't know. I swear. I never go to Julian's villa."

"But you take his money. How does he give it to you? After the women get into the cab you call for them?"

"No. Please."

With a roar, Braden swung the man around, letting go of his jacket. The man sailed across the lobby. A young couple stopped talking and laughing, the woman gasping. An older couple let the elevator doors slide shut without getting inside.

Braden approached the manager.

Oh, no.

Arizona hurried to him, touching his arm. "This isn't the place, Braden."

"The hell it isn't." His furious eyes turned to her. "It won't matter where I do this."

She didn't try to stop him when he resumed his assault. She wouldn't be able to anyway.

The manager had gotten to his feet and pivoted when he saw Arizona's efforts had failed.

Braden caught him easily, long before he made it to the door, hauling him around and slugging him on the jaw. The manager staggered and the young woman gasped

again. The old man with his wife pressed the elevator button again. The door opened and he took his wife inside.

Meanwhile, Braden didn't stop. He slugged the manager twice more, sending the poor man to the floor.

The man with his young wife took out his cell phone.

The manager raised his hand to ward off more beatings. "All right. All right."

Feet wide, fists clenched, Braden stood over him, unaffected by his bleeding face.

The manager took him in from foot to forehead. "I do take money. But only because I have no other choice."

"No other choice?"

"You don't understand. If I didn't cooperate, he'd kill me."

"Since you're making money to oblige him, I'm sure it wasn't a tough decision for you."

The man shook his head. "He'd kill me."

"Why did he take my sister? Why Tatum?"

"She came here looking for the other one."

"Courtney?"

The man nodded, climbing to his feet, wiping his bloody mouth.

"Why did Courtney come here?"

"I don't know."

"What about my sister?"

"I don't know about her, either."

Braden moved a step closer.

"I swear. I don't know! I didn't get paid for that one. She went straight to the villa after asking about Courtney. She didn't stay here."

Now Arizona approached. "What do you mean you didn't get paid for that one? That one what?"

He eyed her hesitantly, and then Braden.

"What's Julian doing with all those women?" Arizona asked.

"He…keeps them."

"Keeps them?"

"Yeah, you know…like a harem." He looked warily up at Braden, who'd gone stone still.

A harem? It made no sense. What did that have to do with stealing laser target designator technology?

Chapter 16

Arizona followed Braden into the police station. He'd cooled down a little since discovering his sister could be held captive with other women to satisfy Julian's perverse activities. Inside the reception area, a black woman looked up and saw them. Braden kept walking, pushing through a swinging half door and continuing on his way.

"Sir?" The black woman headed toward him. "You can't go back there."

Arizona fell in step behind her, seeing Crawford sitting in his office. He stood up and moved around his desk as Braden and Arizona entered the office.

"It's okay," he said to the agitated clerk, who glared at Braden and shook her head as she turned and went back to the front.

"You never went to check Julian's villa and you never went to question Patty Williams, did you." Braden wasn't asking.

Crawford put his hands on his hips, regarding Braden a few too many seconds, a caught man. "Why are you here?"

Braden stepped close, threatening with the sheer energy of his anger. "Cut the crap, Detective. We know you're on Julian's payroll."

"I never took any money from him. I've told you before, I have no evidence on him. I need proof to bring him in."

"You'd risk that? Aren't you afraid like everyone else? Isn't it easier to turn the other way when women disappear?"

Crawford was growing angrier. "I don't turn the other way."

"How does it feel when they end up dead? How does it feel knowing you could have done something to save their lives?"

"If I could have saved their lives I would have." His voice rose.

"I don't see you trying very hard to do that."

Lowering his arms, Crawford went to the office door and shut it. Several faces sitting at the handful of desks averted. Then he faced Braden, barely acknowledging Arizona.

"You don't understand what I'm up against."

"An arms dealer who keeps a harem locked up in his villa?"

Crawford didn't respond.

There was more. Arizona went on high alert. "What else is going on at the villa?"

Crawford didn't stop staring at Braden, stress and angst low on his brow. "You can't beat this."

"Beat what?" Arizona asked.

Braden remained silent.

"Most of the time Julian keeps them for a few weeks, maybe months, and then he gets rid of them when new

replacements come in. But your sister knew things about his organization. She's dangerous."

"You knew all of this and you did nothing? You could arrest Julian." Braden's fists were clenched at his sides just as they had been with the hotel manager.

"If I had proof, I'd arrest him. Solid proof."

"The testimony of my sister and any other woman held captive would be enough proof. You don't go there and free them because Julian pays you not to."

"I told you, I don't take money from Julian."

"Then why not raid his house? You should have done that months ago. A lot of women are dead and they shouldn't be. Why haven't you done anything to help them?"

"Because I can't!" Crawford shouted. "There's nothing I or anyone else can do to stop Julian."

Braden leaned so that his face was inches from the detective's. "Your answer is to give up?"

"You can't save your sister. If she isn't dead now, she will be soon."

Braden brought up his arm and punched him. Crawford's head jerked back with the impact and made him lose his balance. He stumbled backward, holding his jaw.

"Yes, I can. Because unlike you, I'm not a coward. I'm not afraid to stand up to Julian. I'm not afraid." He strode out of the office.

Arizona sent her reproach to Crawford. "You don't deserve to be in law enforcement. People depend on you for protection and you just stand by and allow men like Julian to rape and murder innocent women."

He'd lowered his hand during her admonishment. "This is about more than Julian. His organization is much bigger than you realize. Go home while you still can. I'll get Julian when the time is right."

"The time is right now." She traced Braden's path out of the office, the door open, with workers watching again.

She and Braden went back to the house above Julian's, finding everything just as they'd left it. Braden stood with the binoculars at the window. Nothing would stop him now. He would wait for the opportunity, and probably nightfall, to strike.

"Julian's father is still there," Braden said.

She went to his side and picked up her own binoculars. Carlos Ramirez stood on one of the back balconies that must be off the bedrooms on the upper level of the villa. A man of about fifty, he spoke into a cell phone. Shouting, more like.

"Why is he so angry?"

"Maybe he found out what Julian's been doing in his villa."

Her cell phone rang. She went over to the coffee table where she'd left it. "Lincoln."

"Hey, Arizona. I've got some news for you and Braden. Put your phone on speaker. He's going to want to hear this."

Lowering her phone, she pressed the button to engage the speaker. Braden had lowered the binoculars when the phone rang, curious who had called.

"Braden's here," she said.

He approached, putting the binoculars down.

"I had an interesting talk with my friend. You remember, the one who works for ICE?"

The Immigration and Customs Enforcement agent. "Yes."

Braden sat on the couch. Arizona joined him, sliding the phone to the edge of the table.

"He isn't working the arms dealer case, but he has access to the files. The team did do an investigation of Amer-

ican Freight Forwarding Services. The shipments were done using Tatum's passwords, and they couldn't charge her because she could prove she was nowhere near the company when the transaction occurred."

Things they already knew.

"But he had some interesting information on the arms dealer. His name is Leonardo Gallegos. Ex-military. Left the country five years ago and started up an arms trafficking organization. He's notorious for opening front companies to facilitate deals. The ICE team caught up to him last year and almost made an arrest. He disappeared from France where agents traced him and they've been searching for him ever since. Now he turns up in this American Freight deal, and they've lost him again."

"We have some news for you, too, that you should pass on to your friend," Arizona said.

Braden went on to explain the sex operation Julian Blake was running, and that he paid certain townspeople to either help him or silence them.

"Crawford is dirty?" Lincoln asked.

"I wouldn't say dirty," Braden said with distaste. "Just scared."

"And he's a cop?" Lincoln grunted.

"He said Julian's operation is bigger than we realize," Arizona said.

"If he's involved with Gallegos, it is."

She shared her confused speculation with Braden, his green eyes intelligent and glowing. Could Gallegos be connected to Julian somehow? Was his insurance underwriter job a disguise?

"I'll send over a picture of Gallegos to Arizona's phone. If you catch any sight of him with Julian, let me know."

Arizona ended the call.

"Why would Gallegos come here?"

She retrieved the photo Lincoln sent and sucked in a shocked breath. She showed it to Braden. Around fifty, on the tall side, and skinny, Leonardo Gallegos wore a tan suit and was standing with two other men dressed in jeans and T-shirts. His salt-and-pepper hair was thick and cut short, and he had a well-groomed beard. He looked exactly like Carlos Ramirez.

"Call Lincoln back."

She did. "Leonardo Gallegos is Carlos Ramirez," she said when Lincoln answered. "We just saw him on one of the villa balconies."

Lincoln was quiet for a few beats. "All right. You two stay put. This is enough to bring in the cavalry. Where are you now?"

"At the house we're using to spy on Julian," Arizona answered.

"It won't be long. Twenty-four hours. The ICE team working this are eager to get Gallegos."

Arizona smiled at Braden. That was good news for them, and especially Tatum and Courtney.

"Be ready tomorrow. Don't try anything on your own tonight."

Braden stood and went to the window. She could feel his anxiousness to be proactive. Waiting a day would kill him. But he'd keep watch. And hopefully he wouldn't see anything that made him go there, as Lincoln had warned, on his own.

The upper-level guest room provided the best view of Julian's villa. Arizona had moved the queen-size bed over to the window. A big bowl of popcorn in front of her, binoculars abandoned, she lay on her stomach facing the window. Braden had to stop her from turning on a chick flick. Too much light. It was dark now, and he was watching Ju-

lian's villa. He'd seen servants moving around and a few times Julian and Leonardo.

Arizona crunched on popcorn, moving her feet back and forth in the air. "There's nothing going on down there. It's dark. They probably all went to bed by now."

He put the binoculars on the wide, wooden windowsill. Digging into the bowl of popcorn, Braden rolled onto his back. He dropped kernels into his mouth and crunched with Arizona. She had an amazing ability to make him feel like a kid again. All lightness.

Laughing, she rolled onto her back with him, placing the bowl on her stomach. "A little different than a sleepover but this will do."

He reached over for another handful of popcorn. "I don't do sleepovers. That's for girls."

"You do sleepovers with me."

Sudden vision of her beneath him took over his thoughts. His brief levity faded. "That's different."

She munched another few kernels, looking up at the mural on the ceiling of palm trees and a beach with waves coming in. A bit much but appropriate in a way.

"What are you going to do when this is all over?" he asked.

"I'm not sure." She ate more popcorn. "Maybe quit my job and live off my dad for a while. It's not the same as Macon."

"Where does he fall in the line?"

"He's number five."

"How is he different?"

"He doesn't try to find work or something to do with his life. He's in and out of rehab. Sad. We all hope he comes around this time. He's in rehab right now. He's showing signs. He's started talking about opening a camp for troubled teens."

"Kind of similar to you opening an outdoor experience outfit for victims of violent crimes and their families."

"You and Lincoln," she said with a sigh. But he could tell the idea was more palatable now than before.

"What about you?" She held a kernel of popcorn above his mouth.

What about him? He took the popcorn, and said as he ate, "I'm an engineer, remember?"

"That's right," she teased. "It's just that you seem to like the idea of an adventure club as much as Lincoln."

"And you."

"You like the idea of me?"

He grinned. "You like the idea of an adventure club, too."

When she didn't respond, he rolled his head. Her profile was thoughtful. Was she considering he might be right? That her brother was right? Or was she was thinking of Trevor?

"Why are you so fearless?" she finally asked.

He hadn't expected that. "I'm a man."

She rolled her head toward him. "You know what I mean."

Why was it so important for her to dig that out of him? He rolled his head back upright.

"What happened to you? Something must have. You're too intense in threatening situations."

"Why do you need to know?" His tone bit a little harder than he'd intended. Now she'd really be convinced she was on to something, which she was.

"I don't, I guess. I just think you're keeping something bottled up."

And telling her would somehow help? As though she were that close to him. As soon as that thought came, he

realized she was getting close to him. Closer than Serena had ever taken an interest to accomplish.

"I was almost kidnapped when I was twelve." Hearing the words come out of his mouth felt foreign, and then freeing. He'd never uttered them before. Not to anyone.

Arizona put the paper bowl of popcorn between them as she rolled onto her hip and propped her head on her hand. "Really?"

It must explain so much. Why he was undaunted in finding Tatum. Why he quickly became the aggressor in threatening situations. Why he nearly lost control when someone tried to take his son.

"I was walking home from school when a man approached. He was walking the opposite direction. I didn't think anything of it. I got the highest score on a math test that day, so I was pretty happy and looking forward to telling my parents." He fell deep into the memory, feeling, smelling, seeing as he had back then. "When we were about to pass each other, he grabbed me by the arm and pulled me into a park."

The suddenness of it had caught him off guard. And then fear had set in. He could taste its tinny poison. The way it dried his mouth. The way his surroundings blurred. "He had me in front of him, and forced me to move forward. I didn't realize it at the time, but he was taking me to his car, which was parked on the other side of the park. There weren't many people around. A long distance away was a picnic area. There was a group of kids over there but they never noticed me." That's when it became clear to him what the man was trying to do. "I fought him and started yelling. He put his hand over my mouth and told me to shut up or he'd stick me with a knife. He didn't have a knife, I realized. And his other hand was still gripping my arm, so I turned my head and bit him as hard as I could.

He loosened his hold on me and I twisted away. I ran as fast as I could back toward the street. Yelling. No one noticed. I don't know if the kids over by the picnic area heard me or even saw me. No one did anything."

Arizona remained silent, letting him talk without interrupting. It must be a shocking story to hear.

"He chased me to the edge of the park. I ran all the way home."

And when he'd gotten there, he'd gone to his room. His mom noticed how winded he was and he'd lied and told her he ran home so he wouldn't miss a TV program. Luckily he had a TV in his room.

"What then?" Arizona asked.

"Nothing. I never told anyone."

"You didn't?" She sounded incredulous. "Why not?"

"I was horrified that a pedophile tried to abduct me." He hadn't known what the word meant then, but he'd known what a man trying to take a young boy meant.

"Your parents didn't call the police?"

"They didn't know about it."

"They don't know? Still? To this day?"

"No. I never told anyone. You're the first."

"That's incredible." She stared at him as the import of not only her being the only one he'd ever told, but for him to keep it to himself for so long.

"Did you learn how to fight then?"

"I asked my parents if I could join karate. I'm now a fourth-degree black belt. When I was old enough, I learned how to shoot guns. Blowing things up still had its appeal, too."

She smiled, lifting a weight off him. It was then that he realized keeping the darkest part of his life a secret had eaten at him for too long. The shame he'd felt at twelve hadn't gone away in adulthood. Absurd thoughts plagued

him. Was there a reason why that pervert had singled him out? Had he done something to provoke him? And imagining what the man would have done if he'd succeeded had been infinitely more damaging.

Arizona traced her finger along his face, from his brow down to his cheek, to his lips. "Tough-guy engineer."

"I didn't feel tough for a long time." Her touch began to lull him.

"You should have told someone. Your mother, as soon as you got home."

"I was twelve." And telling her or his dad now would just cause unnecessary pain. "And I'm telling you."

"I'm honored." She kept touching his face.

"You wouldn't leave me alone until I did." His voice was a murmur beneath her soft caress.

"Somebody needed to."

The fact that it had been her reached into him deep, nested and stayed. Maybe now was a good time to remove Trevor from her head. Return the favor, as it were.

He came up onto his hip and used his weight to put her on her back. Getting on top of her, he caged her head between his arms and spent some time looking into her blue eyes. She wasn't startled. She was responding to him and only him, her lids closing with sultry heat.

He savored the sight of her, unwilling to examine too deeply how much confiding in her meant to him. It was enough that a burden he'd carried for so long was lighter. Perceptions he'd had as a boy didn't have the importance they once had. All that mattered was her. This gift she'd given him. He'd give her one back.

Kissing her softly, he made love to her mouth until her breathing picked up and her hands roamed up his arms and looped around his neck. But that wasn't enough.

He kept kissing her, touching her body, running his

hand down her sides, teasing the side of her breast. She moaned and parted her legs, depositing him right where he'd love to be with her, naked.

But not yet. He lifted his head, stopping the kiss until she opened her eyes. They burned up at him, stealing more of his control. He treated her lips to another kiss, then took the attention down to her neck, sucking her earlobe and whispering, "I'm going to make love to you."

"Yes," she whispered back. "Make love to me."

He took her mouth with his, loving the way she said that.

She began tugging at his shirt. If she was going to freeze up on him, it would be when they were naked. He wasn't entering her until he was sure it was him she was thinking of. He was already close to losing control. He needed to be in control until he was sure.

Rising up, he pulled off his shirt and gave her enough room to sit up and do the same. Shirt, bra. Jeans and underwear. He stood to remove the rest of his clothes and came back down to her. Their naked bodies sent shards of ecstasy through him.

He kissed her slowly at first, teasing her again. Her breathing was erratic now. She lifted her hips, her legs open for him, his hardness oh so close. He could feel her wetness against him.

It made him grunt with pleasure. "Arizona."

"Do it. Now."

She was afraid of the same thing he was. Now wasn't the time. She wasn't ready. She could still slip into thoughts of her fiancé. But as she moved her hips and looked up at him with heated wanting, he discovered he couldn't resist. Slowly he did as she asked. They'd gotten this far before.

Embedded deep inside her, he slid back and forth delib-

erately slow. Shivers of sensation rode up his body from his erection, threatening to consume his mind. He went still.

"Keep moving." She grabbed the cheeks of his butt with one hand and raked her fingers into his hair with the other. Her face was fevered, mouth parted, eyes hot for him.

He kissed her softly, caressing her with his tongue. Then he waited until her eyes opened and she looked up at him, drugged with sex.

"Who is inside you?" He pumped his hips slow and deep.

"You."

"Who?"

"You."

"No one else."

She shook her head against the mattress. "Only you. Make love to me, Braden."

He slid excruciatingly slow.

"Oh," she breathed. "Braden."

"Yes," he groaned, picking up the pace.

She began crying out with each thrust.

"Yes."

A final cry burst from her and triumph soaked him. He thrust hard a few more times. It didn't take much. Just knowing it was him who did that to her was enough.

Chapter 17

There was no activity in the house next door. All day, the moving truck was still in the driveway. Lincoln tried not to let his curiosity get the better of him. He had more pressing things to concentrate on—like his sister in Tortola. Calem O'Brien was an experienced ICE agent, and had promised he'd make sure she and Braden were taken care of, and if Tatum and Courtney were still alive, they'd get them out. But it was difficult sitting here in the United States, not being part of the action. Not being proactive. That's why he had to interfere next door. Stack boredom on top of that and he was itching for something to keep him occupied.

Spying on the neighbor did just that.

Hearing a car pull into the driveway next door, Lincoln stood and used his crutch to go to the front window. The redhead got out of a white Audi Q5; nice, and pretty affordable. She probably had a decent job.

Taking a chance, he opened the front door and went

outside. The redhead stopped in front of her Audi and watched him. Didn't say hello. Just stared. Maybe she expected him to interfere again. Maybe she was thinking of what she'd done last night.

He hobbled to his mailbox, hearing her open the moving truck. By herself, unloading it would take a while. Holding the mail in one hand, he made his way back up his driveway.

The redhead still stood there in front of the moving truck. "We should get a few things straight."

Attack mode. He stopped in his driveway, across from her.

"First, I don't want to get chummy with my neighbors. I keep to myself. My business belongs to me and no one else."

Most people who had something to hide took on those habits. Maybe not with this much of an attitude.

"All right. What would you like me to do if your boyfriend starts punching you again?"

"Mind your own business."

"Even if you need an ambulance?" He couldn't keep the bite out of his tone.

"I won't."

She seemed awfully sure. Taking in her slender body, he had his doubts.

"Second," she snapped. "I don't have window coverings yet, so I'd appreciate it if you'd turn away next time you see me through the window."

He lifted his mail and pointed with it. "I apologize for that. I wasn't expecting to see anyone through the window."

"You stood there long enough."

"I..." What could he possibly say to that? He had stood

there awhile, and the reason was that she was hot. "Yes. I did. I'm sorry."

She stared at him as it became clear why he'd stood at the window so long.

The sound of a car pulling up along the street broke the spell, if one could call it that. The lady was a bitch. Once upon a time he'd have been disappointed. Now he just didn't care.

A limo stopped in the street, the sleek body black and shiny, windows impossible to see through. The driver got out and opened the rear door to let his mother out.

"Come get me in about an hour." She patted the black-suited and capped man on the shoulder, not in the least condescending. His mother had a way with servants. She always treated them with respect.

But to those who didn't know her, this entire exchange must seem odd. Even odder, a limo in front of an old house that wasn't in the most upscale neighborhoods in Denver. The houses here were nice, but not in the million-dollar range.

He glanced over at his mean neighbor. She hadn't moved. Would she change her mind about him now? Money had a way of doing that to people.

"How's my Linc today?" His mother kissed him on his cheek.

"Healing."

She took his mail and walked with him toward his door, seeing the redhead, who jerked into motion and disappeared into her garage.

"Is that your new neighbor?"

"Yes. She isn't the social type."

"Hasn't that house been vacant for a long time?"

"As long as I've been here."

"How interesting." His mother hooked her arm with his. "She's pretty."

Yeah, pretty bitchy.

Inside, his mother put her purse down on his coffee table and looked around as she always did. "You should get a maid while you're recovering."

"I don't need a maid. What brings you here?"

"Checking up on you, and…"

And the real reason for this impromptu visit…

"I'm worried about Arizona."

He maneuvered to his spot on the couch. His mother sat next to him. "She's with someone very capable, Mom."

"Braden? I'm not so sure. I know she needs this…to find closure with Trevor. That whole ordeal was so hard on her, but…"

"Braden is capable. He probably knows martial arts better than me."

She relaxed against the couch. "But what if people shoot at them?"

"It should all be over after tonight. Some federal agents are on their way now."

"How do you know?"

"I know. And that's all I'm going to tell you." The last thing anybody needed was the press getting hold of that information. He trusted his mother, but she didn't think like a law enforcement officer.

She mulled that over awhile and then relaxed even more. He'd eased her mind, at least.

"Your father invited the movie stars from his latest film over the Friday after next. You can join us if you like. It'll get you out of this house."

"I'll be there." She liked it when her kids showed up to her events. She may say Dad invited them, but that was her area of expertise. Entertaining at home.

"I'll send the jet."

After enduring her ministrations a bit longer, he walked her to the door. Seeing the redheaded dragon in her driveway again, he stopped on the front porch, giving his mom a hug and watching her get into the limo.

The redheaded dragon watched, too, box in hand.

"Who was that?" she actually had the gall to ask.

"I don't share my business with people who don't share theirs."

Chapter 18

Arizona stopped biting her thumbnail and stared out the window. She'd drifted off into tumultuous thoughts all day. Waiting for the ICE agents was torture. Last night had pushed her into a realm where nothing was familiar anymore. Nothing about Braden had reminded her of Trevor. In fact, he'd done exactly as he'd set out to do. Make her forget Trevor. Now she was afraid of what it meant, where this was headed if she let it continue.

And the smart man he was, he knew what she was thinking and feeling. She'd withdrawn into a shell, struggling to make sense of it.

It didn't make sense that making love with Braden should feel the way it had. It didn't make sense that he should matter that much. She felt like running away.

With any luck, they'd find Tatum and Courtney alive and they could all go back to their lives.

When she realized her instinct carried her toward sepa-

rating with Braden, she lifted her thumb to begin chewing again. Is that what she wanted? Continuing this tied her stomach in a knot. She couldn't bear to go through another loss. And this thing with Braden felt stronger than what she'd had with Trevor. What she'd had with Trevor had been real and all encompassing. She didn't think it was possible to love anyone more than that. While she couldn't call what she felt for Braden love, not yet, their connection was a fireball. Already. That's what didn't make sense.

How could she be afraid of love that hadn't even manifested yet?

Maybe because she was certain it would grow into that. That certainty is what troubled her. She'd been this certain with Trevor. The beauty of it had taken longer, but it was the same. More intense physically, but the same in her heart.

Yes, that frightened her.

Turning from the window, she bumped into Braden. Looking up at him, it was much the same as when she'd first met him. Only now his eyes brooded.

Lifting his hand, he cupped her head and kissed her. Caught off guard, Arizona let him have his way. His other hand glided around her hip to her rear. He pressed her pelvis against him and she felt his growing hardness. The fire lit and roared. She met the fervor of his mouth.

Then just as quickly, he eased off, kissing her softly, almost reluctantly, and then withdrawing, lifting his head.

"Maybe this isn't such a good idea," he said.

Nothing more needed to be said. All their uncertainties remained between them.

"You haven't let him go. You're still afraid." He released her and stepped back.

She lowered her head because he was right. He'd been

right all along. Then what were they doing? What was this all about?

Moving into the living room, she stopped near the three couches on the dark blue rug. She was so confused.

"You were the one who climbed on top of me," she reminded him.

He came to stand in front of her. "Yes, and I proved my point. You can't handle the fact that it was my name you were calling while I was inside you."

Despair pierced her. He'd reduce it to that? To protect himself. And she was ready to let him. Withdrawing felt safer.

He registered her reaction, or lack thereof, and resolve flowed into his eyes, shutting out any possibility that this could go further. No more emotion came from him. He was a hardened man who'd come to save his sister.

Unable to endure the confusion tugging her in opposing directions, she left him standing on the blue rug and went back to the window.

The sound of a door banging open made her pivot.

Four men in gray uniforms ran into the kitchen a second later. Arizona froze. Then frantically searched for her gun. It was on a table, fifteen feet from where she now stood. Two more uniformed men emerged from the hall.

Julian's guards.

Braden had kept his gun on him and now fired at the men in the kitchen. Two went down. The other two took cover behind the kitchen island, but the two who'd appeared from the hallway fired in retaliation. Braden had to crouch behind one of the couches.

When he did that, the men came for her. One had a big hook nose and narrowly spaced eyes. The other was taller and bald and wore John Lennon glasses that looked too small on his big, round face. She'd have to cross their paths

to reach her gun. She ran for it, having her hand around its handle when one of the men chopped her wrist. Pain shot up her arm. She held her wrist while the second man wrapped his arms around her, binding her. The other held a pistol to her head.

Braden remained crouched behind the couch, only his head visible, and the tip of his gun. When the two men behind the kitchen island popped their heads up, he fired.

"Go. Now!" the man with the gun at her head shouted to the one holding her. "Follow and she's dead," he said to Braden.

The man holding her jerked her around, shackling both her arms. Braden took a step toward her, only to be forced to crouch again when the two behind the kitchen island shot at him.

Oh, no! Would they kill Braden?

As she was propelled out of the living room and through the kitchen toward the door where the men must have come, she fought the whole way. Only when the doorway grew too close did she begin to panic. Where were they taking her and what would happen to Braden? As good as he was, he may not be a match for four professionals.

She wrenched and twisted, checked herself briefly as the man with the gun reminded her he still was there. He shoved her through the garage door, making her bump against the man who held her. The big door was open and a white sedan was backed in the driveway, the trunk open. The Hyundai Terracan she and Braden had parked in the garage had its tires slashed.

The hook-nosed man forced her through the garage, toward the gaping opening of the trunk. They were going to put her in there!

"No!" She imagined Trevor facing something similar. She was being kidnapped. Just like him.

Fear and something much bigger fueled her determination. She tried tripping her captor with her foot, entwining hers at his ankles. He easily lifted her and jerked her toward the car. He was much stronger, but she was no quitter.

She dropped her weight. Let him carry her. She was no hundred-pound weakling!

Grunting in surprise, he swore. "Stand up, damn it!"

His grip on her right arm loosened. Just as her spirits lifted, his bald friend appeared in her sight. He'd followed until now.

"You fool!" He grabbed Arizona, jerking her from the other man.

Arizona stomped on his shin. He growled in pain and nearly lost his hold.

"Bitch!"

"She's a feisty one," the other said.

The bald man pushed her back and slapped her.

Dazed, she stumbled and had her hands on the opening of the trunk when she was lifted and dropped inside.

"No!"

From inside the house, she heard gunshots.

"Braden!" She raised her hands to stop the trunk from closing, but all she got was pain.

Ignoring her stinging palms, she beat the trunk, refusing to give in to panic. "Let me out of here!"

The car jerked into motion.

Braden…

"Braden!" she screamed. Were those other men killing him? Or would he kill them? Could he hold them off until the ICE agents arrived? What if they were too late?

The ride to Julian's villa wasn't long. Minutes. But it felt like hours. She was sick with worry for Braden.

The sedan stopped and the engine stopped. Car doors slammed and the trunk latch released.

She kicked it with her foot and rose up. But two more guards were waiting. They each took one of her arms and dragged her out of the trunk. They dragged her feet over the cement driveway as she struggled for balance. The guards continued to drag her into a four-car garage she and Braden couldn't see from the other house. Her arms hurt. She got one foot on the cement floor of the garage and then the other. Finally she had her footing.

But then she was lifted and shoved inside the villa. She fell onto the tile floor of an entryway. As she scrambled to get to her feet, one of the guards opened a door off the entry, while the other lifted her by her arm and then bent it painfully behind her.

"Get your hands off me!" Arizona planted her foot against the wall as he tried to force her through the doorway. She pushed hard.

He staggered back and bumped into the other two who'd put her into the trunk.

"It'll take a lot to tame this one," the hook-nosed man said. He was grinning, no doubt looking forward to the taming.

Arizona wished she could barf all over him.

And it was insulting that none of them felt they had to use their guns to make her go down the stairs. Four against one was enough, she supposed. Is this how Trevor had been taken? Had he been outnumbered?

The guard steered her with her bent arm, lifting whenever she resisted, and shoving her to move down the stairs. When she reached the bottom she saw the hall leading to the commercial kitchen where she and Braden had entered through the servant's door.

She was forced toward the wall of bookshelves and the painting of the sailboat. Beneath the painting and beside a modern, blocky chair with a metal table beside it, one of the guards pressed the wall. A square panel about the size of a light switch cover sprang open to reveal a coded lock.

He entered the number and a door opened inward. Only then did she see the break in the wall that outlined the door frame, concealed further by hip-high wood paneling painted white.

This was where Julian kept his women.

Inside, she took in the sight of a long, wide lounge with a bar at the far end. There were round tables over a polished-wood floor, two pool tables and a poker table. Along each side were closed doors. Six of them. Bile rose up into her throat.

Julian held parties down here, where his guests—all of them male—could drink and gamble and have sex with unwilling women.

The guard wrenched her arm again, shoving her to keep moving.

She was really getting sick of him. Ramming her head back, she made contact with his nose. He yelped and let go.

She whirled around and jabbed his eyes with her fingers. He stumbled back, falling into the man with small round glasses and his friend, hook-nose. The fourth guard whacked her with the handle of his gun. It wasn't enough to knock her out, but it did disorient her long enough for the bald man with round glasses to take hold of her next.

He pushed her into a table. Her thigh stung with the impact and she fell. The bald man kicked her in the stomach.

She curled up and groaned as he bent to lift her, slinging her over his shoulder and holding her legs.

The hook-nosed man opened the middle of three doors on the right side of the room. What would they do? Would she be raped by these animals?

Stepping through the door with her, the bald man pulled her off his shoulder and let her drop to the floor.

As he left and the door clanked shut, it dawned on her that she wasn't alone.

* * *

Damn it! Braden ducked into a hall that ran to the garage and another entry to the kitchen. In the block between this and the kitchen was a bathroom that opened to the hall. At the open garage door, he saw the rental still there and the tires slashed. There were no other vehicles in the driveway. Darkness was descending.

Turning, he spotted movement at the end of the hall. One of the men had moved there. Braden put his back to the wall of the entry to the kitchen just as bullets sprayed the door and pinged the hood and bumper of the Hyundai.

Apparently, Julian wanted Arizona alive and him dead.

Hearing breathing around the corner in the kitchen, Braden knew one of the men was there, waiting to ambush him. He moved, reaching around the corner and grabbing the man's gun hand. The man tried to wrestle free. Braden yanked on his hand and rammed heads with him. The man staggered back and Braden fired. The man fell with a hole in his head, sprawled on the kitchen floor along with the other two he'd shot earlier.

The fourth appeared at the end of the wall in the living room. Braden fired at him, but he moved back behind the wall.

Jumping over the bodies, he went to the kitchen island and ducked as the other man fired from the living room. He was a big blond man with a boxy face and dark blue eyes.

When the gunfire eased, he peered around the island. No sight of the man. Gun ready, Braden moved out from the kitchen, putting his back to the wall and then darting out to face his opponent. No one was there. He moved to the hall leading to the garage. Not there. As he turned, the man was behind him with a chair in his arms, raised high.

As it came crashing down on him, Braden lost his gun. It clattered to the floor. The blond man had put his weapon

in his hip holster. Braden reached for it, having hold of it as the man whacked his wrist. The gun fell.

Braden went down for it, but the blond man stopped him with a punch. Swinging his feet, Braden knocked the man down. The man fumbled for the gun. Braden kicked it.

The man rolled and leaped to his feet. Sidling toward the table, wary of Braden as he followed, the blond man lifted another chair.

What was his deal with chairs?

The big man lifted the chair and threw it in Braden's direction. He easily dodged it and maneuvered so he was close to the hall again.

The blond man lifted a third chair and hurled it at him. Again, Braden avoided it. Next the man picked up a standing lamp and charged, swinging the base at Braden's head. Braden ducked and grabbed the cord, wrapping it once and then yanking. The blond man lost his grip and Braden took control of the lamp, pivoting and driving the metal point at the top of the shade into the man's face. He yelled and Braden swung the lamp around the other way, hitting him again with the base. He went down with a thud that vibrated the floor.

Retrieving his gun, Braden ran through the open garage, and stopped short when he heard vehicles approaching and a helicopter above. The helicopter circled and then disappeared over the horizon of the tree covered foothill.

Who was coming up the hill?

Two white Jeeps stopped in the driveway. Braden was about to take cover when one of the men jumped out with a badge.

"Calem O'Brien. Are you Braden McCrae?"

Braden nearly slumped in relief. "Yes." He approached the man, who was tall and hard muscled, a man who trained regularly so he could be fit when he ran down criminals.

His steel-blue eyes were focused and his dark hair trimmed close to his head. He had on tactical gear. What made a man work for Immigration and Customs Enforcement? The acronym?

Five other men climbed out of the Jeeps and Calem introduced them. ICE was a different kind of enforcement agency. They went after gun smugglers and terrorists. Homeland Security's investigative arm, and one of the biggest agencies in the country, thanks to 9/11.

There was no time to talk about that. Braden told them Arizona had been taken.

Another car drove up the driveway. A dark blue Cadillac. Detective Crawford.

Busy night to be out.

Two of the ICE agents in bulletproof vests and thigh straps pointed mean-looking automatic rifles at Crawford's startled face.

Braden stepped forward. "That's Detective Crawford." What was he doing here?

"I saw the Jeeps head this way and followed."

"We saw him," Calem said.

The detective moved toward Braden. When he was close enough, he extended a file. "These are the floor plans for Julian's villa. There's a section of the basement that's closed off. The only way in is through a secret door. It's marked on the plan."

Braden regarded him a moment. "Why the change of mind?"

"My mind has never changed. I've been waiting for an opportunity to take Julian down for a long time. But you couple a small island police force with a dangerous arms dealer and an unstable stepson, and the pace slows down."

Braden nodded, still thinking the detective was weak.

"I had to make them believe I was staying out of their

way," he continued. "When you showed up and started stirring things up, I kept my cheering to myself." He grinned. "Don't think for a moment that I didn't doubt you'd find out about those murdered women, and that you'd do your own digging. You managed to do what I couldn't. You got the maid to come forward and the hotel clerk to talk. With everyone believing I was taking money from Julian, it was impossible to gain trust. But it was either that or risk being killed."

Braden nodded. Maybe he had needed help. He was one man against a giant.

"Thanks," Braden said, shaking his hand, the blueprints rolled up in the other.

"Let's move," Calem said.

Arizona sat up to discover it wasn't just one other woman in the cell with her. There were two, and the cell was more of a suite. There were two beds, each covered in red satiny comforters. A sitting area was filled with antiques, the butter-yellow settee adorned with red-patterned pillows.

She stared up at a dark-haired beauty with eyes greener than Braden's. "You must be Tatum."

The woman's hyper alertness at the appearance of another woman in the cell changed to curiosity. "How do you know?"

"I'm with Braden. He came here looking for you." She lowered her head when she remembered the last she saw of him, shooting two men and facing off with remaining two other men.

"Where is he? Was he captured, too?" Then she gasped. "Was he killed?"

"No. At least I…" She couldn't finish the thought. "He was fighting some guards off when I was taken."

Tatum relaxed. "Not many could overpower him."

Arizona noticed the other woman again. She sat on a chair next to the settee, watching with a sort of haunted detachment.

"That's Courtney Andrews," Tatum said. "She was brought here before me." Tatum met Arizona's eyes. "I don't think she's had an easy time. They've left me alone for the most part. But her..."

She'd been forced to participate in Julian's harem? Arizona stood and went to the woman. Sitting on the settee, she reached over and put her hand over the one resting on her knee.

"We're never going to get out of here," Courtney said.

"Yes, we are." She didn't explain about the ICE agents in case the room was bugged.

Courtney withdrew her hand. "They're going to kill us." Her pale gray eyes stared in shock at Arizona. "Who are you?"

"I'm Arizona Ivy."

"Ivy?"

Courtney was a woman of average height with long, dark hair that had a natural wave to it. She wore a black sundress that showcased her petite figure and round breasts—something Arizona was certain Julian had intended. She looked up at Tatum, who moved from behind the settee to sit beside her.

"The movie-guy Ivy?" Tatum asked.

Arizona sighed. "Yes."

"I've seen you...on TV."

Braden's sister was amazingly okay for a woman who'd been held captive by a harem freak.

"Yeah. Kind of hard to avoid."

The starstruck light in Tatum's eyes faded into confusion. "What are you doing here?"

"I'm—"

"With Braden. You said that. But…why?"

Her reasons had changed. Now she was here for Braden, to help him rescue his sister. And Courtney, who wore the blank stare of a victim.

"I'm going to take you skydiving," she told the woman.

Suddenly it was all clear. Her father would help her with her start-up, and Braden would—

She stopped herself. Braden would go back to his job and she wouldn't want him to do anything else, but for a second there she'd pictured him going with her on excursions.

"What?" Courtney's eyes had changed with this unexpected idea. "Skydiving?"

Arizona smiled. "You're going to be all right."

"What does skydiving have to do with why you're here?" Tatum asked.

"Nothing." But it had everything to do with her future, and healing. "I'm here because Braden came to see my brother for help in finding you. Lincoln is a bounty hunter and a really good martial artist."

"Braden is a fourth-degree black belt. He said a friend from college taught him. That must be your brother."

Arizona nodded. Lincoln had taught Braden and she'd never known? Her brother never talked about his business. And she'd only met a few of his friends, none of them Braden.

"I still don't understand why you're involved."

Arizona explained about the man in the BMW who'd tried to abduct her.

"Leonardo must have sent him…because of the algorithms."

She had deliberately left out the algorithms. Braden

would be glad to hear that. "Yes. Why don't you tell me what happened?"

Tatum glanced over at Courtney as though asking permission, or in deference of her fragile state.

"I had an affair with Leonardo," Courtney said. "This is all my fault."

Tatum stood up. "Oh, no it isn't, sweetie." She knelt before Courtney and took her hands. "He manipulated you. And he threatened you."

"I thought you met Julian online," Arizona said.

"I did. But then I met Leonardo on a trip here."

"That's when he began using her," Tatum said. "He discovered Courtney's quest to find her father, and when he learned I worked for American Freight, he set his plan in motion."

No wonder he and Julian had fought so much.

Leonardo had stolen his girlfriend, a woman he'd planned to enslave like the other women. As an illicit arms dealer, Leonardo probably worried the illegal trafficking in humans could expose him. "After the arms deal was finished, Leonardo handed Courtney back to Julian," Tatum said.

And Julian must have relished making her pay for betraying him. Arizona saw it all over Courtney's face, the horror of memories suffocating her.

Arizona looked at Tatum. "Why did you take Braden's files?"

Tatum stood up and went to sit on the arm of Courtney's chair. She and Courtney exchanged a glance and then Courtney answered.

"She used the technology to try and save me."

"I came here to make a deal with Leonardo. Courtney for the laser target designator files. He took the files and handed me over to Julian. He wanted to kill us both. We

know too much. But Julian stopped him. When he found out about the missing algorithms, I had to tell him about Braden."

That's why the man in the BMW had appeared. And it was also the reason Tatum's computer hadn't been stolen.

"As sick as Julian is, he saved us."

Only because Leonardo knew Julian would eventually kill them. "Are there any other women here?" Arizona asked.

"There were," Tatum said. "Julian locks them up down here. He likes his women scared. He gives them time to… acclimate." Tatum looked over at Courtney.

Courtney had acclimated, apparently. Accepted her fate. That made Arizona really mad. And then she took in Tatum's indomitable energy and found an anomaly in that theory.

To expand his revolving harem. When he grew tired of them, they disappeared. Murdered. Wouldn't it be safer to keep a few as long as possible, rather than kill them and take more? That begged the chance to be caught. Julian must crave the newness. He had to have new women. That was what he craved. The taming, as the hook-nosed man had said.

Julian preferred scared women. But Tatum was Braden's sister. And Braden was no victim. It was a miracle she was still alive. Maybe it was the challenge she presented Julian. She'd take longer to tame.

The sound of the door unlocking brought all of them standing. Courtney huddled beside Tatum, who put her arm around her protectively.

Arizona moved in front of them as Leonardo entered, Julian behind him.

Where Julian was unkempt in high-priced clothes, his dark eyes as void of life as she remembered, Leonardo

was suave in his tan suit and short salt-and-pepper hair and beard. He'd removed his jacket and now only wore a white shirt with pale blue, thin stripes.

He stepped right up to Arizona. "You."

She refused to flinch.

"You have caused me too much trouble."

"Lenny—"

Leonardo spun to his stepson. "You be quiet. You've caused me even more trouble. This is getting out of control. Your activities have to stop or you'll drag us both down."

"At least let me keep Courtney." He sounded so desperate that Arizona nearly felt sorry for his rotting-toothed hide. What had Courtney seen in him when she'd met him online? She was pretty enough to attract almost any man she desired.

Leonardo leaned to see around him toward the door. "Where is Manuel? I told you to make sure he met us down here. I don't have all night."

"I didn't ask for him yet."

"What?" Leonardo backhanded Julian, who leaned to his side from the impact.

Straightening, he stood up to his stepfather, but barely. "Please. Let me keep Courtney."

Leonardo gestured to Arizona, moving to his side to see her. "This bitch and that idiot of an engineer were camped out at the house above mine. Spying on us! I've had enough tiptoeing around your little…project down here. I've had enough!"

How had he discovered she and Braden were at the other house? Had one of the guards seen them during the day? Possibly…

"Please, Carlos."

"I said no! No more of your sniveling. They all die. All three of them! Now go find out what's taking Manuel so

long. He will do this for us." Leonardo pointed to the door. "Go and get Manuel!"

Courtney began crying against Tatum, drawing Julian's helpless gaze. He was in danger of losing his last sex slave. Courtney didn't matter to him. Only his sick perversion did. What would he do without it?

"Please, Carlos. Spare Courtney."

Leonardo grabbed his arm roughly, jerking him around and forcing him out the door. He'd force Julian to do his bidding and then return with the man named Manuel to finish the job.

Arizona searched the room, seeing bars over the frosted windows. "We have to get out of here."

What if they didn't have time? What if the ICE agents never came?

Just then, the sound of an explosion announced their arrival.

"They're here."

Tatum's bravado began to rejuvenate. "Who?"

Braden ran alongside Calem, behind the smoke grenade they'd ignited. The blueprints Crawford had given them showed a new way in. There was another servant's door on the east side of the villa—the same side that had the secret door. The lock had been quick work for the ICE agents. After encountering a few more of Julian's guards, they'd reached a long, rectangular room and his heart rose up to his tonsils. A bar. A party room, with six doors that had to lead to rooms where Julian held women captive.

Arizona. Tatum. The half sister he'd never met. They were here.

He went to the first door and kicked. It didn't budge. Then he heard Arizona yelling. His sister. Were there only two?

One of Calem's men used another nifty device that ex-

ploded the lock and burst the door open. Shouts of men approaching didn't deter him. He charged in and saw three women and his heart soared.

Arizona rushed into his arms. He kissed her, fierce and brief, noting Tatum's speculation along with her sheer glee to see him and the agents.

Gunfire erupted outside the room. Shouts accompanied it.

The agents returned to the lounge area to fight off the approaching guards.

No time for talking. He let Arizona go to take Tatum into his arms.

"I knew you'd find me," she said.

"Go. Both of you." He set Tatum back from him.

Kissing his cheek, she took Arizona's hand and ran after her to the door. Taking Courtney's hand, he led her out of the room. The ICE agents had Julian and Leonardo on the floor, hands cuffed behind them. It was over. He had his sister. She was alive. He ran outside to the helicopter lowering to the driveway, where there was plenty of clearance, stopping with the women and letting go of Courtney's hand.

Arizona looked at him and smiled. But it was from relief. Now that the search for Tatum was over, what now? He didn't have the answer. Not for himself. And definitely not for Arizona.

Chapter 19

Once all the legal red tape was taken care of, the ICE agents let them go. Courtney had been questioned the longest, and then she'd been released. Leonardo was charged with a long list of export violations. The agents had found a jump drive that contained the laser target designator files and gave them to Braden. Julian had been turned over to Crawford for prosecution. Leonardo had shouted obscenities at him as he was being led to the helicopter. Both men would be in jail for a long time. The agents had told them the BMW man and several others who worked for Gallegos had already been arrested.

Behind Tatum and Courtney, Arizona walked away from the jet her father had arranged for them. Ahead were a throng of reporters. Sometimes even her father's best efforts failed. Braden was behind her and she heard him swear. She was the reason they were here. Jackson Ivy's daughter had just returned from her adventure in Tortola

with a mystery man, who'd gone there to save his missing sister and the stepsister they never knew they had....

The flight back to Denver had been awkward. Braden was getting to know his half sister, who'd regained enough self-esteem to smile every once in a while.

Her father's men created a barrier between them and the line of reporters, and a big SUV with darkened windows rolled to a stop right in front of them. She could kiss her dad. Opening the back door, she let Courtney and Tatum in, and then Braden.

A reporter slipped through the barrier of black-suited men and stuck a microphone under her mouth. "Is Braden your new boyfriend, Arizona?"

She waved the microphone away from her face and a black-suited man herded the reporter away. Closing the back door, she sat in the front passenger seat. The driver backed up and drove off.

Looking back at Braden, she saw the grim set to his mouth, eyes hidden by sunglasses, as were all of theirs. The sense that something had changed between them moved in with a heavy fog around her heart. She faced forward. He wasn't ready for a relationship. He'd protect his son, too.

And she couldn't deny that sleeping with him that second time had scared her. It was silly to be afraid, wasn't it? If she fell in love with him and he either died or left her, what then? She'd have to endure another heartbreak. Maybe she wasn't ready, either. They'd met at a bad time in both of their lives.

She knew some widows who never remarried after the loves of their lives died. Something like that takes years to overcome. At least, that's what she'd discovered. It was taking her years to get over Trevor.

And being kidnapped as he had been hadn't pushed her

toward healing. It had shown her what he must have felt. Only he'd endured that horrible fear longer, and then he'd been murdered. It was so terrible that she couldn't wrap her mind around it. And yet, now she almost could. Did she feel any different than before being taken?

She didn't think so. If anything, she wished Trevor would have been able to fight his way free. Not be a victim. But he had been. She recoiled against that realization. It had been mushrooming in her ever since leaving Julian's villa. In engineering he'd excelled. In self-defense, he was as helpless as a child. It broke her heart in a different way than when she'd lost the man she'd loved. No one should be forced into a situation where they had to fight for their lives. Trevor was a good man. But he didn't have Braden's wherewithal to make his own destiny.

"I have instructions to take you and Mr. McCrae to Evergreen," the driver said to Arizona.

She looked back at Braden. He had to go there because his son was there, but how did he feel about being with her? His thoughts were shut tight to the rest of the world.

"You can drop me off at the United terminal. I'm going to fly to Oregon to see my sister," Courtney said.

"No," Tatum said. "Come with me to meet our dad. It's time, Courtney. We can't put it off any longer."

Her hesitation was palpable.

Tatum gave the driver the address to her and Braden's parents' house. Courtney's dad.

"We'll go there together," Braden said. "After I pick up Aiden."

"Okay," Tatum answered.

And the matter was settled.

"But..." Courtney still wasn't sure.

"Trust me."

After a long stare, Courtney relented.

* * *

An hour later, Arizona was sad to pass through the gate of her family's estate in Evergreen. She didn't like the idea of saying goodbye to Braden. The driver pulled to a stop in front of the mansion. She'd caught Braden looking at her a few times, brooding with whatever weighed him. Was he dreading their parting or was he preparing for it?

She walked ahead of everyone to the grand front entrance. Inside, she greeted Berto, who went to find her mother. Courtney huddled near Tatum, Braden next to them with his hands at his sides. He was so distant now.

Her mother breezed into the entry and gave her a hug. "I'm so happy you're home." Then to Braden, she said, "Jackson had to fly to L.A. It's just me and the staff."

"Daddy!" Aiden came running into the entry, followed by a servant who'd been charged to keep an eye on him.

Braden knelt to take his son into his arms. "How's my man?"

"Come on! I have to show you this!" He tugged at his hand.

"We have to get going."

"They have a whole room of Legos. You have to see what I made!"

Braden let his son tug him along. Reaching Arizona, the boy took her hand.

"You, too, helicopter lady."

His hand was sticky and it didn't bother her. She was flattered that he'd included her. Even though he'd called her helicopter lady. Did he hope to impress her with his Legos? Make her like them?

All the way downstairs, Aiden led them, never letting go of their hands, even on the stairs. She bumped into Braden twice. He hadn't reacted, not outwardly.

Attached to the game room was the Lego room. Aiden ran to the space station.

"See?"

"Wow, you made all this?" Braden crouched to inspect it.

"Not all of it. I want to come back to finish it. Can I, Daddy?"

"We'll see. Come on. We have to go."

"Aw."

"Why don't you come back later in the week?" Arizona suggested.

"No. It's better if we end this now," he said, standing.

The distance in his tone shot through her. She'd withdrawn and now he was. That part hurt. But the part that hurt most was the way he was leaving. And taking Aiden with him. Suddenly, she wanted to experience sticky hands and food fights. And she wanted to buy him a cooler helicopter than the one he had and watch him play with it.

"I'm just going to thank your mother and then go."

Tingles spread with the regret stabbing her. It was that easy for him? She couldn't tell by his eyes. He was impassive and cold. Stiffly polite.

Aiden looked up at Arizona and then his dad, not understanding. Would this be the last time she saw the boy? The strength of her disappointment surprised her.

"Is the helicopter lady going with us?"

"No, not this time."

"How come?"

"She has her own house."

Again the boy looked up at her, his new friend. She crouched to his level. "You're going to go see your aunt Tatum."

"Why can't you go, too?"

The mind of a child was amazing. What had the boy

picked up on that he liked about her? For the life of her she couldn't guess. It didn't matter. He made her feel good inside.

"If you're good, I'll send you a real helicopter."

"I have a real helicopter."

"Yeah, but this is a really cool helicopter. It makes noise and almost flies on its own."

"Really?" She didn't know but she'd find one if it killed her. "Come on." She offered her hand.

He walked with her all the way upstairs, where her mother waited.

"Thank you for watching my son, Mrs. Ivy," Braden said.

Arizona let go of Aiden's hand and he went to his dad's leg.

Arizona's mom swatted her hands. "Oh, no need to thank me. You go on. I'm sure we'll be seeing you soon anyway." She winked at Arizona.

She stiffened and Braden didn't respond.

Animation dimming, her mother glanced between the two.

"Let's go, Aiden. Thanks again." Braden nodded to Arizona. "Arizona."

That was it? She watched him leave, shutting the door behind him without looking back. That was all the good-bye she was going to get?

She went to the door and opened it, watching as Braden climbed into the front seat, his son in the back with Tatum and Courtney, who'd waited in the SUV. The driver drove away from the stone fountain and disappeared around the first turn in the driveway.

Arizona struggled with a rush of intensifying sorrow. Would she never see them again? Braden had been so in-different. It was a deflating end.

"Arizona?"

Reluctantly, she faced her mother. The big house was quiet. But only until she could no longer hold back her tears. They echoed in the gigantic entry.

Walking away from Arizona had torn a hole through his heart, but it had to be done. Both of them had to be sure of what they were doing. He especially. He had a young boy to think about. Women coming and going in his life may not have a positive influence on him. And her withdrawal after sex disturbed him.

The SUV stopped in his parents' driveway and they all got out, except the driver, who simply drove off after doing what the Ivys had instructed. But to him it was like the last of Arizona was disappearing down the street.

"Are you all right?" Tatum asked.

Aiden bounded ahead toward the door. It had been a long drive to Denver. Only an hour, but it may as well have been a lifetime.

"Yeah."

"Did something happen with Arizona?"

"No."

"When are you going to see her again? Did you two make some plans?"

"No."

"No?" She gaped at him with parted mouth, incredulous.

Their mother opened the front door, ruffling Aiden's hair before he ran past her for the toys they kept here for him.

"Are you sure I should be here?" Courtney asked, stopping on the sidewalk leading to the porch.

"Of course we are." Tatum hooked her arm and walked to the porch. "Arizona should be, too."

Braden ignored her. His feelings were too jumbled to explain anything right now. He'd left Arizona the way he had as a tactic to win her. But he wasn't sure he was ready to have her. Being with her felt lasting, like they had what it took to go the distance. But he'd felt this way before with women, and look where that had gotten him.

His mother covered her mouth with her hand, already crying at the sight of Tatum. Tatum let go of Courtney to hug her.

"Hi, Mom."

"Oh, my sweetie. I'm so happy to see you." She braced Tatum's head between her hands, tears flowing, taking in her daughter.

"I'm fine," Tatum said.

"Did he hurt you?"

"Not a scratch." But Tatum looked back at Courtney.

Braden had explained everything to his mother before coming here. His parents weren't the type to take surprises well. Right now, especially. His mother had been hesitant on the phone, but ever the doer of right, she insisted they bring Courtney. She also said she'd arrange for Dad to be here.

"Come in." His mother opened her arm to Courtney. "Come in. You're welcome here."

Courtney smiled bashfully.

In the living room, there were trays of food and a glass bowl of ice and sodas. He took Courtney there and she sat primly and timidly with her hands folded on her lap.

His mother doted on her, nervously, chatting away, offering food.

"I'm sorry if you weren't expecting me to appear in your life," he heard Courtney blurt.

His mother stood frozen, stunned. And then she melted into the warmhearted person he'd grown up with. "Oh,

honey." She sat beside her. "None of this is your fault. We'll work it out."

Braden went to stand beside Tatum, who hadn't wanted to sit, like him. He'd been meaning to get a moment alone with her for a while now. With his mother listening to Courtney talking, this was as good of a time as any.

"So…why did you take the files?" he asked.

She wasn't even fazed, only looked over at him calmly. "Would you have given them to me?"

"No."

"Would you have let me go after Courtney?"

"Definitely not."

"That's why."

"How did you know to leave the algorithms?"

"You said they were needed for the weapon to operate. Remember I asked you if it could be built without them?"

"Yes." And he'd said no.

"You took a big risk."

"At the time I didn't feel like I had a lot to lose."

She'd already lost her job and her reputation.

"Besides, Dad's affair would have killed Mom. I was trying to spare everyone by going alone. I hoped to get Courtney and bring her back. Introduce her without so much trouble going on." She laughed ruefully. "Pretty stupid, huh?"

He shrugged. "But honorable."

Tatum sobered. "How's Mom handling it? Really?"

Of course, she must know he'd told her. "She's pretty upset." Doing a good job of covering it for Courtney, a woman who'd just been kidnapped and raped repeatedly. Their half sister.

"Are she and Dad going to split up?"

"Not if Dad has any power over it."

"I was hoping that would work in their favor. They love

each other. Mom won't throw that away over something that happened before they were married, would she?"

"He slept with her a week before the wedding."

"Yeah, but..."

"And then he knew about Courtney and didn't tell her for years."

"Yeah." She nodded reluctantly. "That is pretty bad."

Just then the door opened and their dad entered. He smelled fresh and looked ready to woo his wife. Their mother stood from the couch, Courtney with her, wringing her hands, her breathing visibly taxed.

"Marlana," he greeted.

She forced a smile. "This is Courtney Andrews."

His dad nodded once, at a loss for words. Then to Marlana, he said, "Thank you for having us here. You didn't have to."

"Yes, I did."

He moved closer, extending his hand to Courtney. "Marlana kicked me out of the house for not telling her about you. I deserved that. I'm so sorry for not being there for you all these years."

"You were. In your own way."

The room fell into uneasy silence. His dad kept looking at his mom for signs of forgiveness, and Courtney seemed to need a rock to crawl under.

"Well...why don't the two of you take a few moments to get to know each other," Marlana said to her husband and Courtney, then she went to Tatum and Braden. "We'll start dinner. It'll take a while. I'm making a turkey and a few sides."

"It's not even Thanksgiving," Tatum said.

"No, but we have a lot to be thankful for. Braden, where's that lovely woman you had with you last time?"

He wished they'd stop asking him about her. He was

having a hard enough time keeping her from taking up real estate in his head.

"She's in Evergreen with her mother."

"Why didn't you bring her with you?"

"He's worried he's going to make another mistake," Tatum said.

"It's too soon, and Aiden…"

"Aiden loves Arizona," Tatum said. "I saw the way they were together. And I also saw how she looks at the two of you together. She's wildly in love with you."

"Your only mistake has been overthinking it, Braden. Take Serena. I told you she was materialistic and you insisted she was a nice girl. You argued with me for an hour over all the things you liked about her. It was as though you felt forced to come up with items to explain to yourself why you loved her."

He remembered his mother telling him that. He'd denied it. And he had worked hard to find things he could say he liked about her. Things that weren't about sex. He could hardly tell his mother the best thing about Serena was the sex.

"What do you like about Arizona?" Tatum asked, pushing him.

Everything.

"She skydives."

"She does?" his mother asked. "Well, you enjoy those things, too, Braden. Have you ever met a girl like that?"

No. "She lost her fiancé four years ago. He was killed and she isn't over him yet."

"Oh, I bet she is. I saw you with her," Tatum reminded him.

"Can we talk about something else?"

"No. Go get her, Braden. So what if it doesn't work out? You don't have to marry her until you're sure."

He stared at her for a long time, Tatum's words replayed in his traitorous mind.

She's wildly in love with you.

Tatum laughed. "You should see your face." She pushed him toward the door. "Just go get her. We'll wait for you before we eat."

Pacing the floor at her brother's house, Arizona bit her thumbnail in front of the Monopoly game spread out on the coffee table.

"Stop that. It's your turn."

"You're milking this for all its worth, aren't you?" She bent and rolled the dice, landing herself in jail.

He chuckled. "That's what you get for negativity."

"You really think I should go to see him?"

"Yes. How many times are you going to make me answer that question?"

"As many times as it takes me to decide."

Using his crutch, Lincoln rose to his feet and hobbled out from behind the couch. "Just go see him."

He crutched into the kitchen, getting a glass of water from the tap even though he had a water dispenser in his refrigerator. Leaning over the sink, he peered out the window.

He'd done that three times since she'd been here. "Who's out there?"

She walked to his side, leaning forward. There was a midsized SUV in the driveway of the house beside his, the back open and full of groceries.

"New neighbors?"

A leggy redhead in jeans and a spandex T-shirt appeared, trekking to the back of her vehicle to reveal a sexy behind, lifting two grocery bags and turning. Squinting her eyes against the afternoon sun, her face was that of a

porcelain doll, petite nose, full lips with perfect bow on top. From what she could see.

"Does she have green eyes?"

He crutched away from the window.

Arizona laughed and followed. "I'll take that as a yes."

Still, he ignored her. Women were usually a sore subject for him. That's why they'd gotten so close over the last four years. They had that in common. "Have you met her?"

"No."

"You want to though, don't you?" Wow. He was interested in someone. That was a milestone.

"It's nothing, A. Just something to pass the time. It gets boring sitting around this house."

Was he glazing the truth? "Something hot to look at while your leg heals?"

He sat on the couch, sullen now. "It's your turn."

Leaning down, she rolled again, turning her head to pin him with a look.

"Stop it."

"I'm still in jail." Kissing his cheek, she moved to the front window, trying to catch a glimpse of this mystery woman. A man appeared next. Big, strapping. "There's a man over there."

"Don't you want to know who it is?"

"It's her boyfriend."

"How do you know?"

"A…" he warned. "Stop staring out the window."

That's when Braden's Subaru rolled to a stop in the street. She sucked in her breath.

"A. Come back here. Let's finish the game this time."

"Oh, my God. Braden is here."

She pivoted and walked briskly over to him. "Braden just drove up!"

"Calm down."

"What's he doing here?"

"He's going to sweep you off your feet."

She put her hand on her forehead, anxiety prickling her nerves.

"You're going to be okay."

Would she?

The doorbell rang.

"Holy crap."

"I'd get the door, but…" He was grinning. How could he grin when they had this phobia in common?

When she didn't move, he shouted, "Come in!"

The door opened and Braden stepped in. Handsome. Intent on something. Her.

"Your mother said you were here."

"You drove all the way to Evergreen?"

"I called her."

"Oh." Of course, he had the number because of Aiden.

He strode into the living room, stopping before her. "I don't have your number or I'd have called you."

"I don't have yours, either."

"We'll have to fix that if we're going to start dating."

Her pulse tightened her vocal cords. "W-we are? W-we're going to start dating?"

"If you're up for it. I just got a divorce. I have a son. And you…"

"I'm ready for whatever is next in my life," she said.

He stared at her.

"With you," she added.

A slanting grin appeared on his mouth. "We don't have to get married right away. We can just see each other."

He made it seem so simple. Or was this a convenient excuse for something that was sure to explode into more than dating?

"Are you sure?"

"No."

She loved his honesty. "We'll take it slow."

His hands slid up her back and down, getting comfortable, adjusting her firmly to his body. "Are you sure?"

"No."

He chuckled.

"You two will be planning a wedding before the end of the year," Lincoln said, spinning the dial on the game.

Arizona smiled, and Braden kissed her, one after another.

"You're not leaving until we finish this game," Lincoln teased.

More kisses. There were no promises for the future, but she didn't need any. Kissing him made all her fears go away. All she needed was him. And when she fell in love, she wasn't going to lose him. She'd fight for him if she had to. Because one thing was sure: she and Braden were not victims. And she was going to make a life out of helping those who needed to get their power back.

Braden broke off the kiss. "You'll have to finish the game another time."

Why? Where was he taking her?

"There's something we have to do first."

Arizona couldn't keep the smile off her face as the plane flew over the city. They'd just finished suiting up into their jumping gear. And now Braden was waiting for the pilot to tell them when to jump. When they received the go ahead, Arizona jumped first, falling into the forward throw from the momentum of the plane, traveling forward for a bit before going down. The wind force created by her falling body grew.

Braden appeared in front of her. She gave him her hands and they turned in a circle. The land below seemed so far

away. Up here, she was like a bird, nothing stopping her from going anywhere. The sense of danger exhilarated her, made her feel alive. Though skydiving was actually relatively safe, the thrill was incomparable.

The therapy worked. It drew her out of her dark shell of mourning and forced her mind in a different direction. It forced her to live, to feel alive. She didn't know if being an adventure junkie helped other people who were victimized in some way or had suffered a loss as she had, but it worked for her, and she was confident she could make it work for others. If not skydiving, then other adventures. Anything to get the person out of their hole.

Inject excitement into their lives, if only for a day. The memory would last and add to the therapy.

A minute or so later, Braden let her hands go and together they released their parachutes. Her free fall slowed abruptly as her parachute opened. She toggled to follow Braden. He seemed to know where he was going.

She knew of a few drop zones in the area, and he was headed for one near the Boulder airport. She'd used it before. And she'd likely use it again when she started her nonprofit organization.

He headed for a small hill, away from the drop zone she was familiar with. This looked like private property. What was he up to? She hadn't questioned him on the way here. She'd only enjoyed the surprise, and the elation that she was going to have many adventures like this with him.

As the ground grew closer, she saw a white-linen tablecloth flapping gently in a breeze. A bucket of ice and a bottle of something. Champagne?

She hit the ground, rolling and coming back up to her feet, releasing herself from the parachute.

Braden landed several feet from her. Out of his chute,

he strode toward her, straps around his thighs and shoulders, removing his goggles and tossing them to the ground.

"It's early for dinner," she said, feeling her big smile.

He held out his hand.

She gave it to him and he led her to the table. He pushed in her chair when she sat.

"Do you have an old-fashioned streak?" But inwardly, she loved this.

Standing near the ice bucket that was on a stand, he lifted out a bottle. Champagne. Of course.

"You know, just because my father is Jackson Ivy doesn't mean you have to be fancy all the time."

Still, he didn't engage in her banter, he opened the champagne without sending the cork flying. Just a small *pop* and it was open.

He poured the bubbly liquid into the glasses and then sat across from her. Sipping, his brilliant green eyes radiated warmth. Brilliant. He was brilliant all right. Brilliant engineer. Brilliant lover.

A van appeared over the horizon of their private hill. It was unmarked. As it came to a halt and two men dressed in chef coats emerged, her delight expanded.

"How did you pull this together?" So fast.

"Your mother helped me."

"My mother?" That didn't surprise her, but…so fast.

"When I called to ask where you were, she questioned me."

The men in chef coats made quick work of setting up a table and removing whatever delicious meal her mother had dreamed up for them to bring.

She sipped her champagne. "What did she ask?"

"If I was going to marry you."

"What did you tell her?"

"I said, 'probably.'"

"And I'll bet that scares you to death."

The servers approached with two plates. The appetizer. Bacon-wrapped dates that smelled delicious.

"Nothing scares me that much."

"Me, either." Not anymore. With him, everything would be an adventure. She wouldn't have time to be afraid. How could she be when she was busy having fun and enjoying his company?

A tiny part of her worried he may not be ready, but a larger part had a hunch that they were more than likely on the same level there. Yes, he feared making another mistake, and yes, she feared falling in love. But what neither of them feared was the adventure they were going to have along the way. He must be thinking the same. Adventure would lead into the scary stuff. Love and marriage. Funny, how she was so sure it would come to that with them. She'd heard of people who said they knew the moment they met their spouse that they were going to marry them.

She and Braden weren't ready to admit that outright—that they both knew they'd just met the one they were going to spend the rest of their lives with—but skydiving was a great first step.

"Is this our first date?" she asked.

"It is now."

"What was it before?" She already knew but she wanted to hear his answer.

"I had to be sure."

That she jumped out of planes? "Satisfied?"

"Very."

So was she. "Where's our second date going to be?"

"It's your turn to pick. Surprise me."

Oh, she would. She'd think of something good. Like

maybe an enchanting chapel. She'd take her time planning. However long it needed to be. Which may not have to be long at all.

* * * *

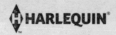

No one believes Nev's disturbing dreams are coming true. But when her life is threatened, Detective Ty Gadney risks it all—including his heart—to find the truth.

Read on for a sneak peek of

COPPER LAKE ENCOUNTER

by Marilyn Pappano, coming August 2013 from Harlequin Romantic Suspense.

He saw her car before it turned into the lot. By the time she'd parked a few spaces down from his, he was there, opening the door, helping her out. Her coffee-with-cream eyes were filled with concern, and she looked graver than he'd ever seen her.

"I'm not going to like this, am I?"

He shook his head. With his hand barely touching her upper arm, they walked across the parking lot and right up to the open door. Her jaw tightened, her mouth forming a thin line, as she looked inside, her gaze locking for a moment on each note. It was hard to say which one disturbed her most. It was the stick figure that bothered Ty, the idea of taking something so simple and innocent as a child's drawing and turning it into a threat. From the tension radiating through her, he would guess it was the knife in the pillow that got to her.

"The crime-scene techs are on their way over," Kiki said. "Does anything appear to be missing?"

HRSEXP0713

Nev shook her head. "The only thing I have of any value is my laptop, and it's in the room safe."

"Do you think this was done by the same boys who sprayed shaving cream on my car last night?" Nev asked, her demeanor calm, her voice quiet with just the littlest bit of a quaver.

"No." Kiki was blunt, as usual. "Gavin and Kevin Holigan are twelve and thirteen. They probably can't spell that well, and besides, this isn't their style."

"Do you have any problems at home in Atlanta?"

Nev smiled wryly. "No. I live with my mother, grandmother and sister. I work at home. I go to church every Sunday and Wednesday. I don't have any enemies there. I don't inspire that kind of passion, Detective."

Those self-doubts again. Ty didn't doubt she believed that. She had no clue what kind of passion she could inspire. He wanted nothing more than an opportunity to show her.

He needed nothing more than to keep her safe.

HRSEXP0713

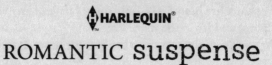

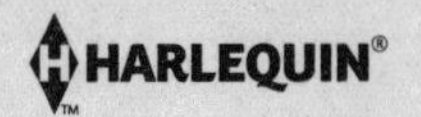

ROMANTIC suspense

COLTON BY BLOOD

The Coltons of Wyoming

Melissa Cutler

Embracing a future with the sweet, sexy pastry chef who's captured his heart means Dr. Levi Colton must settle the score with his past, including the secrets that bind him to Dead River Ranch. Standing in his way is a faceless enemy who will stop at nothing to keep the secrets of the ranch buried...no matter what the cost.

Look for *COLTON BY BLOOD* by Melissa Cutler, the next title in The Coltons of Wyoming miniseries, coming next month from Harlequin® Romantic Suspense!

Available wherever books and ebooks are sold.

Heart-racing romance, high-stakes suspense!

www.Harlequin.com

HRS27834

Dear Reader,

I am excited to bring you a new miniseries about a big family with a famous dad. There will be plenty of trouble to keep the action high and love to keep the heart warm.

In this first novel of the miniseries, meet Arizona Ivy, an adventurer whose last brush with love has left her skittish—the only thing she is skittish of! I chose her to start the miniseries because she's the youngest of eight and at odds with her heritage. Braden McCrae is the perfect man to make her grow. He may seem like an ordinary guy, but underneath his smarts is a man who can't be pushed around.

This was one of my favorite books to write. It's different. Fresh and new. So, here's to wishing you hours of pleasant reading! May it take you away as it did for me.

Sincerely,

Jennifer

"I'm sorry. I shouldn't have let you kiss me. I wasn't ready."

He couldn't take her mind off Trevor. She should be ready by now, and Braden should be able to get her mind off another man.

"Losing him doesn't mean you have to live the rest of your life alone, pursuing a career that will consume all your time."

"Trevor has nothing to do with why I want to be a reporter," Arizona said.

"Yes, he does. You should follow your heart."

"Is that what you did?"

"Yes."

"Then why are you so familiar with guns? And why are you not afraid of dangerous situations? It's like you're ready for battle 24/7."

Had she really picked up on that? Her insight was keen. But he wasn't going to talk about that with her. He didn't talk about it with anyone.

"My sister is missing," he said. "I've never been in a situation like this before."

Ivy Avengers: Family bonds. Family secrets.